# The Ghost Dance

DL Watkins

Copyright © 2021 by DL Watkins

Book cover design by Alejandro Colluci.
Formatting by Polgarus Studio

ISBN 9781737785903 (paperback)
ISBN 9781737785910 (ebook)

Ghostdancebook.com

The Ghost Dance is dedicated to the incredible perseverance and cultural heritage of the Native American tribes of North America.

Special thanks to my family, and all those who provided feedback, editing and support, without whom the book would not have been possible.

DL

# Chapter One

Eight men on motorcycles rode for hours in the dark through the hills of South Dakota. They were all from the Lakota Nation, or Sioux, but their clothing was distinctively modern. The black garb was a hybrid between traditional motorcycle gang and tactical military attire, and they carried differing combinations of backpacks and gear attached to their bodies. They all had one thing in common—a leather vest, which bore a circular insignia on the shoulder of a bird with up-stretched wings.

The riders stayed in a tight, single file formation until they passed the outskirts of Rapid City where the helmeted leader in the front pointed with his right hand to make a turn. One by one the bikes turned off the highway, small sleek machines built for speed with the exception of the one in the rear, a full-sized Harley Davidson with a giant man leaning back against a tall, cushioned seat.

Now that they were away from the competing noises on the highway, the sounds of the motorcycle engines dominated the quiet night as the last few remaining signs of civilization faded away to miles of empty fields, and, finally, to thick forest. The gang turned down a dirt road marked with an old weather-beaten wooden sign that said "Pine Ridge Reservation—five miles." The young leader in the front felt a twinge of anxiety at the thought of returning to his birthplace in Pine Ridge. He took a deep breath of the crisp night air to calm his nerves. Time to get down to business.

The men pulled off the dirt road and walked their bikes along a small trail into the woods before finally hiding them in the undergrowth to keep them out of sight.

"From here we go on foot," said the leader as he removed his helmet and attached it to his bike.

The moon slowly faded out of sight behind the clouds, plunging the forest into a deep blanket of darkness. It was now past midnight, and the only noise was the sound of leaves crunching on the ground as the men walked through the brushy undergrowth of the rarely used trail.

The giant man from the rear hustled to the front to walk beside the leader. He was well over six feet tall and nearly three hundred pounds of muscle. "Red Moon, how old is this one tonight?"

Red Moon whispered back, "Does it matter, Mato?" His deep green eyes burned with intensity as he dismissed the question.

"It does to me if I have to carry him."

"This one is old," said Red Moon. "You'll be fine."

The group made their way through the woods until the trees ended at the back side of a residential neighborhood. There were trailers and small houses spread out in every direction, and street signs that were familiar to Red Moon. A few houses had lights on, but most were dark. On the right, about three blocks away, there was a bonfire burning in a front yard, with a few men still awake, enjoying conversation by the fire.

Red Moon turned to another member of the group. "Adriel, check it out."

Adriel was short, but lean and muscular. His long black hair was captured by a leather binding into a long ponytail that draped down his back. The young man took off his black leather vest, exposing a shirtless torso covered in tattoos. Dark sleeves of intricate artwork covered both arms, leading up to the more distinct images of animals covering his chest and back. Adriel closed his eyes, as if focused in thought, and outstretched his arms to the sky. As soon as his eyes were shut, the tattoos on his back and chest began to shift and blur together like fast moving storm clouds. The jaws of a wolf snarled and swirled on the front of the man's chest, while the feathery wings of a bird flexed across his back. The bird's outstretched wings spanned along the back of Adriel's shoulders, and a beaked head was inked squarely in the middle of his shoulder blades. Adriel opened his eyes quickly, and the tattooed image leaped off his muscular torso, soaring up into the sky.

The shadow bird flapped its wings silently as it flew around the houses and circled down near the men talking by the fire. Red Moon pulled a knife from a sheath on his belt and twirled it impatiently in his fingers while he observed the reactions of the newest members of the gang. They were surprised by the appearance of one of Adriel's shadow creatures, and Red Moon took advantage of the distraction to look carefully for any sign of a firearm. All he saw were the custom weapons crafted by Adriel that Red Moon approved. Some of the men carried guns when he wasn't around, but when they were with their captain, Red Moon had a hard and fast rule—traditional weapons only.

The winged scout finished making its rounds before finally coming back to the edge of the woods and silently swooping down towards Adriel's back. The tattoos began to shift again as the bird rejoined the place from which it had sprung.

Adriel picked up his vest and pointed to a small dark one-story house about one hundred yards to the left. "That's the one. I'm sure."

"What about the men around the fire?" asked Red Moon.

"They are reservation police, but they are tired and drunk. They won't be a problem."

The black clad figures circled around the edge of the trees and converged as an organized unit on the small one-story house. Red Moon made a motion with his hand and the group silently split up. Mato took three men and found a hiding place on the side of a porch by the back door. Mato had the physique of a grizzly bear and Red Moon chuckled to himself as Mato crouched down, struggling to find a comfortable position.

Adriel and Red Moon went to the front door, and it only took a few minutes for Adriel to get it open with a tool that appeared from a pocket in his vest. Two men in the group remained by the front door as guards.

Red Moon quickly moved through the home with Adriel on his heels, and they found their prize asleep in a bedroom in a t-shirt and pajama bottoms. The man was in his sixties and had gray hair, just as described. Red Moon pulled something from his pocket and moved quickly towards the sleeping figure in the bed. He shook the old man and, as he awoke, Red Moon blew a white dust into his face. The old man's eyes instantly rolled back and his head fell into Red Moon's waiting hands. Adriel helped Red Moon lift the man out of the bed and the leader threw the unconscious man over his shoulder.

*The old man was heavier than he looked. Mato will not be happy.*

Red Moon and Adriel went out the back door and handed off the old man to Mato, who effortlessly lifted him up and over his shoulder like a potato sack. The group met up at the front of the house and jogged quietly back to the forest lining the reservation. Red Moon glanced over his shoulder at the men sitting around the fire and noticed that none of them had even moved. Success.

As they got back to the bikes, Red Moon asked Mato to tie the man to Red Moon's body and place him on the motorcycle so it would look like he was a passenger. Mato pulled out a length of black nylon rope from his bag and went to work, quickly finishing his task.

The old man's arms remained limp and it was clear he was going to be asleep for hours. Mato put a helmet over the old man's head and a jacket around his shoulders to hide the rope. Once the work was done, the group mounted their motorcycles and sped off in the night towards their camp.

Red Moon led the line of motorcycles as they retraced their route through the winding roads of the Black Hills. Along the way, Red Moon could feel the heartbeat of the man bound behind him, and it never changed. Slow and steady.

It was only a few hours from dawn when they finally pulled into a gravel parking lot at the foot of a mountain range. Between the parking lot and the mountain were rows of small buildings that formed a compound. This was their home.

Mato helped untie the old man, so Red Moon could dismount and stretch his legs. He barely got an opportunity to prepare himself before the giant man picked up the prize and lifted him up onto Red Moon's shoulder.

"I'll take him to the Crow Keeper," Red Moon said with an air of authority to the others. No one questioned Red Moon's instructions and the rest of the gang tiredly spread out and walked towards the wooden buildings where they lived. Red Moon walked by himself through the large courtyard in the middle of the buildings, and at the end of the giant square, where the open space ended at the base of a mountain, was a stairway of rocks leading down into a cave.

Red Moon was already struggling to carry the still-sleeping old man over his shoulder. He should have asked for Mato's help, but he wanted to be the one to bring back the last one on the list and finish the job. Red Moon was the leader of the *ozuye,* an honorary name given to his group of gang members by the Crow Keeper. Like many of the others in the compound, the Crow Keeper had rescued Red Moon from a difficult life in the reservation and given him a purpose. The life on the reservation was now in the past—no more poverty, pain, and daily struggle. Red Moon would rather die than return to that old life. Now, he was a warrior, fighting to restore greatness to his people.

Red Moon had faith in the Crow Keeper's plan. It was not a blind faith. It was instead a deep commitment, well-earned from Red Moon witnessing fantastic things. Terrible things.

Gas lit lamps guided Red Moon down the steps carved into the stone ground and into the subterranean entrance. The leader of the *ozuye* knew the Crow Keeper would be waiting for his return tonight. The young man carried his burden around a corner, entering a large cavern with a jail cell built into a corner of the room. The Crow Keeper smiled at the sight of Red Moon and quickly opened the door of the cell where five other men and women were sleeping on the cave floor. Red Moon laid the old man down onto the dirt and instantly felt relief in the muscles in his back.

"We got the last one," Red Moon said proudly to the old shaman as he fought to catch his breath.

"No. There is one more," the Crow Keeper replied. "Get your *ozuye* ready for a trip. You leave tomorrow."

# Chapter Two

Keaton Chapa picked his head up from the pillow, awakened by the annoying buzz of his phone vibrating on the nightstand. He looked at his watch—5:17 am. Chapa answered the phone quickly, knowing it was likely not a routine call that early on a Friday morning.

"Morning, Special Agent Chapa," said a familiar voice. It was Wilson Dawes, Bureau of Indian Affairs (BIA) Assistant Director, and Chapa's longtime boss who apparently felt the liberty to call him anytime day or night. "There has been a kidnapping at a reservation, and I am going to need your help. Pack a bag."

"What time do you want to meet?" asked Chapa slowly as his eyes adjusted to the light on the phone screen.

"How fast can you get into the office?"

Chapa thought for a few moments before answering. "I will be there in an hour."

The call ended abruptly and Chapa got out of bed. His walk towards the bathroom was accompanied by the usual aches and pains that marked too many years of pushing the limits of his body. He normally exercised in the morning to get the blood flowing before going to work, but today his grueling routine would have to wait. Chapa turned on the hot water and undressed to get in the shower. The steam filled the bathroom and Chapa's mind started racing.

*I wonder where Dawes is sending me this time.*

After showering, Chapa put on dark khaki pants and a white dress shirt.

He grabbed one of his sport coats and the lanyard with his badge, but had to search for his boots, which were hiding by the side of the couch. Chapa lived alone and liked it that way. No one to tell him what to do.

Chapa's small house was on a few acres in rural Virginia, near the BIA office in Washington D.C. He carefully locked the front door before making his way to a black Dodge Ram pickup parked in the driveway. At first glance, the pickup looked like nothing special, but it was Chapa's most prized possession. The diesel powered behemoth was five years old and had 185,000 miles on it. The truck had so many modifications and repairs there was hardly a single inch of it that remained unchanged from the factory. No one who knew Chapa at BIA had ever seen him driving anything other than a black Dodge pickup. Indeed, he would not admit to ever owning anything else, and to even suggest such a proposition would be nothing less than an insult to Chapa. Some agents would never go out into the field without their preferred sidearm. That was the way Chapa felt about his truck—like his life depended on it. And many times, it had.

The guard waved good morning as Chapa pulled into the BIA parking lot in Washington D.C. After a quick flash of his agent's badge against the card reader, an automated arm lifted with a chirp to allow entry into the parking garage. Although it was still early in the morning, the lot was already filling up and there were not a lot of good options for parking a full-size pickup. Chapa backed into a tight spot between a Lexus and a Land Rover on the third floor and grabbed his backpack.

"Damn," he thought as he looked at his watch. He had fifteen minutes. Chapa opened his door in a hurry and heard the smack of metal against metal on the side of the Lexus. He didn't think twice as he hurried to the building entrance.

Once inside the BIA headquarters, Chapa rushed to the elevator and hit the button for the tenth floor. Chapa got off the elevator and glanced at the sign for his office "BIA - Office of Justice Services (OJS)." The forty-something agent nodded his head at the much younger brown-haired receptionist and scanned his badge again to open the door. She looked up and smiled back casually as he quickly strode into the office.

Chapa had worked hard to advance up the ranks, starting as a BIA police officer after finishing a four year tour in the Marines. His mother was full blooded Cherokee, and Chapa grew up on a reservation in northeastern Oklahoma. He got his last name from his dad, but that was his father's only paternal contribution. Chapa never met his father, and his mother never remarried. She died of an overdose when he was in his early teens and his maternal grandmother pitched in as best she could. As soon as Chapa hit eighteen, he joined the Marines and left Oklahoma. The BIA was a good fit after leaving the military and the work came easy to him because it reminded him of home. After working as a BIA police officer for ten years, Chapa eventually met Dawes and he helped Chapa get a promotion to become a special agent. Instead of handling routine enforcement of tribal law, Chapa now investigated major crimes. He enjoyed the work, but hated the move to Washington D.C. The saving grace for him was that he seldom actually spent time in the office.

For the most part, the job as a special agent required that Chapa go undercover, or spend time away from home investigating murders and violent offenses in reservations across the United States. Chapa had no one to miss him and Dawes knew it, so Chapa always got the tough assignments. He never complained, and made every assignment a personal challenge. Chapa knew that many of the people he had arrested or killed would not have otherwise been caught, but for his work. Very few people cared about crimes committed on reservations against people like his mother, but Chapa did, and viewed himself as their protector.

The door to the conference room inside the BIA-OJS office was open and Dawes was already sitting inside talking with two people unfamiliar to Chapa.

"Come in and grab some coffee!" said Dawes after he saw Chapa's face peek inside the room.

Dawes was sitting at the head of the conference room table, furiously typing out an email on his phone. Dawes was older than Chapa, and dark-skinned with glasses. Chapa had worked for Dawes for over three years now, and they had never once had a personal conversation. Dawes was a mystery, and frankly, that was fine with him. Dawes handled the office part and Chapa took care of his assignments.

Chapa walked in cautiously and looked around the table. There was a young female in business attire rifling through some papers in a folder. Chapa vaguely recalled seeing the woman around the office and presumed she was BIA. A middle-aged man in a dark gray suit was sitting on the other side of Dawes. He had a shaved head, which was obviously intended to mask a receding hairline. Chapa noticed the familiar bulge of a gun under his suit jacket so he presumed the visitor was law enforcement, but the shined shoes and expensive tie screamed desk jockey. The well-tailored man watched quietly as Chapa filled a cup with a black coffee and sat down on the opposite side of the table next to the woman, making sure to keep an open seat between them.

"Keaton, I would like you to meet John Resnick from the FBI, and this is Jenny Anderson from the BIA. They are working on a kidnapping in South Dakota. Thanks for joining us."

Chapa pulled a notepad and pen out of his backpack. The FBI didn't normally get involved in BIA law enforcement matters, so this was going to be interesting. "Morning," Chapa said to Anderson and Resnick as he gave a slight nod.

Dawes turned to Anderson, "Tell him about the kidnappings."

The woman pulled a folder out of her bag and handed it to Chapa. "Three days ago, a council member from the Pine Ridge reservation in South Dakota was kidnapped in the middle of the night. His name is Samuel White Elk," she said, pointing at a photograph. "His neighbor came to see him the next morning and he was gone. No one has heard from him since the neighbor reported him missing and he is not the type to leave his home without telling anyone."

Chapa was surprised about the story so far, and why he was being asked to get involved. An old man going missing for a few days normally didn't warrant the involvement of both the FBI and BIA.

*Who is this person and why is he so important?*

Anderson pulled out a list of names and told Chapa to open his folder. In front of him, he had a similar list of names in his folder along with the police report from the investigation into White Elk's disappearance. Shockingly, the list appeared to have been generated from the Smithsonian Institute, the country's most famous museum that was also housed in Washington D.C.

Anderson continued, "In the last three weeks, there have been six kidnappings in and around reservations in the Dakotas. Some lived on the reservations. Some lived in private homes. All of these people were Lakota and disappeared without explanation in the middle of the night. In some cases, multiple family members disappeared. In other cases, the victims had family in the house or even spouses in the same bed when it happened, yet none of them saw or heard anything. They woke up and, poof, the person was gone."

She paused. "This just didn't make any sense and I have been pulling my hair out trying to find a connection between the victims. And then we found something."

"Actually, the FBI found the connection," added Dawes as he turned to the man sitting beside him. "Since the kidnappings cross state lines, BIA asked the FBI to get involved. Resnick here did several of the investigations personally and discovered what appeared to be a common tie between three of the victims. All three had made prominent claims of being a descendant of Sitting Bull."

Chapa first looked at Resnick then Dawes before smiling about a reference to the most famous historical war chief of the Lakota Nation. "Come on, Wilson. You know that half of the people in that area claim to be related to either Sitting Bull or Crazy Horse. Every truck stop has the world's best cup of coffee and a guy in the gift shop who is related to Sitting Bull. It's a story to sell souvenirs. You can't be serious."

Anderson broke into the conversation. "Don't feel bad. That's what I told Resnick too, at first. We considered the theory an interesting one, but just a random correlation, like being left-handed or a member of the Democrat Party. Then it happened again, when a woman was abducted in Sioux Falls and we were sure it was part of the same pattern. The problem was that the woman's family had no known connection to Sitting Bull."

"Just to prove Resnick wrong, I tried to find a list of living descendants of Sitting Bull. That proved to be harder than you think, as there are frauds and fake claims at every turn. As luck would have it, the Smithsonian museum here in D.C. spent an enormous amount of resources about five years ago tracing the lineage of Sitting Bull because it wanted to return some of his property to his next of kin. I took that list and cross-referenced the names against the list of kidnappings."

Suddenly, Chapa was interested. *No way*, he thought. *This is crazy.*

Anderson was also getting excited. "I ran down each branch of the family tree to see who was still alive in the blood line. Five of the names on that list had already been kidnapped, including the woman in Sioux Falls who didn't even know she was related. And White Elk just made number six. We stationed BIA officers a few houses over from White Elk on our hunch, and two nights ago, whoever is responsible for the kidnappings still got to him. Our officers were watching the house all night when he disappeared."

"They never saw a thing," added Dawes.

*These people are like ghosts*, thought Chapa. *How is this possible?*

Chapa looked down at the list in front of him and saw there were seven names. "So who is the lucky number seven who has successfully avoided the curse of Sitting Bull?" asked Chapa jokingly.

Resnick joined the conversation, pointing to another paper in Chapa's folder. "His name is Logan Iyotake Hatani. He lives in Cortez, Colorado, and he has been tough to find. The Smithsonian had his family's name but never located him because his parents are dead. The kid fell off the radar when he bounced around as an orphan. He is only fifteen and is living with his uncle right now."

Dawes interrupted, "That's enough to get you going. We think the people who are responsible are going to go after the boy and we need to get you guys on the road. You and Resnick are going to go find this kid and make him your shadow. If anyone tries to kidnap him, I would hope that the two of you would be able to stop it. If not, call the local police for backup."

Resnick got up from his seat and turned to Chapa to shake his hand. "I look forward to working with you. Dawes has told me some great stories. Guess I will see you at the airport?"

Chapa shook his hand. "If Dawes has been telling you stories, then you know I don't fly."

The FBI agent grabbed a small suitcase sitting in the corner while Dawes tried valiantly to get Chapa to join Resnick on the next flight out of Washington. Dawes wasted little time since he knew he was fighting a losing battle. Chapa didn't fly. That was non-negotiable and was the price for assigning Chapa to an investigation.

Chapa knew it was a price Dawes was willing to pay, or else he wouldn't have called him. Resnick would need help if the investigation ended up requiring entry to a reservation. Chapa filed out of the conference room behind Resnick, who seemed excited about the assignment.

"Are you really going to drive all the way to Colorado?" asked Resnick, as they entered the elevator.

Chapa slowly nodded his head in the affirmative as he punched the button for the third-floor parking garage. "Indeed, I am."

The BIA agent remained quiet for the rest of the elevator ride, replaying the conversation about Logan in his mind. Guarding a teenager was not a typical assignment for Chapa. Dawes knew something he wasn't sharing, which made him nervous.

A "ding" announced the elevator's arrival at the third floor of the parking garage and Chapa quickly made his exit. "See you in Cortez," shouted Resnick. Without turning around, Chapa waved his hand to acknowledge his partner as his pace quickened. He knew he had a long drive, and it was time to hit the road.

# Chapter Three

Logan walked down the steps of his old mobile home and shut the door behind him. He pulled on the door knob one more time to make sure it was closed. Sometimes, the lock didn't catch. The trailer admittedly wasn't in good shape, but it was a roof over Logan's head and better than some of the foster homes where he had spent time as a young boy. He now lived with his uncle, Hatani, and Logan was happy to have a permanent home—wherever that may be.

Hatani had decided to move the two of them into this valley a year ago for one reason — the solitude. Logan's uncle had no use for neighbors. The two of them were far away from the closest civilization in Cortez, Colorado, and without a car Logan had few options for transportation when Hatani was working—which was most every day. It was summertime, and, more than ever, Logan felt stuck. He had no place he needed to be, so he hardly went anywhere.

Noticing the surprisingly cool summertime breeze, Logan decided against the bicycle, choosing instead to enjoy the walk and take a shortcut on foot across the grassy valley towards his favorite place to hang out during the day. After a short jog towards the tree line behind his home, he pulled out his phone to check the time—10:37 am. Hopefully, his friend Erica would be out today. After Logan got closer to the thick trees that marked the edge of the national forest land, he saw the familiar stream. The boy turned and followed the cold, crystal clear water until he saw his friend Erica sitting on rocks where the river turned to go under the bridge on the nearby road connecting his home to Cortez.

Logan saw that Erica had ridden her bike up the road to their usual place under the bridge in the shade. She lived only a mile away and was his closest friend, although he wouldn't admit it. The pair had hit it off immediately in school after Logan moved into the valley, and was the closest thing to a neighbor. They had spent hours talking on the long bus rides to and from the high school, bonding over a common frustration regarding their lack of personal transportation.

Erica's family life was very different from Logan's. She still had both parents, and even though he knew he shouldn't be jealous, Logan couldn't help it. Sometimes it hurt hearing Erica talk about her family. Making matters worse, Erica was always at the leading edge of every new technology, somehow persuading her parents to buy her the latest electronic gadget or gaming system. Logan desperately wanted to join the digital social scene, but he did not have Wi-Fi in his trailer, and half the time Logan could not even get a phone signal at his place. He spent most of his time outdoors out of sheer boredom, either with his Uncle Hatani or Erica, and it showed. He had a dark complexion and was lean and muscular.

Erica was already sitting on a big rock in the shade under the bridge, with her feet dangling in the crystal clear water. She was scrolling through her brand new iPhone as Logan walked up. "Hey, that's my rock," he said, feigning anger.

"Early bird gets the rock," Erica replied casually without looking up from the screen. Erica was fourteen—almost a year younger than Logan—but she made up for her youth with intelligence. The girl was smarter than Logan, and they both knew it. She made straight As in school and seemed to know something about everything.

The water level in the stream was low, and Logan easily made his way across a path of stepping stones before finally sitting down next to Erica and pulling out his own phone. Unlike Erica's state of the art device, Logan had a hand-me-down from Hatani with a long crack running through the middle of the screen.

*Finally*, he thought, as he saw the bars on the phone proclaiming his newfound signal strength. The area by the road had a much better signal than

Logan's mobile home, deep in the valley surrounded by the mountains. From Logan's perspective, the bridge was the gateway to the world, and a mandatory part of his daily routine. Most days, he would rather spend his time on the rock with cell reception, than in his house without it. Although he would likely be sitting here today anyway, the truth was, it was more enjoyable to have Erica to keep him company. He was glad Erica had decided to spend some time on his rock today.

After making the rounds on all the social network sites and checking the latest sports scores, Logan finally turned to conversation. "What are you doing this weekend?"

"My parents are talking about going into the mountains for some camping. I have to get back later to go to the grocery store with them to get some stuff," Erica said. "My mom is going to text me when she is ready. What about you?"

"Sitting here until my phone battery is dead," Logan replied.

"Sounds about right. You really need to get a job," she said. "Then you could afford Wi-Fi at your house."

Logan looked at her and nodded. "I know, but I need a car first."

He was almost old enough to start driving and that day couldn't arrive fast enough for Logan. Hatani took good care of him, but his uncle worked a lot as a roughneck on oil rigs. That meant Logan was on his own, with only his bicycle for transportation. The closest convenience store was five miles away, and Cortez was double that distance. Without a car, it would be impossible to get to work every day.

Hatani had two old cars at the trailer, but neither of them worked. Logan swore he would figure out a way to get one of them fixed before next year. Hopefully, the red Mustang, he mused to himself.

"Maybe your uncle will get the Mustang running for you," offered Erica with a knowing smile. "I know you want it."

Logan wasn't surprised Erica knew he was thinking about the Mustang. It was all he talked about when the topic came up, which was often.

"I wish," replied Logan with a sarcastic tone. "I don't think Hatani will ever part with that car. He would rather see it rot in the yard than me driving it."

"That's harsh," said Erica. "Actually, you have it sweet because he's never at home. I have three brothers and sisters, so someone is always looking over my shoulder. Trust me, that's worse."

Logan didn't say a word, but all he could think about was how much Erica took her family for granted. Uncle Hatani was the only family Logan had, and he barely knew the man. Making matters worse, Logan didn't know much about his parents either—only that his mother was a member of the Lakota tribe and he was born in South Dakota before she moved to New Mexico. His father—Hatani's brother—was a Navajo from New Mexico and a Christian minister. Hatani told him his parents moved to New Mexico when he was a baby and they died in a car crash. The only thing Logan remembered was bouncing around between state facilities and foster homes until Hatani came back from his jobs overseas on offshore oil rigs and applied for guardianship. For the last three years, Logan had been living with his uncle, first in New Mexico and now in the trailer in Colorado.

"You know," said Erica cautiously, "you could fix that car yourself."

Logan rolled his eyes. "Yeah, right."

Erica pulled her feet out of the water and hopped over to sit down on Logan's rock. "No, I'm serious. Hatani has the tools there at your house and he is never around. You could do it. I would help, if you wanted me to…"

"But I don't know anything about cars. And neither do you."

"That's what YouTube is for," Erica replied triumphantly as she held up her phone. "There is a video for everything!"

The two teenagers both settled quietly into a comfortable position on the rock, and Logan watched over her shoulder as Erica searched for videos on automobile body work.

*She's either crazy or bored*, thought Logan.

After a while, Logan's eyes started to get droopy, and he rolled over to stare at the swirling water. He was almost asleep when Erica's phone buzzed.

Logan could hear the loud voice of the girl's mom speaking Spanish through the phone speaker. He didn't understand many of the words, but he would periodically hear "Mija", which he knew was the name Erica's mother called her in Spanish.

"Gotta go," said Erica as she put away her phone. "Text me if you get reception. I will let you know if we leave town."

Logan was disappointed Erica had to leave so soon, but managed to only get out a simple, "See you later," as she got up from her perch on the rock beside Logan and walked over to her bicycle. Logan watched Erica's long brown hair flow behind her in the wind as she pedaled down the road towards her house. He was back to being alone.

At that moment, Logan heard the sounds of a vehicle coming from the direction of his home. He looked in the distance and recognized the familiar dirty white SUV that turned off the highway onto the road leading into the valley. It was Hatani. *Why is he coming home so early? It was barely past lunchtime.*

Logan jumped off the rock and started jogging back home as worry steadily wormed its way into his mind. *Hatani never came back early. Something was wrong.*

# Chapter Four

Resnick turned his rental car off the highway and drove down the long private road into the valley. He was beginning to wonder if he was in the right place, when finally he saw an old mobile home before the road hit a dead end. The tiny trailer was white with brown stripes painted down the side. As Resnick got closer, he realized the stripes were really just rust stains from water running down the metal frame of the home that had built up over time.

There were a few concrete steps by the front door and a storage shed on the back side of the trailer. Out front in the dirt driveway was a white SUV, caked with dirt, that had recently been driven. The same couldn't be said for the other automobiles on the property.

Under a carport on the far side of the trailer was a brown truck that had been in a bad wreck. The hood was missing and one side had a door that was bent and hanging off the frame. There was a red Mustang parked next to it, which appeared to be in better condition. It was old and in dire need of a paint job, but its character somehow shone through the dents and grime.

The trailer was in a flat clearing, but about one hundred yards behind the trailer was thick brush signaling the beginning of national forest land. To the east, Resnick could see the San Juan mountain range against the skyline.

It had been ten hours since the meeting in Washington, and Resnick was tired. The FBI agent felt the twinge in his lower back that had progressed from soreness to a painful throbbing. He had driven himself to the airport in Washington, waited an hour for the plane, and sat down another four hours on the flight. All of that sitting was followed by another two hour drive in a rental car to get to Cortez. Fearing he would not be able to eat once he got to his assignment, the hungry agent had grabbed a hamburger at a drive-through before heading straight to the address on the paper. After all that, he was desperately ready to get out of the car and stretch his legs.

Resnick scanned the valley and saw there were no other houses in sight. Shadowing the kid would mean staying on the property, and likely sleeping in his rental car. *My back is not going to like that*, he thought to himself.

It was still unbelievable that his partner was going to spend two days driving across the country because he was afraid of flying. *How the hell do you do this job if you are afraid to fly?*

Wondering how long it would be before Chapa arrived, Resnick pulled out his phone and dialed the number provided to him by Dawes back in Washington.

A familiar voice answered on the other end. "Hello, this is Chapa."

"How far away are you?"

"I will be there tomorrow afternoon. You can watch the kid for one night, right?"

"Not a problem. By the way, I hope you brought a mattress. I think we are going to be sleeping in our cars. This is the boondocks out here."

Resnick hit the red button and ended the call. It was time to talk to the boy and his uncle, but he already had butterflies in his stomach at the thought of having to use the cover story that he and Chapa had rehearsed. *No way am I telling them the truth*, he thought. They would never let him hang around the home if he told them why he was really there.

The door on the rental car shut behind Resnick with a soft thunk as he got out of the compact vehicle. The tall FBI agent stretched his legs and slowly took a few strides towards the stairs by the front door. Resnick had called the uncle after he landed at the airport to let him know he was coming. He knew Hatani was expecting him, but the uncle had no idea what the FBI agent was about to say. To be honest, Resnick wasn't all that sure he knew what he was going to say.

He tucked in his shirt, checked his tie, and knocked on the door three times. The door opened quickly and a middle-aged man in worn blue jeans and a blue long-sleeved work shirt stood in the doorway. "Are you the guy who called me from the FBI?"

Resnick pulled out his badge and displayed the familiar FBI logo with his name on it. "Yes, sir, I am Agent Resnick from the FBI."

Most people were impressed with an FBI badge, but this man barely looked at it. "William Hatani, but everyone calls me Hatani. What are you doing all the way out here?"

Resnick peeked into the trailer and put his badge back in his suit coat pocket. "We have received a tip that leads us to believe someone might want to harm your nephew, Logan. Can we talk inside?"

Hatani looked unimpressed, but waved Resnick into the small trailer. Resnick knew that Hatani had a criminal record from years ago, so he wasn't surprised by the cold reception. The uncle had a leather necklace and visible tattoos on both arms that were difficult to make out because of his dark skin. He walked slowly away from Resnick with a gait that suggested an injury. Resnick wondered if it was a work injury or a bar fight. The odds were about equal, thought the FBI agent.

The two men made their way to a round kitchen table where Resnick pulled out a chair and took a seat without being invited. Hatani just stared at him and remained standing.

"I think Logan needs to be a part of this conversation, if that's OK with you," said the FBI agent.

Hatani yelled Logan's name and he came out of his room at the end of a hallway that ran the length of the trailer. Logan had his phone in one hand and earbuds in his ears. He looked nervous as he fumbled with the phone to turn off the music.

"Logan, this is Agent Resnick. He is with the FBI, and he wants to talk to us."

"Nice to meet you, Logan," said Resnick as he shook Logan's hand. "Take a seat. You too, Mr. Hatani. Please."

Resnick launched into his prepared speech. "I am working on a case involving a drug trafficking gang from a reservation in New Mexico. They have a pattern of moving through small towns in the area and kidnapping young Native American males to force them to join their gang. One of our informants has told us that they have their eye on Logan because he is home alone often and they may try to take him."

Both Logan and Hatani had a look of confusion on their faces. Resnick continued confidently with his script, unfazed by their reaction.

"My partner is a special agent from the Bureau of Indian Affairs and he will be here tomorrow. We would like your permission to hang out here and just keep an eye on things for a few days. We will stay out of your way and if we don't see anything suspicious, we'll get out of your hair. If any drug gangs show up, we will hold down the fort until the police from Cortez can get here to arrest the bad guys."

By this point, Logan's eyes were wide, and he had stood up from his seat at the table. "You have the wrong person. Why would anyone want to kidnap me? I don't know anything about drugs."

Hatani looked intently at Resnick and studied him carefully. Resnick wasn't sure if Hatani believed him or not. He was a tough man to read. Chapa and Resnick had agreed beforehand to the cover story, but Resnick always had his doubts it would work and wished Chapa was here right now.

The uncle walked over to Logan and put his hand on his shoulder before smiling and tousling his already unkept hair. "Nothing is going to happen. I am sure this is just a misunderstanding." The uncle paused for a minute. "Logan, why don't you grab a soda and go back to your room? I want to talk with the agent for a little bit."

Logan opened the refrigerator door and picked out a bottle of water. "I will be around the corner if anyone needs me."

Hatani watched Logan walk back to his room and then turned to Resnick. "Look, man, you probably already know, but I'm not the kind of guy who gets along with cops. You know what I mean? I was in a gang when I was younger, and we never kidnapped anybody. How do I know your story is legit?"

"You don't," said Resnick. "The way I see it you have two choices. Option one—you tell me to get the hell off your land, and I will go. Option two—I sleep out in my rental car and keep an eye on your home for the next few days in case you need some help protecting that boy. If our suspicions are right, and all hell breaks loose, you will be glad me and Chapa are here. If nothing happens, Logan will be able to tell his friends he hung out with an FBI agent. It's a win-win."

Hatani moved his hand along his chin and paused as he stared at Resnick. "Look, I don't have room for any visitors and I don't have much in terms of extra food. Today is Friday. I am off for the weekend, but I have to go back to work Monday morning. If nothing happens this weekend, you guys need to give me your card and I will call if there is any trouble. We can take care of ourselves."

"Deal," said Resnick quickly.

They both got up from the table and Resnick shook Hatani's hand again. This time he hung on for a few extra seconds. "I promise you, we're the good guys. If anyone tries to get Logan, they will have to get through me first."

"That makes two of us," Hatani said.

Resnick closed the door and went back down the steps to his tiny rental car. The FBI agent felt relief at finally putting eyes on Logan and convincing the uncle to not kick him off the property. The scenarios he had envisioned on the long plane ride were not so optimistic. Now that he was faced with the task of trying to explain his purpose for being here, he couldn't help but realize how silly it all seemed. Notwithstanding his doubts about the likelihood of kidnappers, the FBI agent followed protocol and slowly walked around the home to map out the surrounding area firmly in his brain. After making his rounds, Resnick opened the door to the back seat of his rental car and stretched out with a backpack as his pillow. Home sweet home for tonight.

The exhausted FBI agent looked at his watch and it was already a little after 9:30 pm. It would be a long night on watch without Chapa. He pulled out his phone to check the signal. Nothing.

As Resnick watched the lights go out in the trailer, he looked around the quiet valley and thought about how the attack might come. All of the kidnappings were at night with no witnesses, so he didn't expect anyone to drive up in a vehicle. Too noisy. No, they would park up the road and come on foot.

He scanned the pitch-dark terrain around the trailer and fixed on the woods about one hundred yards away. *That's where they will come*, he thought.

Fighting against the urge to sleep, Resnick pulled out a power brick and plugged in his phone to keep the battery charged. He turned on his classical music playlist at a low volume and settled in for the night watch. The entire time, all he could think about was a soft bed and what he would be ordering for breakfast the next morning.

# Chapter Five

The visit from Resnick had weighed on Logan's mind all night. Normally, he had no trouble sleeping—his head would hit the pillow and he would be fast asleep within minutes. But last night was different. His brain simply wouldn't shut off.

His thoughts, however, didn't focus on the warning from the FBI agent, but instead kept turning to his parents. Logan missed them terribly, and he wondered whether the gang threat had something to do with Hatani. It was no secret that his uncle had spent some time in prison and run in tough crowds when he was younger. Logan didn't know all the details, but Hatani had shared with him that he had to escape that life by working overseas on oil rigs. Logan's parents died while Hatani was fighting his demons, and it took a number of years before Hatani's wanderings brought him back home and to a place in his life where he felt comfortable taking responsibility for a kid.

But there was something else in Resnick's warning that drew his thoughts back to his parents, and kept demanding his attention. *Why would a Native American gang be looking for me?* Other than Logan's last name, there was nothing about him or his uncle that would announce they were Native American. Most of Logan's friends in Cortez were Hispanic, and his dark complexion allowed him to fit right into the crowd. He knew his mother was Lakota and his father Navajo, but he didn't know anything else about his family history. He couldn't get Hatani to talk about his parents, and didn't even have a photograph of them to keep.

Resnick's warning brought something to the front of Logan's mind that he had never really considered, and now he wondered what it meant. Who was he? Was he a Lakota, or maybe Navajo? He wasn't sure how it worked. Up to this point, he had just been a teenager, and the Native American world seemed far away and irrelevant. Somehow, that world had now found Logan.

He pulled out his phone and checked for a signal. As soon as he picked it up, he saw the words he had been accustomed to seeing all too often in the trailer—no signal. He had hoped to talk to Erica today, but that was looking increasingly unlikely. Frustrated, he threw his phone down on the unmade bed in his small room, and headed to the shower. He needed to get answers, and hoped he could learn more from the FBI agent today.

***

Resnick was eating breakfast at a cafe in what passed for a downtown in Cortez when he saw a message from Chapa flash across the screen. "Just passed Pueblo. Be there in a few hours."

Chapa was setting a land speed record on the trip from Washington D.C., and Resnick was impressed. That was good news, and he was looking forward to the company. He knew Chapa would probably make Hatani more comfortable and he felt he needed to do something to break the tension.

The FBI agent pushed back his chair and left the table. The plate was licked clean, and not a trace remained of the pancakes and bacon he had devoured. Even though his belly was full, Resnick was always planning ahead when it came to food, and his thoughts immediately turned to his next meal while he walked to his car. Since all of the other kidnappings had occurred at night, he felt safe leaving Logan alone in the morning, but he didn't want to push his luck. It could be a busy day, and it may not be safe to leave the boy alone again.

He didn't want to impose on Hatani, so he stopped at a convenience store and picked up some microwave meals, sandwich bread, cold cuts, and drinks. Resnick walked by a can of Folgers and threw it into his hand basket. He remembered seeing an old coffee maker in the kitchen, so he crossed his fingers that it was not broken like everything else around that trailer.

As he walked up front to pay for the supplies, he thought about Logan and made a quick detour. *Better get something for the kid,* he thought. Resnick looked over the candy selection and was momentarily at a loss when faced with the lierally hundreds of options. *When did picking a candy bar become so complicated?* The moment of indecision was followed by a confident smile as he picked up a Twix bar. Resnick always liked those, so if the kid didn't want it, he would eat it. Problem solved.

By the time he ran his errands in Cortez and drove back to the trailer, it was almost lunchtime. Resnick knocked before pushing open the door and announcing his return. "I'm back and brought some food if anyone wants something."

Logan and Hatani barely acknowledged Resnick and were sitting in the living room watching soccer on television. The uncle sat in his recliner wearing a white undershirt, flanked by Logan eating potato chips and wearing the same attire. "Thanks, we're good," said Hatani.

Resnick brought the groceries into the kitchen and started to put them away. As he got to the candy bar, he pulled it out of the plastic bag and tossed it to Logan. "Here, kid. Hope you like it."

Logan snatched the Twix out of the air and wasted no time peeling off the wrapper. He handed one of the bars to Hatani, then got up to approach Resnick.

"So, are you going to just hang around here all day?" asked Logan. Hatani hadn't moved from the game, and Resnick was impressed Logan was brave enough to initiate conversation with an FBI agent by himself.

"My partner from the BIA will be here soon. We'll stay out of your way, but we will be right outside. If something is going to happen, I expect it will be at night, so just do whatever you normally would do today."

"That sounds really boring for you," said Logan.

Resnick politely excused himself to go back to his rental car, which now doubled as a command post.

*That kid is right,* thought Resnick. Back to the boredom. Long hours sitting, waiting for something to happen, but hoping it didn't.

Resnick turned his classical music back on as he settled into the driver's seat. He really hated this car, he thought to himself. His six foot four inch frame could barely fit into the seat, even if it was pushed back as far as it could go. The FBI was Resnick's life, but he had rarely left the office over the last twenty-two years. He had never been particularly athletic, and his lack of exercise was catching up to him as he aged.

Over the music he thought he heard a noise. It started as a faint rumble of a motor, then got louder as the noise approached his car. Someone was coming. Resnick unfolded himself out of the cramped seat and passed his hand over the holster under his arm as a matter of habit. He looked over the now open car door and saw a black pickup rumbling up the long drive way. *This has to be Chapa,* he thought.

Resnick walked up to Chapa's driver side window after the large truck parked next to his rental car. Resnick flashed a smile. "Come on in, partner. I will introduce you to the Hatanis."

Chapa followed Resnick into the trailer and Resnick made the introductions as if he was introducing friends at a party. "Guys, this is my partner, Special Agent Chapa. He is law enforcement for the Bureau of Indian Affairs."

The new visitor was not as cheery as Resnick, and Chapa's demeanor remained stern as he exuded authority. Hatani got out of his seat and shook his hand. "Nice to meet you."

"Same here. Thanks for allowing us to stay in your home for a few days," replied Chapa.

Logan stood up and peeked at Chapa's BIA badge hanging around his neck. "Where are you from?" the boy asked.

Resnick expected Chapa to say Washington D.C., but Chapa somehow knew that was not the question being asked by Logan. Chapa's demeanor finally softened. "My mother was Cherokee. I grew up on a reservation in Oklahoma."

Logan's eyes lit up. "My mother is Lakota. She is from Standing Rock, but we moved away when I was very young."

"Looks like we have something in common. We are both from the 'res'," said Chapa, as he moved into the kitchen and eyeballed the sandwich bread. He turned to Hatani and Resnick. "Do you mind if I make a sandwich? I haven't eaten anything in two days."

"Help yourself," said Resnick proudly. "I picked that up for you. I figured you would be hungry when you got here."

Chapa sat down at the kitchen table and made himself two sandwiches and pulled a bottle of soda from the refrigerator. After watching the BIA agent take a couple of bites, Hatani finally came over and sat beside him.

"So how did you and Resnick end up working together? Aren't you in different agencies?"

Chapa looked up at Resnick and he nodded. "We are following a drug gang that has committed crimes on a reservation in New Mexico and crossed the border into Colorado to sell drugs. Started off as my case at the BIA, but once they left the Indian land and crossed state lines it became a federal case."

Hatani listened intently and studied Chapa as he attacked the sandwich. "Seems like a lot of trouble for a gang to come way out here. How would they even know anything about Logan if they are from New Mexico?"

"There are drugs in Cortez just like every other town, and they have to get them from somewhere. They come up here, sell drugs and talk to people in town. We believe they are coming back this weekend and one of our informants says they are looking to kidnap Logan."

Hatani kept up the questions. "Sounds like some really bad folks. What is the name of the gang?"

Chapa slowly finished chewing his sandwich and looked straight into the eyes of Hatani before answering in a calm measured tone, "Local offshoot of the Native Mob. I know you have heard of them. Look—all you need to know is we have to keep an eye on that boy. I did not come all the way out here from Washington to waste your time. I promise you that."

The BIA agent got up and pushed in his chair. "I appreciate the food, but I have some work I need to do in case we get visitors tonight." Chapa walked out of the trailer and back to his pickup without saying another word. Resnick looked on, unsure of what to do next, before finally deciding it was best to follow Chapa out the door.

# Chapter Six

Logan looked down at his phone as he heard the telltale noise of a text message. Wow, he thought as he sat on the couch, I have a signal today.

It was Erica, and she was looking for him. "Want to go to the creek? We stayed in town this weekend."

Logan hastily typed out a message on the phone. He couldn't wait to tell Erica about his visitors and his pulse was pounding with excitement. "Yes! Be there in a few minutes. I have something to tell you."

The teenager jumped out of the couch and ran to his room to find his shoes. As he flew down the cramped hallway, he yelled to Hatani that he was going to the creek on his bike to see his friends.

"I am not sure it is safe," Hatani replied. "You just heard these guys say a gang is looking for you. Check with them first."

Logan's heart sank as he realized that he might not be able to share the crazy events of the last twenty-four hours with Erica like he planned. He quickly located his bicycle and walked it over to Chapa's truck nervously, where the BIA agent was reading over the file again from the meeting in Washington. For some reason, Logan found Chapa intimidating. The BIA agent had an air of authority, and a hard edge. Resnick, however, was different. He didn't *feel* like a cop.

"I am going to the creek to see a friend. Is that OK?" asked Logan. Chapa looked up from his papers without saying a word. The BIA agent stroked his stubbly chin with his hand, thinking about how to respond to the question.

Logan knew the answer was not going to be good, and turned away from Chapa's disapproving gaze.

Resnick heard the conversation and chimed in to break the awkward silence, "Is it a boy friend or a girl friend?"

Logan was embarrassed and answered quickly, "She is a girl, and only a friend."

Chapa finally said, "Tell you what. Leave the bike here and Resnick and I will give you a ride to the creek. Otherwise, no deal."

Logan was not excited about having company on his trip, but then realized that would be the best way to convince Erica he was telling the truth. He wouldn't need to convince her—he would bring her proof.

Resnick opened the door to the passenger side of Chapa's truck and waved Logan into the back seat. Chapa put his files away and backed up quickly, throwing dust in the air as he turned around to drive back towards the highway. After making it to the highway, Chapa followed Logan's directions to the bridge where Erica would be waiting. It was only a five minute drive, and no one said a word.

As they got closer to the creek, Logan saw a familiar brown-haired teenage girl sitting on the rocks with her feet in the water. "I will get out here," said Logan.

"Say hello to your girlfriend for us," cracked Resnick.

"We will be parked on the side of the road so we can see you," said Chapa, as he flashed Resnick a dirty look.

Logan turned red as he jumped out of the pickup and took off in a jog down towards Erica. As he approached her, he saw the puzzled look on her face.

"Who gave you the ride?"

"You are never going to believe it," said Logan. "Those guys in the truck are with the FBI and the Indian police."

Erica laughed. "They are in a Dodge pickup. No way that is the FBI and there is no such thing as Indian Police. Who are they really?"

"They showed me their badges and I think they are the real deal," said Logan. "They told my uncle that some New Mexico drug gang is coming through Cortez and an informant told them they might try to kidnap me."

Erica's tone suddenly went from dismissive to curious. "That sounds like bullcrap to me. So, what is the dynamic duo doing here—just watching you?"

"Basically," said Logan.

As Erica and Logan debated the legitimacy of Resnick and Chapa's credentials out of earshot, the two agents relaxed in Chapa's pickup, brainstorming on the best way to avoid a potential kidnap attempt.

Chapa spoke first. "So, tell me about last night. Did you see anything?"

"Nothing," said Resnick.

Chapa pulled the folder from Washington out of his backpack again and studied it while Resnick chewed on a protein bar from his supply run earlier in the day.

"All of the kidnappings were at night, right?" asked Chapa.

"Yep."

"So, if you were going to take Logan from that trailer at night without anyone hearing you approach, how would you do it?"

Resnick stopped chewing and looked deep in thought. "You could hear a car coming up that road into the valley, so I would ditch my vehicle somewhere by this highway and approach through the woods. They would be exposed as they approached the trailer across that field, but it would be dark and hard to see them unless there was a full moon."

"Agreed," said Chapa. "Any guess as to whether there is a moon tonight?"

"I bet you already know the answer to that question," said Resnick.

"Yes," said Chapa. "Tonight will be cloudy with almost no moon. We need to be ready, and I have a plan."

After Chapa explained his plan, Resnick wondered out loud what these kidnappers would do if they ran into resistance. So far, they had captured their prize every time. Someone who was that good would either turn around at the first sight of a problem to avoid being caught, or have the ability and firepower to achieve the objective at any cost. After agreeing on the plan, Resnick leaned his head back and settled in for a quick nap. He would not be getting much sleep tonight, but at least he wouldn't be in the back seat of that rental car.

As Resnick napped, Chapa rolled down the windows and took a breath of fresh air. He smelled rain, and it gave him a feeling of dread. Chapa normally did not get nervous, but today was different for some reason. He envied Resnick's ability to fall asleep.

A few minutes later, Logan waved at Chapa to come pick him up. Chapa turned the key in the ignition and the pickup fired its engines.

"Can you give Erica a ride home?" asked Logan. "It's looking like rain, and she just has a bicycle."

"Sure. Throw it over the side and get in the back seat," answered Chapa.

Logan strained to throw the bike into the bed of the truck, but refused to ask for help. He finally got it in the truck, and piled into the back seat next to Erica.

Erica smiled at Logan and piped up, "I hear one of you is with the FBI?"

Chapa looked at Logan disapprovingly as if he had shared a secret he was supposed to keep private. "Not me—the guy sleeping to my right is FBI. I am a Special Agent with the Bureau of Indian Affairs."

Erica smiled at Logan again as she sprang her trap. "That's really interesting. By the way, I was wondering what federal department the BIA falls under. Isn't it the Justice Department?"

Chapa laughed out loud. "I like this girl," he said to Logan. "She's smart."

Erica looked flustered that her plan had not worked. She was so sure she would be able to trip up Chapa and expose him as a fraud. Logan looked at her and just shrugged his shoulders.

The sun was already getting low in the sky and Chapa's demeanor turned sharply, after allowing himself the momentary lightheartedness. "By the way, Erica, it is Interior, and I promise you the badge is real. We better get you home. Logan and I have some things we have to do tonight."

# Chapter Seven

Red Moon accelerated his motorcycle as he climbed the steep incline of a hill near Cortez. The gang of *ozuye* followed behind him, ignoring the rain that was soaking their bodies. Red Moon was searching for the landmarks that would lead them to the last piece of the Crow Keeper's plan, but the rain clouds blotted out what little moonlight was available, making it hard to see through the helmet.

Finally, he saw the stream that marked the edge of a valley. In the distance, he could make out a dim porch light marking what he knew would be their target. Time to get off the road, thought Red Moon. The rest of the way would be on foot.

Mato was the first one off the road and walked his bike into the forest for about five minutes to ensure it was not visible.

Adriel carefully hid his own bike and approached Red Moon, making sure to keep his voice low so the others could not hear their conversation. "This is the last one, right?"

"Yes," said Red Moon confidently as he tried to assure Adriel.

"Good. We are a long way from home, and I don't like it," said Adriel.

"Adriel, he is just a boy. It will be over quick as long as we don't wake the uncle." Red Moon knew his friend was nervous. That was just his way.

It was past midnight and the rain had finally slowed down. The thunder and occasional lightning in the distance was still a constant reminder, however, of the storm that had just passed. The group moved confidently through the forest towards the glowing light in the distance, until they could finally see the source—a lone lightbulb. It was not much, but it cast a pale light down the front side of the small trailer, illuminating the front door.

"Have a look around and take care of the light," Red Moon said to Adriel.

Adriel tossed his vest on the ground, and the tattoos immediately shifted on his back and chest. The shadow of a bird jumped off his skin and launched up into the sky with the almost inaudible sound of its wings slicing through the rain. Against the night sky, the shadow bird was invisible as it navigated the strong winds left over from the storm, guided by Adriel from behind the cover of the tree line.

Red Moon watched his friend intently as he appeared to struggle with control of his winged scout in the rain. Adriel momentarily opened his own eyes and glared at Red Moon while he cursed in Lakota.

"I can't see anything up high. I will have to get closer."

After making a quick pass around the trailer, Adriel's bird took a steep dive from the sky, aiming towards the lightbulb hanging by the front door. The fast moving shadow sliced the top of the bulb with its wing as it flew by the door. The top part remained screwed into the fixture and separated cleanly from the bottom of the bulb, which fell towards the ground as the light snuffed out silently. The bird instantly turned in mid-flight and caught the falling bulb with its talons before the damaged piece could hit the ground.

The bird flew into the clouds and back to the edge of the forest before finally dropping its package into Adriel's hand and reclaiming its place in the mosaic of animal art on his back.

"There was no one outside and the white SUV is in the driveway as we expected."

Adriel tossed the object in his hand to Red Moon. "And I took care of the light."

Red Moon calmly discarded the broken lightbulb into the grass and waved to the group. "It's time. Let's go."

The *ozuye* quickly crept across the field away from the cover of the trees towards the trailer. As they converged on the small mobile home, the gang split into two smaller groups without saying a word. Adriel went with Red Moon to the front door, while Mato led a group around the back and took cover by the dilapidated carport, which doubled as a junkyard.

Adriel turned the doorknob on the front door and it pushed inward without any effort. Adriel looked back at Red Moon and smiled at the ease of entry. This would be over quickly.

Once they were inside, Red Moon took the lead as the pair moved through the living area past the kitchen. Red Moon quietly walked down the hallway that spanned the length of the trailer, focused on his objective, sleeping behind one of the two closed doors at the rear. Red Moon opened the door into the first room and quickly determined that the room belonged to the uncle. It was equally obvious that no one was inside.

Red Moon looked at Adriel and he could tell Adriel was thinking the same thing. Something was wrong. *The SUV was out front, so where was the uncle?*

Adriel pulled one of the many small tomahawks out of his belt and twirled it in his fingers nervously as Red Moon opened the door to the last room in the trailer. Red Moon peered in and cautiously stepped over the threshold before looking around for signs of life. It was a small room, barely eight by ten feet in area, and it was clearly a teenager's living space. Clothes were everywhere on the floor, and the bed against the far wall was unmade. On the left was a small closet with two sliding doors on the front, one of which was partly open.

In the dark it was hard to tell if there was someone under the crumpled blankets and pillows, but Red Moon's head was screaming this was a trap. Adriel went left, and Red Moon approached the right side of the bed as Adriel poked the covers with his tomahawk. The blankets collapsed, and it became obvious there was no one in the bed.

The partly open closet door slowly slid open the rest of the way and Resnick poked his Ruger pistol into the back of Adriel. "Sorry, the boy isn't here. Just us FBI agents."

"Kill him," said Adriel in Lakota, turning his body sharply to avoid the knife that immediately flew from Red Moon towards Resnick's gun hand.

Resnick was fast enough to block the knife with the Ruger, but the momentary break of concentration allowed Adriel to leap away across the bed to join Red Moon. Resnick began emptying his pistol as the two raced out the bedroom, interrupting the silence with the unmistakable sounds of gunshots fired in rapid succession. After one of the loud pops, there was the distinctive noise of a bullet hitting flesh and Red Moon quickly realized he had been hit in his side. He dropped one hand instinctively to feel the fast developing bruise, but there was no bullet hole and it did not slow him down as he raced out of the trailer behind Adriel.

Taking advantage of the sudden retreat, Resnick chased the two kidnappers through the trailer, flipping on every switch he saw, bathing the home instantly in light. He was calling for help.

# Chapter Eight

Hatani was sitting in Chapa's pickup looking through binoculars at the trailer when he saw the light go out on the porch. He was parked in the lot of a vacant shop on the highway that Chapa had identified earlier in the day on the way to drop off Erica. From the elevated vantage point, Hatani could see his trailer through binoculars down in the valley. The plan was for Hatani and Logan to stay away all night, in case there was a kidnapping attempt. Chapa also wanted to hide the agents' cars away from the home, and, in the dark, he figured no one would notice anything out of the ordinary about a couple of vehicles parked next to the building.

Logan had fallen asleep hours ago and was lying in the back seat, covered up with a blanket.

"Wake up, Logan," Hatani said quickly as he turned to give the boy a push.

Logan slowly got up from his nap and looked over his uncle's shoulder down into the valley. "I don't see anything," he said.

"Exactly."

Hatani pulled out his phone and texted Chapa and Resnick. "Be ready," he typed. He put the phone back in his pocket and crossed his fingers that one of them would have enough cell reception to get the message. He desperately wanted to be there to learn more about the people responsible for the kidnappings, but he had reluctantly agreed that it simply did not make sense to leave Logan as a sitting duck in that unsecured trailer. They needed to move him away, and Hatani preferred not to let him out of his sight.

Chapa and Resnick agreed to stay behind in case anyone tried to snatch Logan in the middle of the night. They decided that if the agents got into trouble, the best way to signal Hatani was to turn on the lights, which would be visible through the binoculars. The more lights, the more urgent the need for help. Cell service was spotty, and this method was the best idea they had under the circumstances. It was a good plan, thought Hatani.

Hatani continued to scan the distance with the binoculars, but he was too far away to see anything now that the light had gone out on the porch. *Something wasn't right.*

Logan was wide awake and increasingly anxious. "What's going on? Do you see anything?" Hatani ignored him, so Logan looked intently at his phone to keep checking to see if he had any texts from the agents. Nothing.

As Logan kept asking questions, Hatani saw the lights inside the trailer flip on, starting at the bedroom and then spreading throughout the trailer. The place was lit up like Christmas.

Hatani turned to Logan. "I have to go back home."

"But I thought we were supposed to call the cops if the lights turned on?"

Hatani reached over and picked up a shotgun that was laying in the passenger seat. He had been in bar fights on three continents, but never shot a gun at another human being. *Could he do it?*

The adrenaline racing through his body was spiking his heartbeat, and he was torn by a mixture of fear and curiosity about what might be happening right now at his home. It wasn't long before curiosity won the battle in his mind. He had to know, but he also had to find a way to keep Logan safe.

"The Cortez sheriff will take forever to get here. Anyway, I don't need them. I can take care of myself. I don't want to leave you but you can't come with me. I need you to run as fast as you can to Erica's house. It is dark and no one knows to look for you there. Just find a hiding spot near the house and you will be fine. If you don't see me before the sun comes up, knock on their door and ask for help. Do you understand everything I just said?"

Logan was speechless and didn't know what to do. "But that wasn't the plan…"

"Look, I don't trust these agents. I have to go back and see what is going on, but I have to know you are safe."

Logan's hand moved down to open the door then paused and looked back at Hatani. "I don't want to run away. That's my home and I should come, too. I can help."

"I know you can. But if someone down there is looking for you, we have to keep you away. So right now I need you to do what I said. Can you do that for me?"

Logan reluctantly opened the truck door to go out into the rain. "Yes," he said. "I got it." He pulled up his hoodie and made a mad dash behind the building towards the street leading to Erica's house.

Hatani watched as Logan faded into the mixture of rain and darkness. He had made a promise to his brother that if anything happened, he would raise Logan. When that promise was made, he never thought he would actually be called upon to be a parent, and certainly never contemplated having to protect the boy from criminals.

He turned the ignition on the truck and gunned the accelerator as he peeled out of the dirt parking lot and onto the highway. He knew it would only take a few minutes to get back home, but that could be an eternity in a fight. He had to see if what the agents said was true and find out who was looking for Logan.

# Chapter Nine

Hearing the gunshots, Chapa peeked out of his hiding spot in the trunk of the red Mustang parked under the old carport. The sounds of the rain hitting the carport had almost put him to sleep, but the cramped quarters made him just uncomfortable enough to keep him from a deep slumber. Now he was wide awake and he lifted the lid of the trunk just in time to see the lights suddenly turn on inside every room in the trailer. With the benefit of the newfound light, he could also see four men standing guard on the back side of the home. One of them was huge.

Chapa pulled out his Sig Sauer 357 revolver, and carefully climbed out of the tight confines of the Mustang. The men outside were focused on the activity inside the trailer and never noticed him creeping out from the cover of the carport in the dark. "Stay right where you are or I will shoot. I am a Special Agent with the Bureau of Indian Affairs and you are all under arrest."

Once the words came out of his mouth, the gang turned in his direction and Chapa could see that the men had no intention of complying. Mato immediately pulled a short metal rod off a pack on his back and pushed a button. The rod extended into a five foot staff with a sharp point on the end. He next yelled out something in a language Chapa didn't understand and the remaining men ran towards the front of the trailer.

Chapa quickly realized that these kidnappers were not going to give up without a fight, and that the two agents were outnumbered. While his mind was processing the situation, his eyes remained fixed on Mato's spear. As soon as Mato made his move, Chapa's finger squeezed the trigger, firing off three quick rounds. None of the bullets found their mark, and Chapa ducked to the ground as the projectile launched by Mato shot over his head like a rocket. When he looked up, Mato was gone.

Two more gunshots rang out from inside the trailer, signaling that Resnick was still alive. Chapa sprinted from his cover under the carport, up the small set of concrete stairs, and rammed the back door of the mobile home. The old flimsy fiberglass easily buckled under the charge from Chapa, and the agent found himself on the floor, looking up at Resnick at the other end of the hallway.

"Who are these guys?" Resnick shouted from his position near the front door while he reloaded his pistol.

Chapa raced up to Resnick's side, remaining crouched behind the living room furniture along the way. "I don't know, but there are more outside."

At that moment, Chapa heard a familiar noise approaching up the long driveway. The loud rumble of the engine in his truck was now unmistakable.

\*\*\*

Outside the trailer, Red Moon and Adriel had taken cover behind Hatani's SUV as shots rang out behind them from Resnick. The FBI agent peeked around the doorframe as a knife came whistling by his ear thrown from one of the *ozuye* in the dark.

Hatani raced up the driveway in Chapa's truck and his headlights illuminated Mato and his group rounding the front of the trailer.

The pickup slammed to a halt and Hatani left the lights on as he opened the driver side door of the pickup and hid behind it as a shield. He looked around quickly and saw no trace of Chapa and Resnick.

Hatani pumped the shotgun and shot a blast into the air as he stepped out into view of Mato and his group. "Get out of here!" he shouted.

To Hatani's surprise, no one ran away. Instead Mato turned and faced him while clutching what appeared to be a metal spear. There were at least six men now surrounding Mato and they looked and moved like a military unit. *This does not look like any reservation drug gang I have ever seen*, thought Hatani.

Hatani decided that his only chance was to shoot first, so he aimed at Mato and pulled the trigger on the shotgun. Instinctively, Mato jumped to his side and was only sprayed with a few pellets. The giant man closed the distance surprisingly quickly and swung the spear towards Hatani's head. He had no choice but to block the downward swing with the shotgun, which felt like being hit by a freight train. The blow knocked Hatani down onto one knee as he struggled to avoid falling onto his back.

The other *ozuye* closed ranks to cut off Hatani's escape route, but allowed Mato space to handle the fight himself. It was as if they knew better than to interfere. Logan's uncle was strong, but he was no match for Mato. The behemoth kicked Hatani in the side and knocked him to the ground. The impact hurt Hatani and he felt immediate pain in his shoulder, which bore the brunt of the fall as he slid across the wet grass. Through the dirt and rain that now covered his face as he lay on the ground, the realization set in quickly that he had to do something fast or he would be dead within minutes. Luckily, Hatani had somehow held onto the shotgun and he decided to do something crazy. From the ground, Hatani took a random shot at one of the other men watching the fight from a distance. Hatani squeezed off another shot in the general direction of one of the black clad figures and heard a sharp cry denoting a successful hit.

Mato looked to his injured comrade and then turned back to face Hatani. There was now no doubt of Mato's murderous intent. Hatani quickly turned the weapon back towards Mato, but it was too late. Before he could pull the trigger again, Mato swung the spear and knocked the gun out of Hatani's hands. Watching his last line of defense fly off into the rain, Hatani immediately rolled on the ground to get out of range of the vicious blows from Mato, which he expected to rain down on his head at any moment. As he rolled, Hatani's necklace fell out of his shirt and flashed in the moonlight.

The rolling only bought Hatani a few seconds, and instead of hitting him with the spear, Mato lunged forward and grabbed Hatani by the neck so he could choke him. The giant's hands began squeezing the life out of Hatani, but Mato suddenly stopped and stared at what he saw around Hatani's neck. Hatani's necklace had a small black stone on the front with a symbol carved into it with silver etching. The symbol was a bird with outstretched wings to the sky, within an oval circle. Mato clearly recognized something about the stone and was taken aback. Hatani, likewise, was surprised that he was still alive.

"Where did you get that necklace?" bellowed Mato.

Hatani realized in that moment that he was only alive because of the jewelry around his neck and decided to tell the truth. "My sister," he gasped. "She gave this to me before she died."

Mato looked lost in thought for a moment and then gunshots rang out from the front of the trailer from Chapa and Resnick. Mato dropped his victim roughly into the dirt as Chapa called out Hatani's name. The calls went unanswered as the gang ran towards Red Moon and Adriel, leaving Hatani unconscious on the ground.

The *ozuye* gang was now together hiding behind Hatani's truck as bullets from the agents' guns shattered the windows above their hiding spot, raining glass down on their heads. Adriel yelled at Red Moon angrily, "The boy's not here. We must leave!"

Red Moon reached around his back and released two latches on a small carbon fiber bow that had been resting flat across his back. He pulled on the ends and it expanded, making the wire string taut. Red Moon reached down towards his boot and removed an arrow the size of a crossbow bolt that was stored in a ring around his leg that held five more arrows just like the one he removed. As soon as the gunshots stopped, Red Moon stood up and shot an arrow over the hood of the SUV towards one of the headlights on Chapa's pickup. The carbon steel arrow shattered the glass casing and pierced the socket, extinguishing the light. Within seconds, another arrow flew towards the other headlamp and the front of the trailer was again cloaked in total darkness.

Chapa heard the crack of the headlight, followed immediately by another crack before everything went dark outside. Realizing the kidnappers were making an escape, Chapa immediately stepped out the front door and emptied the last few rounds in his gun.

As Chapa ducked behind the door to reload, a whistling noise filled the air and a metal spear flew through the front door, embedding itself deeply in the wall on the far side. Chapa looked at Resnick and he knew they were both thinking the same thing—this was a warning sign against pursuit.

Chapa dropped to the floor, exhausted and silently conceding that chasing the kidnappers in the darkwould be suicide. He looked up at Resnick. "Find Hatani. We have to make sure Logan is safe."

# Chapter Ten

The two agents scanned the ground outside the trailer with their flashlights until they saw a figure slowly getting up off the ground. Logan's uncle was covered in dirt and his arm was scraped and bleeding. There was an ugly red bruise on his neck.

Both Chapa and Resnick raced to Hatani and Chapa helped him get up. "You are tougher than you look," said Chapa.

"Can you walk?" asked Resnick.

Hatani nodded his head affirmatively and they walked back to the front of the home and sat on the ground. After waiting a few seconds for Hatani to collect himself, Chapa began interrogating him. "Where is Logan?"

"He is safer than us right now. He is probably playing on his phone outside that girlfriend's house."

"I hope you're right," said Chapa as he crossed his arms. "Why did you come back yourself instead of calling the police?"

Hatani looked down to avoid Chapa's judgmental stare. "I had to see what was happening myself. He's... my responsibility. I had to do something, and I have never trusted cops."

Resnick was a bundle of nervous energy, still high on the adrenaline from the shootout. He was pacing in front of the trailer, scanning for movement while putting a new clip in his handgun. "Cut the guy some slack, Chapa. We needed the help and it's not over yet. Do you think they are coming back tonight?"

"I don't believe they will be back tonight, but they are still out there and may be watching us to see if we lead them to Logan," said Chapa. "I don't like it, but I think the smart thing is to sit right here until morning and then go pick him up. Some of them are hurt. I know I hit at least one and we will have a much better chance if the fight is in the daylight."

"I shot one, too," said Resnick. "I heard it hit his chest at point blank range, and he didn't even fall down." He put his clip back into his gun with a forceful push from his palm. "Who are these guys?"

"I should be asking you that question," said Hatani. "You lied to me. That was not a bunch of punk kids just rolling through Cortez. Who are they really... and why are they looking for Logan?"

Chapa looked at Resnick and the FBI agent nodded. Chapa paused as if thinking about what to say. "We don't know much and what we do know sounds crazy so we didn't think you would believe it. The part about someone looking for Logan was true. Over the last few months, there have been kidnappings. Most of them have been from reservations around South Dakota. They have been men and women. Old and young. No connection between them other than all of the people who went missing are bloodline descendants from Sitting Bull."

Hatani looked confused at first, then his right hand moved slowly up to his necklace, clutching it tight.

"We told you it sounded crazy," said Resnick.

"No. I believe you," said Hatani quietly as he looked down at his necklace. "And I think I know something about who they are."

Now it was Chapa and Resnick's turn to be confused. "OK. I'll bite. Who are they?" asked Resnick.

Hatani held up his necklace with the symbol of the bird with upstretched wings. "Logan's mother gave me this before she died. I remember she gave one to Graham, too, my brother. It seemed important to her, and it reminded me of my brother, so I've kept it. I honestly didn't think much of it until today, but I think it has something to do with a cult up in South Dakota." As Hatani spoke, Chapa and Resnick leaned in to get a closer look at the necklace in the dim light. "When I was fighting the big guy tonight, he saw my necklace and I saw the same symbol on his vest. He could have killed me but he didn't. That means there is a connection, right?"

Resnick looked confused. "A cult?"

"It was like a religion, I guess, but Graham called it a cult. Logan's mother, Tolulah, never told me much. She was into all of the old stories about power over animals and the spirits. I thought she was just a little weird, but I didn't think anything of it."

Hatani replaced the necklace and was now rubbing the darkening bruise on his neck where Mato had grabbed him. He seemed to be getting frustrated. "I wish I could remember more."

"How did your brother meet Logan's mom?" asked Chapa.

"She met Graham when he traveled to the Standing Rock reservation to preach. They eventually got married and she left the cult to come back with him to New Mexico. I thought it was funny because they both believed so strongly in completely opposite things. He was a Christian who went to church, and she was always dancing with the old women and talking about the native traditions. My brother thought he would convert her, and Tolulah was sure Graham would join her thing."

After several moments of silence, Resnick looked to Chapa. "I am out of my league on this one. What do you think?"

"I don't know what to think, but this is the first connection we have between Logan and this gang." Chapa paused and turned to Hatani. "Is there anyone who could tell us more about this cult?"

"There is a place where someone might be able to help," said Hatani. "After they moved back to New Mexico, my sister would tell me about trips to Mesa Verde with Graham and Logan. The way she talked about the place made no sense because I always thought it was an abandoned ruin, but she talked about meeting friends there and how it was a beautiful city. She called it Anasazi and was always talking about how Graham hated the place but Logan loved it.

"Since my brother hated it, I assume it had something to do with this stuff. I know it is crazy, but I think we should pick Logan up and take him there. It is not far, and I believe we can find it."

Resnick waved at Chapa to step away from Hatani to talk, and they walked together back to Chapa's pickup. "None of this makes sense to me, but I can't stay here forever to protect Logan and no one is going to believe this story if we ask for backup. If we stay here, there is a good chance the commandos come back tomorrow night, or the next night. I don't see a downside to taking a road trip to see if there is a safe place where Logan can hide out. Once Logan is safe, we can get some help and track down the bad guys."

Chapa reluctantly agreed. Staying at the trailer was a bad idea. They needed to get Logan somewhere safe, and if they could accomplish that goal and find a lead on the identity of those who attacked them earlier in the night, that would kill two birds with one stone.

The two agents walked over and sat back down by Hatani. "Looks like we are going to Anasazi," said Chapa. "I hope you know the way."

"I can get us there," replied Hatani, but the shakiness in his voice cast some doubt on his own confidence in the statement.

Chapa sat on the front steps all night next to Hatani, too high on adrenaline to sleep, and constantly scanning the darkness for any sign of movement. As the orange rays of the morning sun finally peeked out over the horizon, a flock of crows took flight from the power line over the trailer.

Hatani had long ago dozed off, and the noise of the crows taking off awakened him and also pulled Resnick out of his peaceful slumber leaning up against a front tire on Chapa's truck.

"It's time to go," said Chapa. He had already removed the arrows from the headlight casings on his truck and was digging through his back seat for duct tape for temporary repairs.

The BIA agent turned to Resnick. "The kid will be hungry, and we have a long drive. Load up some supplies from the trailer and let's get Logan."

# Chapter Eleven

R ed Moon was in pain. The *ozuye* leader gingerly massaged the deep
bruise and swelling near the ribs below his heart. This was not the
first time he had been shot. It hurt—a lot—but the skin was
unbroken. *It would heal*, he thought. *Just like the other ones.*

Two of his companions, however, were not so lucky. They were not
different like Red Moon. They hadn't been changed by the Ghost Dance.

Red Moon had gained favor quickly after joining the Crow Keeper when
he was a teenager in South Dakota. His father was a bully and his mother was
a drunk, leaving him on a collision course with a life of crime like many on
the reservation. Before finding the Crow Keeper, he was a nobody. Now, he
was part of something that would change the world. At first, he thought the
Ghost Dance was just like other religions, lots of talk, where everything had
to be taken on faith. Then, he discovered that the Crow Keeper was different.
His powers were real and those who believed could receive that power, too.
Red Moon was definitely a believer, and so were Adriel and Mato. They had
been through the Ghost Dance and experienced the change first-hand. He
didn't have much patience for those who weren't brave enough to follow in
their footsteps, and he showed it.

Back safely in the woods near their motorcycles, Adriel was dressing a
gunshot wound on one of the men's legs, while another member of the group
tended to one who was pale and barely conscious. The pale one had a nasty
gunshot wound to his stomach that would not stop bleeding.

The band of Lakota had retreated to their hiding place in the forest, but two remained behind at the edge of the woods as scouts to watch the trailer. They were now down to six, and two were seriously injured.

Red Moon covered up his wound with his vest and walked over to the group. "That boy is around here somewhere. The agents will eventually lead us to him. We just have to be patient."

Adriel finished his work wrapping the wound and stood up before speaking. "We are far from home and are low in numbers. Fighting the FBI in the daylight is risky, especially without guns."

This last comment was a sore spot for Red Moon and Adriel knew he had hit a nerve based on the changed expression on Red Moon's face. "Guns are for the weak," said Red Moon. "We are *ozuye*—or have you forgotten?"

"I haven't forgotten," said Adriel before kneeling back down next to the man whose bandage was already soaked in blood. "But these men are not like you or me. They die if they get shot."

Red Moon knew Adriel was right, but the Crow Keeper was not one who would tolerate failure. He shouted at Adriel as he walked away to think: "You know the *Khanji Kipa*. Maybe I will let you tell him that we were beaten by a couple of *wasicu*."

Mato was trying to stay out of the argument, but he knew he had something he needed to share with Red Moon. "The uncle was not a *wasicu*. He had a necklace with the symbol of the Ghost Dance," he said, pointing to the sigil on his shoulder. "They knew we were coming too. Maybe they even know who we are."

"None of that matters now," said Red Moon. "If we bring the boy back to the *Kipa* he will know what to do."

Red Moon knew the sun would be coming up soon and they had to be ready for whatever would happen next. He waited for Adriel to finish supervising the first aid on the injured men, then gathered the remaining *ozuye* and told them to spread out on the roads around the area and search for the boy.

"Mato, Adriel, come with me. We will watch the road to the trailer. They have to come out that way and if they do, they may lead us to him."

Red Moon and his two lieutenants drove out of the forest away from the rest of the group as the sun's first rays peeked out over the trees. He knew Adriel's shadow bird would allow them to watch the road without being seen. The leader of the *ozuye* had never failed the Crow Keeper. He was determined to keep it that way.

# Chapter Twelve

Logan looked at his phone while he lay uncomfortably on the concrete floor of Erica's garage. It was 5:30 am and he was wet and dirty. It would be light soon.

After being hastily kicked out of Chapa's pickup, he ran for almost thirty minutes in the dark, darting quickly between buildings and trees to remain unseen.

Wet and tired, Logan had carefully made his way to Erica's small brick house and found shelter through an unlocked door on the side of the garage. It kept him out of the rain and allowed him to slowly drift off to sleep as he clutched his phone on his chest waiting desperately for word that never came.

It was getting close to dawn, and he had woken up a few minutes earlier, noting the lack of any messages on his phone. Logan couldn't help but wonder whether he would lose his family for a second time, and he got a sinking feeling that he might really be alone for good.

Logan's fear suddenly felt overwhelming and the boy decided that he had waited long enough. He thought about Erica being only a few feet away and desperately wanted to talk to her and get her advice. She would know what to do. He didn't want to call her in the middle of the night in case Hatani came back quickly, but it was now almost morning and he had not heard anything. *Hatani told me to get help in the morning*, he rationalized.

Logan dialed Erica's number on his phone and brought it to his ear. It rang for what seemed like an eternity and then went to voicemail. *She is asleep*, he thought. He tried it again and again, each time letting it ring until voicemail picked up. Finally, Erica answered groggily, "Hello?"

"Erica, it's me. I have been hiding in your garage all night and I really need your help. Something happened and Hatani told me to run to your house. I haven't heard from him all night and I don't know what to do."

"So that gang was really looking for you?"

"I guess."

"It is Sunday so my parents are asleep. I will be outside in a minute. "

After what seemed like an eternity, the side door to the garage opened and Erica's familiar face appeared. It was clear that she had taken the time to fix her hair and put on some makeup, as well as getting fully dressed. She shone the light from her cell phone directly into Logan's eyes. "I'm here," he said.

Logan could tell from her reaction that he must have looked like a crazy person, but he didn't care as he grabbed her and pulled Erica into a deep hug. "Thank you," he said, as the emotions of the whole episode started to well up inside him.

Erica seemed taken aback at the hug, but she awkwardly reciprocated. "You're all wet," she said.

The pair sat down on the floor in the dark and Logan recounted everything that had happened since Chapa had given her a ride home the previous day. Erica listened intently and asked lots of questions—most of which Logan could not answer—until the sunlight finally peeked under the garage door.

"I think we should call the police," Erica said after listening to the story. "We don't know if it is safe for you to go home, and if you stay here, I have to tell my parents what is happening."

As the two debated their next move, the familiar sound of a truck engine rumbled closer to the enclosed garage. The noise stopped moving and Logan heard a vehicle door slamming shut. Logan and Erica tumbled out of the garage to see that the sun had indeed come up and Chapa and Hatani were standing in the driveway.

Hatani ran to Logan and grabbed him in a bear hug. "I'm so happy to see you. We had a tough night."

Logan was happy to see his uncle but was taken aback as he noticed that Hatani looked like he had been in a fight. He glanced at the truck idling in the driveway and noticed that both of Chapa's front headlights were shattered and were being held together with duct tape.

Resnick waved casually from the back seat. "Hey, kid, I'm still here, too," he said.

Erica smiled as she watched the family reunion, but her attention was suddenly drawn to three motorcycles in the distance coming up the road. Remembering Logan's story, she immediately began to get worried. "Look. Someone is coming!" she shouted.

The three riders were now picking up speed as they closed the distance to Erica's driveway. Resnick jumped out of the truck and climbed into the bed to be in a better position to shoot at the approaching motorcycles. Hatani and Chapa quickly piled into the front seat and Hatani yelled at Logan, "Come on!"

Logan grabbed Erica's hand. "Stay here! I have to go."

"No way," she said, as she followed Logan into the back seat of Chapa's pickup. The truck was already backing out of the driveway when the two teenagers closed the door. The three motorcycles were now only a block away.

"Dammit," said Chapa as he saw Erica pile into the back seat with Logan. "You really should have stayed at home."

"I wasn't going to stand out there by myself!" she shouted.

Chapa spun the truck around and sped off down the road towards the highway. Logan wasn't exactly sure where he was going but it was clear Chapa was determined to get away from civilization and head towards the mountains.

"How did they find us?" yelled Hatani.

"I don't know. We drove in circles for half an hour before coming here. I was sure we didn't have a tail."

Chapa continued. "Hatani—I need you to navigate. We need to get to Anasazi now."

The truck was not built for speed, but it had unexpected power for such a large vehicle. Chapa looked at the rearview mirror and noticed that the three motorcycles were nonetheless slowly gaining on them.

"Logan, open up that back window so I can talk to Resnick."

Logan followed the directions and the sliding window opened, immediately filling the cabin with the sound of rushing wind. Resnick peeked his head in the cab. "Is that as fast as this thing can go?"

"I have a present for you, Resnick," yelled Chapa. "Logan, get off the seat and pick up the cushion."

Logan and Erica maneuvered off the seat so Logan could pick it up, and the boy's eyes widened as he saw a cache of weapons and supplies. "What do you want me to give Resnick?" he asked loudly over the sound of the wind.

"Give him the rifle," Chapa replied.

Logan pulled a 30-06 rifle out of the compartment under the bench seat and handed it through the window to Resnick. Without being asked, Erica searched the compartment quickly and found a box of ammunition and passed it through the window. Logan looked surprised that she could spot the right box.

Hatani pointed to a sign up ahead noting a turn towards Mesa Verde National Park. "Turn here," he said.

Chapa made a sharp turn onto the highway leading away from the town and into the mountains. He looked into the mirror and saw that the three riders took the turn and were still gaining. The road ahead was a series of winding switchbacks climbing towards the higher elevation, which would make it difficult to increase speed.

Resnick had already loaded the rifle and was calmly kneeling at the back of the pickup's bed. He carefully examined the rifle's mechanisms and rested the barrel on the back of the gate. The agent took a couple of deep breaths and sighted in the riders who were following in pursuit. The motorcycles went in and out of sight as the truck flew around the sharp turns on the highway and over the bumps in the road. Resnick waited patiently, using his strength to keep the rifle steady until he could hit a straight away with enough time to take a shot.

Red Moon was in the front of the pack with Mato and Adriel flanking behind him on each side. He pressed his motorcycle to speed through the increasingly sharp turns, when a shot rang out and a bullet from Resnick's rifle hit his front tire. The spokes on the front wheel shattered, momentarily causing Red Moon to lose control. The motorcycle swerved erratically until Red Moon pulled up the damaged front wheel of the motorcycle so only the rear wheel remained on the ground. Riding on one wheel, Red Moon waved up Adriel and jumped onto his motorcycle as he let go of the damaged bike. The riderless vehicle raced off the side of the road and crashed into the ravine below.

Erica yelled out encouragement. "Good shot!"

Emboldened by his success, the FBI agent reloaded and refocused his marksmanship skills on the remaining two pursuers.

The next shot from Resnick's rifle narrowly missed Mato who was now in the lead. Logan was watching the action intently, trying to think of a way to somehow help the FBI agent.

Red Moon barked out orders in Lakota and Adriel pulled up beside Mato. The *ozuye* leader leaned over to take the handlebars of Mato's bike as the two slowed down in unison.

In a fluid motion, Mato rose off the seat of his motorcycle, grabbed a metal rod off a latch on his back and clicked a button on the handle. The metal rod extended, and the spear tip jutted out from the end. The big man reached back and launched the spear before the truck could turn a corner and escape the danger.

Chapa never saw the projectile coming because he was watching the turns. Resnick flattened himself into the bed of the truck just in time to avoid the spear. The FBI agent managed to yell, "Get down!" but his words were hard to hear over the sound of the wind.

Logan saw the spear and immediately pushed Erica down towards the floor of the back seat. Hatani didn't hear Resnick's warning over the sound of the wind and never saw the spear as it passed through the back window like a bullet and landed with a thud in the back of his seat. Hatani immediately felt an excruciating pain on his left side and looked down to see that the spear had gone cleanly through the seat and was now lodged in his lower back. He unsuccessfully tried to pull his body off the spear, which prompted a primal scream unlike anything Logan had ever heard from his uncle. Logan remained shell-shocked at the sight of the growing bloodstain on his uncle's shirt, while

Erica pulled on the spear from the back, finally dislodging it from his uncle's body.

Chapa looked over at Hatani then quickly refocused his attention on the road. "Logan, I need you to look in that seat and find something to help Resnick. We need to get away from these guys now or your uncle is not going to make it."

Erica picked up the back seat to help Logan look again for something helpful. *There has to be something else in here we can use*, thought Logan. Erica excitedly pointed to several cans of motor oil and shouted "Oil slick!"

Logan grabbed the oil and threw it out the back window into the bed of the truck and shouted at Resnick. Resnick wasn't paying attention as he prepared to take another shot on the two remaining riders who were again approaching quickly.

After looking back at Erica, Logan decided that he had to do this himself. He climbed through the open window and flopped awkwardly into the bed, hitting his elbow with a thud on the metal floor as he landed. Logan fought through the momentary jolt of pain, and quickly grabbed the two containers of oil and started unscrewing the lids.

Resnick took another shot at Mato, but a last minute turn by Chapa caused the bullet to narrowly miss and hit the pavement. Resnick heard a noise behind him and turned to see Logan crawling through the bed of the truck with the cans of motor oil in his hands. He nodded at Logan approvingly and said, "Nice thought, but I have a better idea. Tell the girl to find a lighter."

He next put a hand in his pocket and handed Logan his knife. "Put the top back on and cut off the bottom. We want it to spill quickly all over the road."

Logan went to work cutting up the oil containers and oil started to spill on him every time the truck rounded a corner. Pretty soon, his hands were covered with motor oil, and he began getting nervous at the prospect of Resnick using a lighter.

Resnick turned to look for the next corner, before yelling, "Get ready" to Logan.

He pulled out the lighter Erica had found in Chapa's cache and kneeled forward with the rifle on his knees. Resnick started shooting wildly towards the trailing motorcycles, hoping to distract them and slow them down.

As Chapa made the next sharp turn, the side of the mountain momentarily blocked the view from the riders. "Now!" said Resnick.

Logan leaned over the back of the pickup and turned over the bottles in both his hands releasing a fountain of motor oil to gush out over the road. He ducked back down as Resnick clicked the lighter and threw it at the growing oil slick.

Mato was the first to see the fire, but it was too late. His motorcycle went through the fiery liquid and immediately swerved uncontrollably as he hit the brakes. Adriel saw Mato slide, but he was moving too fast to avoid the same fate. Red Moon jumped off the bike and rolled across the pavement towards the rocky wall carved out of the mountain. The road didn't have guard rails, and Adriel's motorcycle slid right off the road and plunged down the cliff side, smashing into the rocks.

Logan watched the fiery wreck over the back gate of the truck, but he quickly lost direct line of sight once the truck rounded the next corner. He sat next to Resnick as the truck climbed the winding road into the mountains, catching an occasional glimpse of smoke marking the accident scene. Resnick never said a word, keeping the rifle ready, looking for some sign they were still being followed. Once he was sure the riders were gone, he put his hand on Logan's shoulder and smiled as he turned his back and slumped down in the bed of the truck.

The feeling of celebration was short-lived for Logan, and he immediately turned his attention back to his uncle. He carefully made his way back to the sliding window and squeezed into the back seat so he could check on Hatani.

# Chapter Thirteen

It took a while for Chapa to slow down and feel comfortable they were no longer being followed. Logan had pulled the spear completely out of the seat, and Hatani had covered his wound with a bandage from Chapa's glovebox. Hatani was hurt badly, but he would survive.

They were getting closer to Mesa Verde and still had no idea how to find Anasazi. Hatani turned and looked at Logan. "We need your help. Do you remember Anasazi? Your mother took you there when you were young. She told me something about a beautiful city in the canyons near Mesa Verde National Park."

Logan closed his eyes and fought back the urge to cry. It had been a long time since he thought about his mother and father. He struggled to remember his mother's face, but it was a fleeting memory that made him wonder how much was real and how much was his imagination. He opened his eyes just in time to see a large rocky tower on the ridgeline of the mountain ahead. "Hey, that's Chimney Top," he said casually.

Everyone looked in surprise at Logan. "What is Chimney Top?" asked Erica.

"That's the way," said Logan confidently. "I used to love saying that word. I remember my mother laughing at me as I would shout 'Chimney Top, Chimney Top' when we drove up this way in the car." Logan smiled as he finally wrapped his mind around a memory of his mother.

Chapa saw the cutoff ahead that led towards the mountain ridge, and he turned onto the dirt road. It soon ended at the top of the ridge and a large iron gate that said "No Trespassing. Area Managed by Bureau of Indian

Affairs. Violators will be Prosecuted."

Logan remained convinced they were on the right path, so the group left Chapa's truck behind, and they continued on foot up the dirt road towards what looked like the ruins of an ancient stone city. Logan walked ahead with Erica while Chapa kept Hatani at his side. "You doing OK?" Chapa asked, looking down at the blood on his bandage.

"It hurts, but I will be fine," Hatani replied.

Erica reached over and grabbed Logan's hand, which immediately set off alarm bells in Logan's head. *Was she scared? Or maybe excited?* She didn't say anything so Logan kept quiet as well. After the dangerous events on the road, he was worried that she would be angry at him for getting her involved in this mess. How could he say that he was glad she was here with him? He figured the safest thing to do was just not say anything at all.

Resnick followed behind them all, still carrying the loaded rifle at his side. He had made clear that, based on the last few days, there was no way he was leaving it behind at the truck.

They reached the end of the road at the top of the ridge and the ruins of an old stone tower finally came into full sight. It was about fifty feet high at its tallest, but part of it had fallen down over the years. The inside of the tower was open to the elements and there was a large room that had been weathered and overgrown in places by grass. The tower was connected to a larger set of ruins containing multiple structures, many of which had nothing left but partial walls made of crumbling stone.

"There is nothing here," said Resnick as he looked around. "This is just part of the national park. There has not been anyone here but tourists for hundreds of years."

Logan looked determined as he scanned the ruins for something that looked familiar to him. His eyes settled on a round structure that looked newer than the rest of the ruins. "There," he said, pointing to the outline of a circular structure jutting out of the ground ahead. Logan ran past the tower, with Erica on his heels.

Hatani saw the structure identified by Logan and turned to Chapa and Resnick. "I think it is a Kiva."

"What the heck is a Kiva?" asked Resnick.

"It is an underground room where the Navajo and other tribes in this area gathered for ceremonies. Kind of like a theater with a fire in the middle and a hole up top for the smoke to escape."

Logan was on the move again as he climbed down a ladder into the giant underground arena. The rest of the group followed, straining to see as their eyes slowly adjusted from the bright sunlight outside to the underground chamber lit only by the sunlight seeping in from the hole in the roof.

Unlike the rest of the ruins at Chimney Top, this underground Kiva looked much newer and well kept. There was a level below the ground that circled around the Kiva like the mezzanine of a baseball stadium, with six stone stairways leading down from the mezzanine level to the bottom floor. All of the stone floors were clean and the craftsmanship of the rock walls looked light years ahead of the old crumbling construction outside. There were decorative figures of animals carved into what appeared to be murals along the ceiling and walls of the mezzanine level.

In the middle of the bottom floor was a large fire ring made of stone, but inside the outer stone ring was a liner made of gleaming silver metal. Other than the ladder up to the ruins of Chimney Top, there appeared to be only one other way out of the Kiva—a hallway at the far end of the bottom floor of the circular structure.

The group made their way down and gathered around the fire ring on the bottom floor of the Kiva. Logan stared at the hallway as if digging deep into his memory bank. "I think… I think it's that way," he said slowly.

Erica asked, "Are you sure? It looks dark."

Almost on cue, the Kiva momentarily plunged into darkness as a sliding door sealed off the upper entrance, cutting off any traces of sunlight. A fire erupted in the middle of the Kiva, causing everyone to step back to avoid the flames. Out of the darkness of the hallway across the floor, a tall figure stepped into the Kiva. He was immediately followed by a group of men in brown uniforms who assumed positions around the circular floor to block all of the stairways leading up to ground level. They were trapped.

"Who are you, and why are you here?" the man asked calmly but firmly as he approached the group. Logan looked at the man and he somehow looked familiar. He had short cropped gray hair and a cane with the head of a horse carved in silver on the top. Based on his formal attire, he could pass for a business executive, but his style was certainly unique. The suit was a dark maroon color and the coat went down almost to his knees. Beaded bracelets circled one of his wrists and he had an earring in one ear. A long draping necklace hung from his neck on top of his dark shirt.

Logan stepped forward without fear. "My name is Logan Iyotake Hatani. I came here with my mother Tolulah Hatani years ago, but now she is dead. My uncle and I have come because we have nowhere else to go and we need help."

Hatani stepped up beside Logan. "Tolulah gave me this necklace before she died and I saw the same symbol on some men who tried to kill us today. They are trying to take Logan and we need help. We had nowhere else to go." Hatani removed his necklace and held it up near the fire. The etched symbol of the soaring bird was illuminated in the light of the flames and the outline seemed to glow red in the light.

The man stepped forward and smiled. "Tolulah Hatani and little Logan. It has been a long time since I have heard those names. I am glad you found this place again, and rest assured you will be safe within Anasazi. Please follow me."

Chapa looked at Resnick and breathed out a sigh of relief. Erica ran up to catch Logan as they all merged into a single file to enter the hallway at the end of the Kiva. The group walked quietly down the dark passage, lit only by torches on the walls. As they walked through the corridor built underneath the ground, they rounded a corner and their view opened up into a bright plaza. Logan's eyes had to adjust again, this time from the darkness to the glare of the sun, except it was not sunlight and they were not outside. Instead, the sunlight was reflecting off the white stones of a city built directly into the mountain. Every inch of the city, including the streets, seemed to glitter in the light as if the stones were lined with gold.

"It's true. Everything Tolulah said was true," whispered Hatani.

Logan looked on in amazement at the sight of the golden city, and somewhere in the recesses of his mind, it looked familiar. The light entered through hidden openings in the rock cliffs surrounding the edges of the city, and was magnified and reflected by the crystalline nature of the stones. For those inside the city, it was if they were standing in direct sunlight, yet they were hidden underground. Like the much smaller structures in the nearby National Park, the buildings were carved out of the rock walls and were built in all shapes and sizes. The entire city was interconnected in a maze of structures that fit into an open cavern that was at least one hundred feet high. Not surprisingly, the architecture was dominated by Adobe styled structures favored by the Navajo in the area, but there were notable exceptions. A classic fountain served as a centerpiece in a Spanish style plaza and some taller buildings incorporated ornate metal and glass into their design. It was as if thousands of years of architecture were mixed together in one place.

The man who greeted them in the Kiva waved at the golden city with his cane. "Welcome to Anasazi—one of the four remaining ancient cities in North America."

# Chapter Fourteen

Logan looked around as the group entered the streets of Anasazi, and he saw men and women of all ages walking casually through the city. It was a familiar place in his memory, yet somehow unlike anything he had ever experienced. Logan had seen traditional Native American clothing in pictures and videos, but never anything like what he saw in Anasazi. This was modern. The colors were breathtaking, and every outfit was different. Some of the men and women had feathers in their hair. The women had ornate jewelry of all types and carried colorful purses and pouches. Many of the men wore suits like the man who greeted them in the Kiva, and some had hats of all colors and sizes.

Something else also stood out to Logan. He was not an expert on Native American tribes, but he immediately noticed the diversity of the occupants of Anasazi. He recognized the look of the local people in New Mexico and Colorado. Some of the men and women, however, were taller and had lighter complexions. They looked like what Logan had imagined when he thought of his mother's people, the Lakota, and other northern tribes.

At that moment, a couple of young girls in white dresses walked by and began pointing at the group. The mother grabbed the girls' hands tightly and pushed them away. She said something to the girls in a language Logan didn't understand and they giggled. As the girls melted into the crowd in the plaza, Logan noticed that one kept turning around and staring at Erica. He could only imagine the spectacle created by their entrance.

Behind them, the guards from the Kiva materialized from the corridor and

Logan could now make out the details of their uniforms. They all wore a leather band around their head, but, unlike everyone else in Anasazi, they looked like they would blend into the outside world. They had loose fitting button down shirts and pants that were a dark brown color, and were wearing tactical boots. They easily could have passed for members of the park service. None of them had guns, but they all appeared to have knives and other tools on their belts.

One of the guards had a distinct red band around his head and strode quickly past the group to catch up to the man who had welcomed them in the Kiva. "This way," he said, pointing to a stone staircase leading up to the second story of a building carved into the rock wall of the cavern. It had a round domed ceiling made of a mud and hay mixture.

The group arrived into a large central room with wooden beams circling the ceiling and smaller rooms connected in every direction. There were several antique chairs in what appeared to be a living room and a few stone benches against the walls. Bookcases lined the room, filled with not only books, but objects of all shapes and sizes. There were stuffed birds and animal heads on the walls. "Please sit down," said the man with the red headband.

Logan, Hatani and Erica sat down on the chairs and made themselves comfortable. Resnick took a seat on a stone bench off to one side, while Chapa remained standing.

The gray-haired man entered the room hastily, but with a smile. "My name is Zuma," said the figure from the Kiva. "I am the Caretaker of Anasazi."

"This is Kinzi," he said, pointing to the man with the red headband. "He is the head of the Anasazi Guard."

Chapa spoke up first. "My name is Keaton Chapa and I am a Special Agent with the Bureau of Indian Affairs. This is Special Agent Resnick and we were working on an investigation into a pattern of kidnappings of men and women that were the living descendants of Sitting Bull. That investigation led us to believe Logan might be next, so we came to Cortez to protect him and ran into a gang last night. They almost killed us, and Hatani—Logan's uncle—is hurt. We need to get him medical attention and leave Logan somewhere safe so Resnick and I can track down the ones responsible for the attack."

Zuma seemed unsurprised by the bizarre story, and instead turned to Hatani. "You mentioned a necklace in the Kiva. Tell me about the symbol on the necklace," asked Zuma. "Where else did you see it?"

Everyone looked at Hatani, and he seemed embarrassed by the sudden attention. "The men who attacked us had the same symbol on their vests. When one of them saw the symbol on my necklace, he stopped fighting. He could have killed me, but he didn't. That's all I know."

Kinzi looked at Zuma nervously, then crossed his arms.

Zuma nodded affirmatively, as if they were having their own private conversation. "I believe these men are followers of a cult that is trying to resurrect the Ghost Dance, a religious movement that has been dead for over a hundred years."

"Ghost Dance. That's what Logan's mother called it, too," recalled Hatani.

"She did not believe in the same things as these men," said Zuma. "Tolulah loved the culture and traditions of her people. The Ghost Dance is a part of that culture and one that she explored like everything else, but you have to understand she was looking for the good in a power that has been used too many times for evil."

"So, this is all about some type of magic?" asked Resnick.

"You can call it that if you like," said Zuma. "Many of our people have found ways to connect with the spirit world and to gain insight or strength from their ancestors. Some by design, and some by luck. But this power was not intended to be used for war. When war came to our people over a century ago, many of us decided that the only way to coexist in peace was to go into hiding. Others believed the Ghost Dance would bring back the spirits of their ancestors and provide power to defeat their enemies in battle."

Zuma waved his cane around for dramatic effect. "Initially, the Ghost Dance was successful as Sitting Bull and Crazy Horse won a great victory at Little Big Horn. But, as we knew would happen, these victories only steeled the resolve against our people, and hundreds of innocent men, women and children were massacred in retaliation. The Ghost Dance was declared illegal, and everyone who pursued its power was hunted down and killed, including Sitting Bull."

"But what does that have to do with Logan?" asked Chapa impatiently.

"Sitting Bull was a war chief, not a medicine man. The Ghost Dance was started by a powerful Paiute shaman named Wovoka. Before Tolulah died, she told me something that I did not believe at the time. She told me that a new Lakota shaman had somehow discovered Wovoka's secret and was building a new following. They called him the Crow Keeper."

Logan was now confused and angry that his mother might somehow be at fault for the attack. "My mother… was a member of this cult that is trying to kidnap me?"

Zuma looked at Logan and answered with the compassion of a father talking to a son. "No! She left South Dakota and came here to keep you safe. No one, including me, believed her stories about the Ghost Dance. Shortly after your mother moved here, she was killed along with your father in a crash in the mountains. I never saw you again."

He put his hand on Logan's shoulder and squeezed tightly. "You should know that your parents loved you very much. I am sorry they are gone, but you and your friends will be safe now at Anasazi."

Zuma looked back at the group. "This is your hogan, or house. You can get clean and change clothes. You will find bedrooms off this central room, and I will send someone to tend to Hatani's wounds."

As the mysterious man in the suit walked towards the door to exit, he paused at Resnick's bench. "I would like the two of you to speak privately with Kinzi. Please tell him everything you know about the men who attacked you last night. In exchange, he will do what he can to help with your investigation."

Chapa hesitated, unsure whether it was a good idea to leave Logan alone in a new place. Sensing his hesitance, Zuma pointed at the guards outside the Hogan. "I assure you Logan is quite safe under our Guard's protection."

While Chapa and Resnick considered Zuma's request, Erica turned to Logan with a sudden look of worry on her face. "I have to call my mom. She is going to freak out when she wakes up and discovers I am gone."

Logan pulled out his phone and saw the familiar but dreaded words, "No service."

"You can't call her from here. Phones don't work."

Erica, of course, insisted on checking her own phone and quickly confirmed the same result. She sat down dejectedly in one of the antique chairs, contemplating her predicament in silence. A few seconds passed before her face suddenly brightened. "You know, this is the first time I have actually been on my own away from my parents. As crazy as it sounds, I think this is kind of exciting."

# Chapter Fifteen

An old man in a black wide brimmed hat walked slowly out from the cave entrance into the early morning sunlight. He had many names, but he no longer used his birth name. Over time, he had acquired a different one. *Khanji Kipa.* The Crow Keeper. Of course, he knew the name was not flattering, but it generated fear. Fear was a tool the Crow Keeper found helpful.

He walked over to the cages filled with crows outside his home. It was a bizarre bird sanctuary, with home-made wooden cages of all shapes and sizes strung together and connected, housing hundreds of black birds. Some of the cages were so big that a person could walk inside, while others were small and housed a single bird. Crows were coming and going from the cages that were open to the sky outside the cave, and the scene had the hustle and bustle of a busy airport.

The Crow Keeper walked around the cages throwing food on the ground for the birds to eat. As he methodically made his rounds, he put his ear up to the cages and the birds seemed to be whispering to him. Sometimes he would whisper back something into the openings on the side of their heads, or scratch the neck of a crow. Tending to all of the cages would take hours of his time each day, but the man never hurried his work. It was the most important part of his morning, and he never altered his routine.

They were more than just his pets. The crows were a spy network, ranging far and wide, always watching and reporting back to their keeper.

The old man stopped at one of the large black birds who had just arrived at the network of cages. He bent over into the cage listening to the noises from the old bird. The Crow Keeper's dark weathered face contorted into an angry frown at whatever news was being conveyed by the feathered messenger.

The Crow Keeper finished his walk through the maze of bird cages, refilling his small pot with feed multiple times along the way. The sun was now even higher in the sky, and it was getting warm.

He turned his old body and slowly walked back into the cave where the temperature almost immediately began to drop. The naturally chilled cave had now been the Crow Keeper's home for decades, making the heat of the day unbearable in large doses.

The old shaman shuffled down the gravelly path, which eventually turned into a floor made of stone. Soon, the sunlight was no longer helpful in illuminating the path and the Crow Keeper picked up an old gas lamp and carried it the rest of the way down into the cold damp lair.

The Crow Keeper made his way into a larger part of the cave where there was a fire burning in the middle of the naturally carved-out space. The smoke drifted up to the ceiling and out of the cave through an unseen natural chimney. There were stalactites hanging from the ceiling and the drip of water occasionally broke the silence.

In one corner was a large cage like the ones keeping the crows outside. This one, however, was made of metal and had people inside. As the old man came into view, a few women started screaming and crying for help. The Crow Keeper threw bread and some dried meat into the cage and passed a pan of water through an opening at the bottom near the rocky floor. He ignored their cries and instead sang songs to himself in Lakota to drown out their screams. The people in the cages seemed terrified of his haunting voice, and several began sobbing uncontrollably as if a loved one had died.

Ignoring the jailed men and women, the Crow Keeper sat down on a blanket draped across a rock next to the fire and filled his pipe. He puffed on the pipe and stared into the flames. He knew Red Moon and his band of *ozuye* warriors had failed to capture the last one he needed for the upcoming Ghost Dance. The boy had help and they were now in Anasazi. The *ozuye* were on their way back to South Dakota and would not be able to overpower the defenses of Zuma's city. *It was now time for a different approach,* he thought. *I must make the boy come to me.*

The old shaman puffed on the pipe and dreamed of the possibility that Sitting Bull would soon join him in his fight. *This time it will be different,* he thought. *The world is different.*

This time, they would have the element of surprise. If he successfully brought back Sitting Bull, the word *would* spread and followers *would* flock to his movement. The Crow Keeper already had hundreds who were living in the compound outside the cave, and the number seemed to grow bigger every day. The followers of the Ghost Dance will soon be too strong to be defeated again. *This time, it will be different.*

# Chapter Sixteen

C hapa was initially hesitant to let Logan out of his sight again, but after some convincing from Kinzi, and seeing that Hatani was now getting medical attention, he finally agreed. The two agents quietly followed Kinzi to another building across the city, still in awe at the sights and sounds around every corner.

Kinzi finally stopped at a stone structure, like the others, built directly into the rocky walls of the mountain cavern. This part of the city, however, was closer to the outside world. They could now hear birds chirping as they walked up a stone staircase and entered the headquarters of the Anasazi Guard. Chapa watched as men and women came and went from the building, all wearing a head band like Kinzi and the other guards they saw in the Kiva. Unlike the ones at the Kiva, Chapa observed that some guards in the headquarters wore sidearms on their belts.

The pair followed Kinzi up even more stairs to a tower where guards watched over the city streets, and protected a staircase carved into cliff walls that appeared to go down into a canyon. Chapa bent over, out of breath at climbing the stairs, and used the momentary break to look out into the canyon. A faint sparkling barrier disrupted his view. He reached his hand out to touch the glimmering curtain, and it went right through the barrier without any noticeable effect.

Kinzi led the pair into an office at the top of the tower and sat down behind a desk with a stone top. He pointed in front of him and Chapa and Resnick sat down on wooden chairs with decorative cushions that turned out to be surprisingly comfortable. Chapa couldn't help but take in the surroundings and quickly surveyed the walls. Hanging behind Kinzi was an ornately carved spear with bright stripes painted on the handle. A circular shield made of stretched leather hung on the other side of the room. Both Chapa and Resnick felt at ease as they realized Kinzi and his guards were the closest thing the city had to law enforcement. He was one of them.

Chapa spoke up first and recounted the basic facts of the investigation into the kidnappings, including the attack at the trailer, and the chase on the highway. Kinzi listened intently, asking a few questions along the way. The head of the Anasazi Guard was professional, and never interrupted.

After Chapa finished his account, Resnick finally cut to the chase and asked the question that had been bothering him all day. "So, what the hell is actually going on here? Are we really dealing with hidden ancient cities and Indian commandos? I can't report that back to the FBI."

Kinzi smiled reassuringly at them. "Relax. Your government already knows about us. Most of us come and go from Anasazi and the outside world all the time. Hell, I served in the Army for twelve years before coming back to the Navajo Nation, and most of my Guard are former military. The outside world doesn't bother us and we don't bother them. The barrier you saw prevents outsiders and satellites from seeing past the edge of our city, and if anyone touches it, like Chapa did, we will know about it instantly."

Kinzi looked right at Chapa. "We have an arrangement with the Bureau of Indian Affairs at the highest level. They keep curious tourists away from places like Anasazi, and we peacefully turn away the few who are curious or make a wrong turn and end up on our doorstep. I promise you—anything you report about us will be covered up, just like UFOs being covered up as weather balloons."

Chapa was losing patience with the talk about politics. "Look, I don't care about your city. I just want to stop whoever is trying to kidnap Logan, and hopefully rescue the ones who have already been taken."

Kinzi leaned forward in his chair. "You have to understand that this is bigger than Logan. There is so much more to the situation than what you know. There has always been a battle for the hearts and minds of the tribal nations. The ones who attacked you want to start a revolution and retake what was lost. Here in Anasazi, we only fight to protect our peaceful but secret coexistence. We are two sides of the same coin, with the only difference being tactics. For those who have remained true to the old ways, they have to pick a side, and I fear a war is coming."

As Kinzi talked about war, his demeanor hardened. The casual conversation had quickly taken a serious turn, and Chapa wondered whether Anasazi was really the safe haven it had initially appeared to be when they first arrived. His thoughts returned to Logan, who was alone in the city without protection.

Chapa and Resnick exchanged worried glances. "Look, I don't know anything about a war," said Chapa. "I have a case I need to solve, and we can't stay here long. Can you tell us where those men who attacked us came from?"

"They are from South Dakota, and they call themselves the *ozuye*," said Kinzi. "That is all we know."

"What about this cult and the medicine man Zuma mentioned," said Resnick. "How do we find them?"

Kinzi stood up from behind the desk signaling an end to the conversation. "You will have to follow the trail back to South Dakota. That is all the help I can provide."

Chapa looked at Kinzi suspiciously and Resnick waited to see if his partner would press harder for answers. This was the reason Chapa was here—to deal with tribal officials like Kinzi.

"Thanks," said Chapa, deciding against offending their host with more questions. "We will leave in the morning and take the others with us."

"Do what you like," said Kinzi. "But the safest place for Logan right now is in Anasazi. The *ozuye* will not attack this city."

As they walked out of Kinzi's office, Resnick leaned over to Chapa. "Did you hear what he said? If these secret Indian cities of gold are real, and being covered up by the government, that means UFOs are real, too, right?"

Chapa couldn't help but laugh and Resnick soon followed. It felt good after the tumultuous events in the last twenty-four hours.

# Chapter Seventeen

After eating lunch, Hatani was quickly snoring peacefully in a bed off the main room in their hogan. Zuma had sent a woman who rubbed a salve on his wound, before bandaging it up and giving him some medicine to help him sleep. Logan and Erica took advantage of the opportunity to finally have a private moment and walked out of the house onto a balcony that overlooked the narrow stone-laced street below. This was the first time they had been alone since the attack that morning.

"So, are you really thinking about staying here?" asked Erica.

"Yeah, for now," said Logan. "Seems like the smart thing to do. I can't have people risking their lives to protect me out there. Hatani almost died getting me here safely."

"This place is beautiful," said Erica, nodding her head affirmatively. "Too bad, no one will believe me if I tell them about it when I get back. They will think you and I ran off together or something weird."

"I heard Chapa and Resnick say they were going to take you back tomorrow. Hopefully, they can come up with a story for your parents. They seem to be good at that."

As they people-watched on the street below, they saw Zuma walking purposefully towards their building. Walking by his side was a teenage girl with long curly red hair that extended down her back. The first thing the teenagers noticed about the girl, however, was a large bird perched on her shoulder. The bird had a beautiful white underbelly with brown feathers on its back and wings. A bright yellow beak constantly darted in every direction, taking in the stimulus of the crowd. It seemed remarkably well-behaved and was not leashed or restrained in any way.

Zuma and the red-headed girl turned to walk up the stairs and Zuma saw Logan and Erica watching from the balcony as they approached.

"Hello again," he said as he neared their balcony. "This is my daughter Tia," Zuma added, as he put his hand on the girl's shoulder. "She was dying to meet you because we don't get a lot of outsiders her age visiting our city."

"I'm Logan and this is my friend Erica," volunteered Logan as he shook her hand.

"*Ya-at-eeh*," said Tia warmly. "That means hello in Navajo."

Erica gave it a try, fumbling the pronunciation of the greeting. "Ya—tee."

After a moment of awkward silence, Erica pointed at the bird on Tia's shoulder. "What is the bird's name?"

Tia smiled from ear to ear at the prospect of talking about her bird. "Her name is Jini and she is a falcon. I have had her since she was a baby."

Almost on cue, the bird shrieked loudly, startling Erica as Tia rubbed her stomach. Logan laughed, "I think he likes you."

Zuma cleared his throat. "You will all have plenty of time to get to know each other tonight. The reason I came back is to invite you and your companions to dinner at the Kiva. It is tradition for all of the tribes in the City to gather together for a meal and short ceremony before nightfall."

"Yes, please come!" added Tia excitedly. "You can sit with us."

Logan looked at Erica. "We have nowhere else to be. I think we can make it."

Erica just shrugged. "Sure."

"It's settled," announced Zuma. "You will find suitable attire in your rooms, and you will be a guest of the Navajo Nation tonight."

"Oh, I brought you something," said Tia. She had been carrying an old leather bound book, which she handed to Erica. "My father told me that you were talking about Sitting Bull and the Ghost Dance. I thought you might be interested in the letters of the man who killed Sitting Bull. We had a copy in the Anasazi library and I thought you should read it so you understand what happened."

Erica's eyes lit up when she saw the book. "Thanks," she replied. Logan looked over at her and just rolled his eyes as Erica was already thumbing through the pages.

"We'll see you tonight," said Tia, making a point to look at Logan as she made the comment. Zuma took her hand and the two walked back down the stairs out of the hogan. Logan watched them as they blended into the crowd in Anasazi and disappeared from view. A few minutes later, Chapa and Resnick came bounding up the stairs from their meeting with Kinzi.

"Zuma invited us all to dinner tonight at the Kiva," said Logan.

"No way. We are leaving tomorrow," said Chapa quickly. "I don't think you should stay here."

"C'mon, let's go to the pow wow. We aren't leaving until tomorrow. You have to eat sometime, and I bet the food here is great," replied Resnick.

Chapa glared at Resnick, but eventually relented. "We will go with you guys tonight but don't get too comfortable. Remember—you are coming back with us tomorrow." He then turned and followed Resnick up the stairs to the main part of the house.

"I don't think that's culturally appropriate," Erica said firmly as she shook her head in disgust at Resnick.

The two of them went upstairs to Logan's room and Erica settled into a chair while Logan laid down on the bed. "So, what's in that book she gave you?" asked Logan.

Erica was quiet for a few minutes as she read through the pages of old letters trying to find the ones on Sitting Bull. "I found it," she said suddenly, pointing to the page.

"What did you find?" asked Logan.

"These are letters from a man named James McLaughlin, who worked for the BIA and ran the reservation where Sitting Bull lived. I read about this in school. This is the guy who had Sitting Bull killed." Erica continued reading, and suddenly her expression changed. "This is crazy," she said.

"What?" asked Logan, his interest now piqued.

"I will read it to you," replied Erica.

*Standing Rock Agency, October 1890*

*I trust that I may not be considered an alarmist and believe that my past record among the Sioux will remove any doubt in this respect, and I do not wish to be understood as considering the current state of excitement so alarming as to apprehend any immediate uprising or serious outcome, but I do feel it is my duty to report the present craze and nature of the excitement among the Sitting Bull faction over the annihilation of the white man and supremacy of the Indian, which is looked for in the near future and promised by the Indian medicine man. This is known among the Sioux as the return of the ghosts.*

*They have been promised that their numbers will be reinforced by the Indians who are dead, and that the gunpowder on hand will not pass through the skin of the Indians who follow the medicine men. It would seem impossible that any person, no matter how ignorant, could be brought to believe such absurd nonsense, but many in this agency actually believe it, and the numbers are growing. Sitting Bull is a high priest and leading apostle of this latest absurdity. He is the chief mischief maker and it is infecting those who believe in his power. Something must be done to stop the Ghost Dance.*

"Wow," said Logan. "So they killed Sitting Bull because of the Ghost Dance?"

"Sure looks like it," said Erica, still reading through the pages. She paused for a moment before getting excited again. "Here is the account of Sitting Bull's death."

"Read it," begged Logan.

*Standing Rock Agency, December 1890*

*I made known to Lieutenant Bull Head and Sergeant Red Tomahawk the plan of arrest and the desire to take Sitting Bull alive. Ten policemen entered one house and eight entered another to be sure of finding him early in the morning. Sitting Bull said, 'I will go with you but first I will put on my clothes and favorite headdress.' He then requested that his favorite horse be brought to the house and saddled for him, which was done by one of the Indian policemen. Sitting Bull caused considerable delay and began abusing the policemen, which provided time for his supporters to arrive at the house. Lieutenant Bull Head and Sergeant Red Tomahawk walked on either side of him as he exited the house, so as to prevent his escape. At this moment, two supporters rushed the policemen and shot Bull Head. Before dying, Bull Head shot Sitting Bull, but only wounded him. The supporters opened fire, fatally wounding Red Tomahawk, and allowing Sitting Bull to break free and run away from the policemen. Red Tomahawk managed to fire his rifle before he died, and killed Sitting Bull. The fight then became a melee with thirty-nine policemen against one hundred and fifty Indians. Once the supporters realized Sitting Bull was dead, they were driven back and disappeared.*

*I wish to publicly commend the bravery and the fidelity of the survivors and sincerely regret that the taking of life was necessary.*

"There is also a photograph of Sitting Bull," said Erica, holding up the book for Logan to get a closer look. "Look at his headdress. Do you notice anything?"

"The symbol with the bird!" replied Logan.

"Exactly. This has all happened before one hundred years ago. And now history is repeating itself."

"So, what does it say about Wovoka, the medicine man Zuma mentioned?" asked Logan.

"Not much," said Erica. "It says that Wovoka learned the secret of the Ghost Dance in a vision during a solar eclipse and used that power to help Sitting Bull's army."

"What happened to Wovoka? Was he killed with Sitting Bull?"

Erica slammed the book shut and put it down. "It doesn't say what happened to him. It's like he just disappeared."

She began to frown and twirled her curly hair nervously while she paused to think. "There's something else, Logan."

"What?"

"It may just be a coincidence, but I'm pretty sure I remember reading somewhere that there will be another solar eclipse in a couple of days."

Logan was stunned by yet another connection to the past. There were now too many to ignore, and a worry was building in the back of his mind. He thought that making it safely to Anasazi would be the end of his problems. Now, he realized that he might be caught up in something bigger than he imagined. The danger was far from over.

# Chapter Eighteen

At the appointed time, Logan and his companions met in the main room of their hogan to make the trip to dinner. It was now approaching dusk, and the streets were filled with the sights and sounds of people headed toward the Kiva. Even Hatani had managed to wake up and seemed to be recovering from the spear wound well enough to brave the short walk.

Chapa and Resnick had defiantly insisted on remaining in their street clothes. Hatani had already changed into fresh clothes from Anasazi when his wounds were cleaned, and Logan and Erica similarly decided to wear the clothing left for them by Zuma.

Logan had changed into a white knit shirt with black and red stripes around the neck and waist of the shirt. It was loose fitting and didn't have a collar, which suited Logan just fine.

He had chosen to wear the clothes left by Zuma but couldn't bring himself to change shoes. As he walked out of his room, the first thing Hatani noticed were Logan's beat-up Nike's peeking out from under the pants.

"I see you are too cool for the moccasins. You know, they really are comfortable, Logan," Hatani said as he wiggled his toes in his own moccasins from his seat on the floor.

"Here, I have one more thing to make the outfit perfect." Hatani stood and walked over to Logan before removing his necklace and putting it around Logan's neck. "Your mom would want you to have it, and if it keeps those killers away you will need it more than me." Logan had never known about the origin of the necklace before the attack, but now he realized the value of the last remaining object in the world that had a personal connection to his parents. He needed that connection, and he couldn't help but smile at Hatani's generosity.

After a few back-and-forth exchanges with Hatani, Logan looked around and asked if anyone had seen Erica.

"Get used to it, kid," said Resnick.

Moments later, the small talk came to a screeching halt as Erica finally walked out of her room. Logan's mouth dropped as he had never seen Erica in anything other than a t-shirt and shorts, or maybe blue jeans if she intended to "dress up."

Erica was now wearing a royal blue Navajo dress that extended down to her feet. It had a maroon and white "v" shape across her chest up to the shoulders, and matching bands of stripes around the bottom of the dress. It was tapered at her waist, and she had added a small leather belt. A large turquoise barrette peeked out from her neatly combed brown curly hair.

As Erica entered the room, she twirled around, and the dress flared out like a flower petal spinning in the wind. Logan winced as he saw that Erica had decided to ditch her tennis shoes for a pair of moccasins.

Resnick smiled and looked over to Logan. "Looks like the lady is ready for her dinner date."

The group left their newfound quarters and joined the crowd of people in bright clothing walking in the streets of Anasazi back towards the Kiva. Chapa and Resnick noticed the stares and whispers of those in the crowd who were, no doubt, wondering about the identities of the two men who had decided to dress for the event in their law enforcement attire.

Once they all entered the Kiva for the second time, they were blown away by its transformation. The once dark amphitheater was now lit up by torches around the room, with a fire burning brightly in its center. The people from the city were making their way up to the mezzanine level where food and drink of all types were displayed on tables. The Kiva was one big cocktail party with people milling around in groups and the din of hundreds of simultaneous conversations filling the air.

Resnick was the first one to bravely take a step towards the stairway leading up to the food, and the others soon followed behind him. Once they climbed the stairway, they entered the mezzanine level, which was filled with people holding plates or cups of drink while they talked. Resnick made a beeline for one of the tables, and began piling food on his plate, starting at a section that seemed to have every variety of meat one could imagine. Resnick quickly moved onto other tables, adding roasted peppers and squash to his plate, and a piece of warm bread that smelled like it was right out of the oven.

As Chapa went behind Resnick with a more judicious eye and a lighter plate, he commented, "I am surprised you didn't start with dessert."

"They have dessert, too? Where is it?" he asked quickly. Chapa laughed and shook his head.

Erica and the two members of the Hatani family moved towards the food line as well but were soon interrupted by a familiar girl with a falcon on her shoulder approaching quickly towards them through the crowd.

"I have been looking for you!" Tia said excitedly as she gave both Erica and Logan a warm hug. "You look beautiful!" she said to Erica.

"You, too," replied Erica.

Whereas Erica was dressed in dark and earthy tones, Tia stood out like a brilliant star in the darkened Kiva. Her white blouse had shiny sequins in a pattern across the neckline and around the bottom. Tia wore a skirt that had three layers ranging from white, to silver, and finally gold. A small silver tiara was wedged in her red hair. Jini was now wearing a small matching white vest, which he kept picking at with his beak.

"This is my Uncle Hatani," said Logan.

"Glad to meet you," said Hatani as he started filling his plate behind Resnick and Chapa.

"After you eat, come find me and my father. We will be saving you a seat in the section for the Navajo Tribe," she said, loudly enough for everyone to hear over the noise. "Since Anasazi is within the Navajo Nation, it will be the biggest section."

Tia next turned to Logan and Erica after eyeing the mounds of food on Resnick and Hatani's plates. She bent over to whisper, "Just so you know, it is kind of rude to eat a lot at these ceremonies. Hurry up and eat, then come down to the Kiva. Zuma is eager to introduce you to everyone."

Logan and Erica ate quickly and left the three older members of their group who were busy looking for the mysterious dessert table. The two teenagers walked down one of the stairways into the Kiva and looked around at the hordes of people searching for seats on the rows of benches lining the giant arena. The stairways sliced the Kiva's seating into seven sections, with one clearly being larger than the others. It was impossible to cut across the rows filled with people, so the two ran down to the floor of the Kiva and across to the section where they could now see Zuma and Tia waving for them to approach. At the front of the stairway to the Navajo section was an ornately carved wooden pole with a light brown flag. Since there was no wind in the Kiva, it was hard to make out all of the details on the flag, but Logan saw a rainbow over what appeared to be a mountain with clouds on each of the four sides.

"Welcome to the Blessing Way ceremony," said Zuma as he invited them to take a seat at the front of his section near the floor of the Kiva. "Tonight, you will be guests of honor of the Navajo Nation."

"Are those what the flags are for?" asked Erica, pointing at the flag with the rainbow.

"Yes," said Zuma. "Each of the seven tribes in the Great Council has a place in the Kiva which is marked with its own Nation's flag. Because the Navajo are the hosts here in Anasazi, all guests and members of smaller tribes are welcome in our section of the Kiva, which is why it must be larger than the others. It is the tradition."

"The Kiva is a circle, so no Nation gets a better view of the ceremony than the others. We are all equal in the Kiva."

"To our right is the Cherokee Nation. They are one of the largest Nations and their section is always filled to capacity. On the left side of us is the Apache people. They are our cousins and were once a single tribe with the Navajo. The remaining tribes represented in the Kiva are the Choctaw, Lakota, Chippewa, and Blackfeet."

Logan sat quietly listening to Zuma and watching the Kiva fill up with people. He noticed that he was starting to discern subtle patterns distinguishing the different tribes from one another. The Apache did actually look a lot like the Navajo. The Lakota and Cherokee were taller and had higher cheekbones. The Lakota had long black hair and seemed to look more distinguished. Every time he looked at one of the Lakota, Logan thought about his mother and what she must have looked like when she came to the Kiva when he was a baby.

The Blackfeet were dressed in heavier, darker clothing than the other tribes, more suitable for cold climates. Many of the Chippewa men wore distinctively colorful hats. They also seemed more stern-looking and quiet than the other men in the Kiva.

Logan scanned the Kiva, taking in all the new sights and sounds while Erica and Tia talked about the different flags and what they represented. Erica had a million questions and wanted to know everything about the different Nations in the room. As Logan watched the activity in front of him, Hatani, Chapa and Resnick quietly took a seat in the row behind him.

Suddenly, a distinguished middle-aged woman with brown hair approached the Navajo section from across the Kiva floor. Her eyes never left Logan as she walked up to within only a few feet before pausing and turning to his right. "Zuma," she said. "I am so glad to see you again."

Zuma stood and nodded to acknowledge the graceful woman as she also bowed slightly. "Good evening, Magaskawee. We are honored that you are here with us tonight for the ceremony. What brings you to Anasazi?"

"The shopping, of course," Magaskawee said with a smile before turning quickly to Logan. "This must be Tolulah's son. We have heard so much about him."

Logan shifted nervously in his seat and didn't know what to say. "Yes. Tolulah was my mom. Did you know her?"

Magaskawee looked at Logan, then to Zuma, and back to Logan. "Yes. Tolulah was Lakota, and we grew up together. You are Lakota, too, Logan. Why are you not sitting with us?"

Logan and Hatani looked at each other worriedly and were suddenly intimidated by this woman.

Zuma rescued them from the awkward silence. "Magaskawee, you know the tradition. They are our guests in the city and have graciously accepted my personal request to attend the Blessing Way. Tonight, they will be treated as brothers and sisters of the Navajo."

Magaskawee kept her focus on Logan but smiled to lighten the mood. "Of course, I understand. Logan, I hope you come to find me sometime so we can talk about your mother. She would have wanted that."

The sound of drums filled the air and the people on the Kiva floor began moving quickly towards the staircases. Magaskawee looked at Zuma. "It was good to see you again. It is time for me to rejoin my people." She took one last look at Logan before turning and racing across the floor towards the staircase by the Lakota flag.

Logan could not help but be relieved as she walked away. At the same time, he also felt fear as he suddenly realized that his presence in Anasazi was clearly not a secret.

# Chapter Nineteen

T he drums signaling the start of the ceremony continued in the background as people scurried around in the Kiva to get seated. Zuma leaned over to Logan, "Do you know anything about the Blessing Way ceremony?"

"No …. I don't remember this at all," replied Logan.

"It really is quite the experience," said Zuma. "The Blessing Way is normally a long dance that can last for multiple days and tells a story of our people. Tonight's dance is just a small part of that full ceremony and is intended to bring good fortune and prosperity to our visitors here in Anasazi."

"I don't speak Navajo, so I probably won't understand it," replied Logan.

Zuma smiled. "The dance is not about the words. It is about the connection to our past. Focus on your connection to your parents and then open your mind. Perhaps, if you are lucky, one of your ancestors will speak to you during the ceremony."

As Zuma finished his last sentence, there was a sudden quiet that descended upon the Kiva. A single file line of dancers walked out onto the Kiva floor and fanned out purposefully into positions around the central fire pit. The dance troupe was made up of both men and women, young and old, and they were dressed in bright Navajo clothing.

At the front of the procession onto the Kiva floor was a man and a woman who were leaders of the ceremony. The male leader wore a vest made up of colorful beads. The female leader had a rainbow colored dress, and was adorned with elaborate necklaces and earrings.

Logan stared at the ornate carvings on a wooden staff held up by the man in the front, but the spell was broken by the noisemakers which erupted in the hands of the female leader. Suddenly, drums started from an unknown source and the dancers began to move in rhythm around the fire pit, chanting words that Logan didn't understand. The lead dancer pointed his staff at the pit, and it erupted in a blue flame with orange tips that flickered towards the ceiling. Logan peered through the darkness and noticed there was no firewood at the base of the flames. The fire seemed to come from nowhere and the flames danced in tandem with the movements of the dancers. It was as if the man was controlling the fire with his staff.

The dancers moved in formation around the Kiva floor, sometimes circling close to the fire and sometimes circling closer to the audience. The Blessing Way was filled with chants and intermittent songs led by the woman with the noisemakers. Her voice was loud yet beautiful, and the repetitive rhythm of the ceremony made Logan relaxed.

It had been an incredibly long day and Logan was fighting to keep his eyes open. He noticed that Tia had also closed her eyes and was already swaying with the music. Logan watched the dancers move in faster and faster circles until his eyelids drooped, and this time they closed for good. In that moment, he lost all sense of time and space.

Logan opened his eyes and he was in the Kiva like before, but there were now figures moving in the flames. The shapes in the fire moved closer and emerged into view. He gasped as his parents' forms emerged from the flames. Was he dreaming? They smiled at him warmly and he felt himself smile in return. Behind them were people he did not recognize and in the back of the flames was a shape that instantly made him feel a sense of dread. The shape was moving quickly, and Logan saw that it was a warrior on a horse riding towards him at full speed. The warrior stared directly at Logan, raised up his spear, and let out a blood curdling war cry. The last thing Logan saw was the warrior thrusting the spear towards his heart.

Logan recoiled in fear and closed his eyes at the last minute before jerking them open once again. Suddenly, he was back in the Kiva and there was nothing in the flames. The dancers were slowing down, and the dance was complete.

Zuma looked over at Logan and noticed that he was drenched in sweat. "You saw something, didn't you?" he said matter-of-factly.

Logan hesitated. "I… I don't know. Maybe. I think I fell asleep and saw my parents."

"Whatever you saw, you were meant to see. Visions are a gift and should not be taken lightly. Come, Tia. We must let our guests get some sleep. I am sure they are tired."

Tia joined Zuma and they headed towards the exit of the Kiva. Tia waved goodbye to Logan. "I am glad you could join us tonight!"

Logan walked next to Erica as the five companions left the Kiva to return to the hogan. "Uh. Did you see … something … in the fire?" he asked Erica.

"No. Did you see something?" she replied.

"No. Nothing," said Logan dismissively, even though he knew that was untrue as soon as the words left his lips. As they walked back through the city streets now lit by torches instead of the outside sun, Logan was deep in thought. In fact, he could only think of one thing all the way back to his temporary home. The warrior in the fire who was coming for him with the spear. The warrior that he somehow knew was a Lakota named Sitting Bull.

# Chapter Twenty

Although Anasazi was bright and illuminated during the day, it was quite different at night. Without the sun, and shielded from the glow of the moon and the stars, the city built into the mountains of Mesa Verde was pitch black. The thick darkness was broken up only by the occasional torches outside buildings, which created ghostly shadows in the dim light reflected onto the stone walls and streets.

After the ceremony at the Kiva, the group had made their way back to their bedrooms at the hogan and fell asleep almost immediately. Chapa and Resnick were in adjoining rooms on one side of the central great room, while Hatani and Logan were fast asleep on the other side. Logan was so tired that he was sprawled out on the bed in his under shirt without even a blanket. Erica enjoyed her own private room on an upper level above Hatani and Logan. While they all slept in exhaustion after a day filled with danger, a fresh guard assigned by Kinzi stood watch at the front balcony entrance to the hogan.

The howl of a coyote was nothing special to the guard, as the sounds of nature often made their way into the city. It was nighttime, after all, and coyotes were nocturnal animals. First the howls were faint, but the guard noticed that the noises seemed to be drawing closer and approaching from multiple directions. It was odd, but it sounded like they were communicating.

The guard walked to the edge of the stone steps leading towards the street and scanned below. It was hard to see anything in the darkness of Anasazi, but he thought he saw a glimpse of a quick movement in the light of one of the torches. The guard peered intently, and saw nothing. He heard the howl of a coyote again, and this time the noise seemed to come from only a few yards to his right. He turned reflexively towards the source of the noise, and a hard blow to his head sent him crumpling to the stone floor.

Inside, Logan was awakened by a howl from a wild animal that seemed so close it had to be in his room. He sat up in the bed and searched for the source of the noise as his eyes adjusted to the darkness. Logan caught a glimpse of hind legs and a tail running through the central room towards the outside stairs, so he stumbled out of bed and threw on his shoes to follow the dog-like animal.

Logan quickly made his way into the open-air balcony, where he saw the guard lying on the floor with blood seeping from his head. Although he was rattled by the sight of the injured guard, the next thing he saw was even more disturbing. In the dim light from the torches, Logan saw Erica running down the street following two of the largest coyotes he had ever seen.

"Erica!" he yelled at her desperately, but she never even turned her head. His friend just kept running.

Logan raced down the steps and turned to follow Erica, but she had a significant head start. Although he had been through parts of Anasazi in the daytime, the streets all looked the same after dark. He was forced to make educated guesses on a few turns and soon realized that he had lost Erica's trail. She was gone, and he was all alone in the darkness.

*Why would Erica run away in the middle of the night? It doesn't make sense.* Logan took a deep breath and fought back despair as he wondered why these things kept happening to him. He looked around the darkened buildings in the city and thought about asking for help but had no idea where to start.

Logan decided he needed to get help from Chapa, so he started wandering back through Anasazi in the dark looking for a familiar landmark to guide him back to the hogan. As he turned a corner, he saw a plaza he had never seen before with a water fountain bubbling in the center. Sitting on the edge of the fountain was Tia, alone without the now familiar bird on her shoulder.

Logan ran up to Tia and words began flying out of his mouth. "I am so glad to see you! Something terrible has happened. Erica is gone. I heard a coyote in the middle of the night, and I woke up to see her following two of them through the city. I tried to chase them, but I couldn't keep up. They were too fast."

As Logan hurriedly shared his story with Tia, he noticed something different. She was not looking him in the eye and instead looked blankly off towards the ground. Tia seemed embarrassed to see Logan.

He stopped talking and slowly came to the realization something was wrong. It was the middle of the night and Tia was out alone in the dark acting strangely. "Tia. Are you OK? Do you need help?"

She finally spoke. "Logan. I don't need any help. I am blind. I see through Jini's eyes when she is with me, but when I break the connection I can't see. She is my guide during the day and, in exchange, I give her freedom at night to hunt mice and do what she wants. Sometimes I sleep, but I mostly spend time in the city at night. I don't mind the darkness. It gives me comfort."

Tia paused as if waiting for Logan to respond, but he just looked at her, digesting this new information. "I didn't want to tell you earlier that I'm blind. Does it matter?" she asked. "Some people don't understand… And it's complicated."

"Of course not," said Logan. "I'm just… surprised… and confused. How do you see through the eyes of a bird. Is that some type of magic?"

"Something like that," Tia answered. "I'm not sure how it works, but I have had the ability ever since I was a small girl. You can probably tell from looking at me, but I'm not Navajo. I was brought to Zuma from the outside when I was young, and he helped me understand my gift."

Tia turned the conversation away from herself and back towards the missing girl. "I know what happened to Erica," she said slowly.

"Where is she?"

"I don't know where she is, but I know who took her." Tia paused and she suddenly looked very worried. "Skinwalkers," she whispered.

Logan had never heard of a skinwalker but he figured that was not good news. They would need help and he needed to get back to Chapa and Resnick.

In the dark of the night, a shriek suddenly pierced the silence above Logan and Tia. Tia looked up wildly in the air. "Jini!" she cried out. "Jini!"

In the dark, Logan could barely make out the outlines of two birds fighting at the top of the cavern walls above the plaza. He could hear the distinct "caw" sound of a crow, and it looked like the black bird was being viciously harassed by Tia's falcon Jini as the crow divebombed in Logan and Tia's direction. The crow dropped a small piece of rolled-up parchment paper at the feet of Logan and flew away swiftly towards the canyon outside the city. Jini landed on Tia's shoulder and Logan noticed that her pupils dilated and the blank faraway stare in Tia's eyes immediately went away.

"Open it," she said hastily, pointing towards the paper.

Logan picked up the paper and unraveled the twine on the outside. The scrap of old-fashioned paper had a message inscribed in a chalky black ink that was unfamiliar to Logan. "If you want the girl to live, come alone to Hovenweep. Nightfall tomorrow." Under the inscription was a roughly drawn map, showing a trail from Anasazi to Hovenweep.

Jini peered over Logan's shoulder so Tia could read the paper through the eyes of the bird. "I know of Hovenweep," she said worriedly. "It is not safe. It's not within the tribal boundaries of any Nation, so you will have no protection. Whoever took Erica will just take you, too, or worse."

Logan knew Tia was right. Whoever was looking for Logan had taken Erica to lure him out into the open. That much was obvious. Logan played out the possibilities in his mind as he sat next to Tia in the deserted plaza with only the sound of the water bubbling behind him in the fountain. Logan knew he might get both him and Erica killed if he went to Hovenweep, but he also knew that if he remained in hiding at Anasazi, Erica would most assuredly die.

He had no good options, but finally settled upon his choice. He knew what he had to do. Hovenweep was not that far, and he could make it in a day. He would try to find a way to rescue Erica, but he had to leave now, and he needed help.

Logan put his hand on Tia's hand. "Tia. Come with me to Hovenweep. If I tell my uncle or the two agents, they won't let me go. I need your help to get out of the city. You know the way and can help me figure out a way to defeat the skinwalkers."

Tia listened to Logan's desperate plea in the darkness. She admired his bravery and loyalty to Erica. She also felt jealousy in the back of her mind as she wondered whether Logan's passion for rescuing Erica was about more than just chivalry. Above all, however, she was excited by the opportunity to leave the city and experience an adventure of her own. Zuma never let her out of his sight, and she desperately wanted to prove she could handle herself, even with her blindness.

Tia pushed Logan's hand away and stood up. "Logan, you have no idea what you are dealing with. You will be hopelessly outmatched by whatever is waiting for you at Hovenweep."

Logan's heart sank as he feared his best chance of making it to Hovenweep and returning alive was now slipping away.

"I will help you sneak out of the city tonight, but we must leave a trail for Kinzi to follow. My father will send him to look for us and we will need their help. We will be far enough ahead that they will not be able to stop us from getting to Hovenweep. If you want my help, those are my terms."

"Deal," he replied. "But we have to go now before the sun comes up."

Tia smiled and her pulse was now racing with excitement. "Wait here," she said as she ran off towards one of the buildings lining the plaza, which Logan assumed was her home. Within minutes, she returned wearing hiking boots, a backpack slung over her newly added parka, and an object in her hand.

"We need supplies for the trip. And you need to protect yourself." Tia handed Logan a leather sheath with an enclosed knife that had to be at least six inches long. "It is one of the knives from my father's collection. Wear it, and don't be afraid to use it."

# Chapter Twenty-One

After accepting the knife, Logan followed Tia as she quickly and expertly led him out of the city. He found himself balancing precariously on a rocky path carved into the cavernous walls above the city of Anasazi that was obviously not meant for travel at night. The path could not have been more than a few feet wide, but it was impossible to tell exactly because of the darkness that surrounded him on every side, including down. The void was occasionally broken up by slivers of light reflected from the torches below to remind him just how high he was above the stone streets, and how an almost certain death awaited him if he slipped.

Logan ducked his head to avoid a rock as the path turned sharply into a cave that required him to kneel down to continue. He focused his concentration on copying Tia's every step and movement. With the benefit of Jini's high powered eyes made for hunting in the dark, Tia could navigate her way at night much faster than Logan. Logan also got the distinct impression that this was not the first time Tia had snuck out of Anasazi in the dark.

Tia picked up her pace in the cave as the danger of falling off the ledge was no longer a concern. The passage through the mountain ended at the edge of a cliff in a canyon and a trail down to a river, which could be heard gurgling in the distance. Logan followed Tia as she nimbly climbed down the steep trail towards the sound of flowing water. At the bottom, Tia pointed towards a corral and a large set of stables posted alongside the fast moving white water.

"Horses," she whispered. "Anasazi's golden stallions are some of the fastest in the world."

Logan continued to follow Tia's lead as he had never ridden a horse in his life and had no idea what to do. Tia quickly pointed out two saddles for Logan to grab while she walked through the stables and picked out the matching horse for each of them. Tia was a regular in the stables and chose two horses that she knew from personal experience were the fastest. She guided Logan in tacking up his mount and left to ready her own horse. After fixing her saddle, Tia walked over to the door to the stables and pulled out her own blade from a hiding place in her boot. In the dark, she quickly carved "Hovenweep" into the wood frame of the door on the stable from which she had removed her horse.

Tia saddled up and Logan looked back towards the top of the ridge and the crumbling tower now visible on Chimney Top in the moonlight.

"You ready?" asked Tia.

"I think so," Logan replied. "I just have no idea how to get on the horse."

Tia guided Logan's movements as he put one foot in the stirrup and swung his body up and over onto the saddle. "Grab the reins," instructed Tia. "Now just hold on and squeeze with your legs to maintain your balance. These horses are trained to follow the leader, so you won't have to do much."

As promised, Logan's horse fell in line behind Tia and the two horses took off in a slow trot following the river to the West. "Do you need the map?" asked Logan.

"No," said Tia. "I know the way, but it is a long ride so get comfortable."

As Tia's horse picked up speed, Jini launched off Tia's shoulder and flew up into the sky. Logan lost sight of the falcon in the dark, but knew the bird remained close by and was guiding their way.

After a few hours of riding along the river, the morning glow began to illuminate the sky and the surrounding mountains. Logan could see they were almost out of the canyon and the cliffs on each side were getting smaller. Soon, the horses were trotting on what looked like the familiar plains near his home in Cortez, and he knew they were headed in a familiar direction.

Thinking of his home in Cortez made his thoughts turn to Erica. Her parents would be sick with worry and would have already called the police by now. He wondered to himself whether he did the right thing by striking out alone instead of waiting for help from his uncle and the agents. Thinking about the need for help brought an idea into his head. Logan pulled out his phone and turned on the power. His heart missed a beat with excitement to see that he had reception, so he immediately typed out a message to his uncle along with Chapa. "Erica kidnapped and taken to Hovenweep. Had to leave immediately with Tia to follow. Need help."

Up ahead, Tia remarked, "You know I can see you, right? What are you doing on your phone?"

"Texting my uncle to let him know I'm OK."

"Phones don't work in the city. I left a more low-tech message for them to find. They will see it when they notice the horses are gone, and my father will send Kinzi to follow us."

Logan realized that when Jini was in the air, Tia would have a full three hundred and sixty degree view of the area. She saw him texting on his phone behind her without even turning her head.

"By the way, has anyone ever told you it is creepy that you have eyes in the back of your head?" said Logan.

"Someone has to keep an eye on you," Tia joked as she laughed nervously.

"Could you see at all before you had Jini?" asked Logan.

"I was born blind, but I quickly figured out I could see through the eyes of animals—it just came naturally to me. I can communicate with them, too. My parents didn't understand my gift and thought it was witchcraft when they found me playing with a mouse when I was a baby. Somehow, I ended up at Anasazi and I have been raised ever since by Zuma. He is the only parent I have ever known.

"When I was ten, Zuma brought me Jini. I remember seeing myself through her eyes for the first time and feeling her fear of being in a new place with someone she didn't know. I felt her soft feathers and it was strange because I could not see Jini through her own eyes to appreciate how beautiful she was. But somehow I knew she was beautiful just by touch.

"So, what happened to *your* parents?" asked Tia.

"It's a long story," said Logan dismissively.

"We have a long ride," Tia responded quickly.

Logan recounted the crazy events over the last few days and the confrontations with the gang, first at his home and then again on the road to Anasazi. He shared everything he knew about his mother and father, his mother's necklace, and the speculation that he was descended from Sitting Bull.

"Do you still have the necklace?"

Logan touched his hand to the rock around his neck. "Yeah. I need all the help I can get. So, when are you going to tell me about skinwalkers and Hovenweep?"

"Those are long stories," replied Tia.

"We have a long ride," quipped Logan.

# Chapter Twenty-Two

The arrival of dawn in Anasazi brought chaos as Chapa woke to find Logan and Erica missing, and a contingent of Anasazi guards tending to one of their own, lying injured on the terrace.

Hatani was pacing back and forth, yelling at no one in particular. "How did this happen? We were supposed to be safe here!"

Chapa was already beating himself up for letting his guard down. He walked over to Hatani and reassured him. "We will find Logan."

"First, we need to find that Kinzi guy," said Resnick, who was already dressed in his now wrinkled suit and standing nearby. "He must know something."

"Speak of the devil," said Chapa.

He pointed to the door as Kinzi and Zuma came racing up the stairs past the guards into the great room where Chapa and Resnick were standing with Hatani. Kinzi now had a gun on his hip and was leading the way. Zuma, however, looked like he had just woke up, with an unshaven chin and disheveled hair. He had an anxious look in his eyes and the air of authority from the previous day had evaporated.

Kinzi spoke first, establishing that he was in charge of the situation. "I know Logan and Erica are missing, but we have also discovered that Tia is gone. I believe she helped Logan and Erica sneak out of the city last night and they left on horses stolen from the stables on the canyon floor."

Chapa was immediately skeptical. "OK ... but who attacked the guard outside?"

"I don't know," replied Kinzi. "Maybe Logan."

Hatani shook his head and he started pacing again, stopping only a few inches away from Kinzi as if looking for a fight. A bloodstain was growing noticeably bigger on the side of his shirt, where it was covering the bandage from the spear wound.

"Logan didn't attack anybody. You cops are all the same—even here. How do you know that the person who attacked the guard didn't take Logan and the horses, too?"

"I don't," said Kinzi with remarkable calm in his voice. "But, if they were after Logan, why would Erica and Tia be missing, too? Why wouldn't there be any sign of a struggle or break-in at Tia's home? All three of them were being friendly last night and the evidence points to them choosing to leave, not an abduction. Tia knows about the stables and is an excellent rider. She could have helped them sneak out of the city and steal the horses."

Hatani stood tensely in front of Kinzi for a few moments as if he wanted to argue. In the awkward silence, Chapa wondered if the boy's uncle might actually strike Kinzi and was relieved when Hatani finally walked away and collapsed into a chair.

Kinzi continued, "My guards are preparing horses as we speak. We will follow them and bring them back."

Resnick piped up. "Fine. Chapa and I are coming with you."

"When was the last time you rode a horse?" asked Kinzi.

Resnick shrugged. "I don't know. Never?"

Kinzi looked over at Chapa. "And you?"

"It has been a while," Chapa admitted.

"That's what I thought. Look, my men are experienced trackers, and you will only slow us down. We don't have time to argue. Every minute I stand here talking to you gives them more of a head start. Logan is my responsibility now."

Kinzi turned to Zuma and touched his arm. "I will bring Tia back, too. All of them. Don't worry." The leader of the Anasazi Guard raced down the stairs, leaving Zuma behind to deal with Hatani and the agents. It was a remarkable transformation from the previous day, as Zuma suddenly looked old, and mustered only a half-smile as he assured the others that Kinzi would get them all back safely.

"Kinzi knows what he is doing," he said confidently.

Chapa was not convinced but immediately knew there was nothing more they could do in Anasazi. "We have to go, too," he said to Zuma.

Zuma nodded his head and walked outside to the balcony. He was staring off into the distance as if he was looking for something. His suit from the day before was now replaced with a loose-fitting shirt and pants, but he still carried the formal wooden cane with the sculpted horse head. It was now clutched tightly against his chest.

Resnick nudged Chapa. "We need to report Erica missing and get word to her parents."

Chapa nodded, then turned to Hatani. "I think you should stay here. You are in no condition to travel, and Logan might come back."

Hatani didn't seem happy to stay, but he nodded his approval. "Thank you for everything you have done," said Hatani.

"Heal up and we'll see you soon," said Resnick.

The two agents said goodbye to Zuma, then backtracked through the city, out the Kiva, and through the ruins of Chimney Top. Chapa was delighted to confirm his pickup was still parked right where he left it at the end of the road. "She is a sight for sore eyes."

"Except for those busted headlights," said Resnick.

"It has seen worse, trust me."

The two of them piled into the pickup and headed back down the winding roads through the mountains towards Cortez. Once they were clear of Anasazi, Resnick decided to speak freely. "Do you believe that story about the kids overpowering the guard and sneaking off last night?"

"Hell no. Do you?"

"Nope," replied Resnick. "I saw the gash on the guard's head. No way Logan did that."

"None of it makes sense. There are pieces of the puzzle that are missing, and I intend to find them."

Chapa pulled out his phone and was disappointed to see he still had no reception. "It's Monday morning and Washington will be wondering what is going on. We need to get back into cell range at Cortez and check in."

The two agents rode in silence back to Cortez. Chapa dropped off Resnick at the Cortez police station to check in with local law enforcement on what they knew would be a frantic search already underway for Erica. Resnick planned to continue the cover story related to a drugs gang from a local reservation. An assurance from the FBI that they were on the case and following a lead would at least do something to calm the hysteria of Erica's parents.

While Resnick dealt with Erica's situation, Chapa stopped by a local auto parts store to pick up two new headlights for his beloved pickup. While they were being installed at a garage, he pulled out his phone and saw that he had a text message from Logan. He read it a couple of times, then made a call to Assistant Director Wilson Dawes.

Dawes picked up almost immediately and seemed eager to get an update. "Morning, Chapa. We have been waiting to hear from you. How is the investigation coming?"

"Not good. Our hunch proved to be correct, and we ran into some trouble at Logan's home in Cortez. We were attacked by a group of men Saturday night, and we barely fought them off. We hid Logan in a safe house, and when we picked him up yesterday, they attacked again. I believe they were Lakota, and they were very well-trained."

"So, where is the boy now?" asked Dawes.

Chapa thought about his words carefully since he knew his story was about to take a turn into the unbelievable. "Sir, we took Logan to a place called Anasazi near Mesa Verde. Have you heard of it?"

There was a long pause on the other end of the line.

"Continue," said Dawes without ever answering Chapa's question. Chapa filed away the strange evasiveness but figured now was not the right time to push that issue.

"We thought we had found a safe place for Logan, but he went missing last night, along with a friend of his from Cortez, and a girl from Anasazi." Chapa continued catching up Dawes on the meeting with Kinzi, the theory that the three of them had run away, and Chapa's return to Cortez to figure out their next move.

"I agree with this Kinzi guy. You did your job. You fought off the kidnappers and left the boy in a safe place with his uncle. You don't need to waste your time on some teenagers running away for a horse ride. You have a lead and need to follow it to South Dakota. We have six other missing people and you need to find the gang who attacked you before they do more damage."

Chapa momentarily considered arguing with Dawes over whether Logan had really gone on a "horse ride", and whether the disappearance was related to the kidnapping attempt, but he knew Dawes would not change his mind once it was made up. "Yes, sir, understood."

"One more thing, Chapa," said Dawes. "I would keep this Anasazi place between you and me. No need to mention it in your report."

Chapa recalled Kinzi's words about the BIA's knowledge of the city and the agreement to secrecy. *I guess he was right*, Chapa thought to himself.

"I have to go," said Chapa, ending the call. He was not big on reports anyway, and it sounded like no one would care if this one ever got done.

Chapa admired his newly replaced headlamps and headed back to the police station to pick up Resnick. The concrete building was not very large, and Chapa doubted the police officers inside had much experience in dealing with the FBI. That would play right into Resnick's hands, and he figured Resnick would not get much push back on his story.

He parked the truck in the parking lot by the door of the police station and waited. A few minutes later, Resnick appeared and hopped into the front seat. "Erica's situation is handled," he said grimly.

"You alright?" asked Chapa.

"I talked briefly with Erica's parents, the Guzmans, and that was tough. The local cops had already connected Erica's disappearance with Logan and found the scene at the trailer. It actually proved to be helpful as they immediately bought the drug gang story. I told the parents that we believed she was still alive, and the FBI was working to get her back. I didn't tell them everything, but I didn't lie to them either."

Chapa nodded affirmatively. "You did good."

"So, what did the BIA say about our next move?" asked Resnick.

"Dawes told me to go to South Dakota," said Chapa.

"That's about what I expected. Did you tell him about Anasazi?"

"Yes, sir. And Kinzi was right. He didn't want to hear it."

Resnick whistled loudly. "I knew it. Damn conspiracies. You know what that means, right?"

"No, what?" Chapa asked.

"UFOs are real, man!"

This time there was no laughter from Chapa and he remained focused on the task at hand. "I don't know about that conspiracy, but I know about another one. Kinzi wasn't honest with us." Chapa handed Resnick his phone, so he could read the text message from Logan.

The truck's gearshift yanked into reverse and Chapa roared out of the police station parking lot toward the highway. It was already midday, and he knew they had to make a quick decision on whether to follow Logan or leave the rescue mission to Kinzi.

Resnick put Chapa's phone down on the console after reading the message multiple times and turning it over in his head. "Chapa, this changes everything. We can't go to South Dakota. I just looked that girl's parents in the eye and told them I would get their daughter back."

Chapa punched the accelerator to the floor and looked at his watch to check the time. "Glad to hear it. Looks like we agree that our investigation just became a rogue operation."

# Chapter Twenty-Three

The sun was now high in the sky and Logan and Tia had put some miles on horseback between themselves and Anasazi. Logan discovered that Tia was a treasure trove of information about the Navajo culture, and there was an entire world that he never knew existed.

Tia had kept her promise to share what she knew, starting with Hovenweep.

"Are you afraid of Hovenweep?" asked Logan.

Tia answered without hesitation, "Yes, and you should be, too. It was abandoned for a reason. There are evil spirits in that place."

Logan noticed that Tia's mood had changed. Her horse was galloping a little faster, and Jini had retreated from the sky and taken her familiar spot upon Tia's shoulder. He wasn't convinced about evil spirits, but Tia clearly believed. She was afraid.

"Zuma told me that the place will always be sought after by those who look to learn its secrets. He said terrible things had occurred at Hovenweep— killings, dark ceremonies, and witchcraft—things that I didn't need to know about."

"And skinwalkers?" asked Logan.

"Yes," Tia said quietly. "He mentioned them, too."

Tia stopped talking for a moment and that was fine with Logan. He decided that he was actually enjoying the experience of riding a horse for the first time. If he didn't get killed tonight, he might try it again sometime. There was something about the feel of the horse underneath him and the ability to break into a run at any moment. It was exhilarating, but also felt somehow familiar—like he was re-discovering something he had done in the past.

Every so often, Jini would take off from Tia's shoulder and soar up into the clouds for a survey of the surrounding area. When the bird was on Tia's shoulder, her head was constantly moving, darting left and right in response to every sound along the trail. Tia always seemed to be more comfortable after Jini's scouting flights, and more willing to talk.

"I know you want me to tell you about skinwalkers, but it is very hard to explain to people outside our tribe."

"Well, can you tell me how they got Erica to follow them last night?" asked Logan.

"Skinwalkers are said to have the power to change into animals. The Navajo name is '*yee naaldlooshi*'. It means, 'he goes on all fours'. The coyote is known to us as the trickster and I believe that explains what you saw," said Tia.

"Zuma told me that a medicine man was looking for me because I am related to Sitting Bull. Do you think these skinwalkers and the medicine man are working together?"

"The answer to your question is I don't know. I have never seen a *yee naaldlooshi* before, and certainly don't understand their motivations. They are known to exist, but it is considered bad luck to speak of them. What you would call witchcraft is a part of the natural world to our people. It is part of the Navajo ways, but it is neither good nor bad. The skinwalker is someone who has twisted those ways and used them for an evil purpose."

"So how do we kill it if we run into one at Hovenweep?" asked Logan.

Tia shook her head. "I don't think you understand. If this really is a *yee naaldlooshi*, we will not be able to kill it." Tia seemed frustrated that her pessimism was not fully understood by Logan.

Logan was not backing down. "Anything can be killed. There has to be a way."

"I have heard that the skinwalker will die if you say its full name in its presence. Others claim they can be killed with weapons made from precious metals like silver. These stories are probably not true, but it is the legend. It is not like people are going around testing the theory out on skinwalkers and living to tell about it."

"Good point," replied Logan with a smile. He looked ahead and saw the path was getting steeper as they left the river and headed back into the mountains. A giant mesa loomed ahead on the right and Logan thought he had seen that before somewhere. He pulled out the map to Hovenweep dropped by the crow and saw the mesa marked on the map.

Logan crumpled up the map and put it back into his pocket. He had never done anything this adventurous before in his life, and the reality was setting in that he may have underestimated the danger. "I think we are getting close. Have you been here before?"

"Yes. Zuma took me there one day and showed me the castle towers. He told me I had nothing to fear as long as he was with me, but to never set foot inside by myself. Lucky for you, I didn't listen to him."

*Perfect. Just perfect. How are we supposed to fight skinwalkers at a place like that?* thought Logan.

"I think we should try to get there before dark. It is our best chance," Tia replied. She kicked her horse to pick up speed and Jini launched from her shoulder for another round of scouting.

Logan's horse increased its pace to match Tia's, and he looked up to watch Jini float on the wind as she circled ahead. He could not help but wonder whether skinwalkers were real, or if Zuma just liked telling Tia scary bedtime stories. In the back of his mind, however, there was a growing acceptance that the world was not as he had imagined, and that was both exciting and deeply troubling.

# Chapter Twenty-Four

Kinzi bent forward in the saddle, eyes focused on the trail ahead as he galloped full speed through the flat lands of Colorado. Riding with him were two of his guards from Anasazi, and all three were riding the fastest of the remaining horses in the stable after Tia took her pick. Time was of the essence, and Zuma would never forgive him if he returned without Tia. Zuma plucked that blind girl from obscurity and she was now the most important thing in the world to him.

The Navajo on Kinzi's right was a young but skilled guard who he knew would be useful in a fight. Riding in front of Kinzi was an old and weathered member of the Guard named Diamondback. Unlike Kinzi, who preferred a modern military uniform, Diamondback dressed like a cowboy. He wore a bright red bandana around his bald head to protect it from the sun. He usually went shirtless, and his dark skin had seen more than its fair share of the sun, but today he was wearing a loose cloth shirt that flapped in the wind. Kinzi didn't know the man's birth name as it was common for Navajo to take different names throughout their lives—almost like a nickname.

Somehow, the Diamondback name just stuck, and as far as Kinzi knew, no one had ever called him anything else. At first, Kinzi thought the name came from the man's affinity for rattlesnakes, or just plain old toughness, but he quickly learned the real reason for the moniker. Snakes are fierce hunters, and diamondbacks are some of the most ruthless and capable. A diamondback's senses are extraordinarily strong, including the ability to sense vibration and the body heat of their prey. Even blind diamondbacks have been known to survive in the desert, and to be able to stalk and ambush rodents for food. Right now, Diamondback was on the hunt for Logan and Tia, and they were not making it particularly hard to be followed.

Even without the skills of Diamondback, it was obvious to Kinzi they were only following two sets of horse tracks. There was some speculation earlier in the day that perhaps one of the horses was carrying two riders, but that theory was quickly dismissed by Diamondback. "Only two riders," he declared firmly, casting doubt on the initial conclusion voiced by Kinzi to Zuma and the others at Anasazi that all three of the missing teenagers had left together. The old tracker could determine the weight on the horses by the depth of the tracks in the dirt, and he was never wrong.

Kinzi had been thinking about the best way to stop the riders ahead, and decided that he had two options. They could announce their presence and hope the two kids stopped and voluntarily turned around, but that was unlikely to work. Once they realized they were being chased, they may try to run away or hide. Diamondback had suggested a different strategy. With their faster horses and superior riding skills, they would try to circle around ahead of them in the hills and cut them off without warning. Kinzi knew, however, that this strategy had one major flaw—sneaking up on a falcon who could see for a great distance in every direction would be exceedingly difficult. Only Diamondback could pull off a stunt like that successfully.

Diamondback had easily spotted the turn off from the trail by the river towards the path into the mountains. "We are getting closer," he said to Kinzi and the other guard. "We must now go up that hill so we can see them more clearly when they wind back through the canyon. They will not be able to see us because of the trees on the ridge."

Kinzi and the others expertly guided their horses up the rocky terrain, weaving between the trees and rock outcroppings to stay shielded from the canyon below. Diamondback was constantly scanning the sky for any trace of Tia's falcon, and sniffing the air periodically to catch a scent from Logan and Tia's horses.

The three guards from Anasazi finally caught their first sight of the riders below them as they came out from behind a giant boulder near the top of the ridge. Diamondback raised his hand quietly to signal they should stop. The men left their horses behind the boulder and laid down at the edge of the rocks. "Watch the bird," hissed Diamondback. "She flies then she rests. We must wait for her to fly again, then come down in front of them while she is resting. That is the only way we can avoid being seen."

Diamondback escorted the two guards back to their horses and instructed them to wait out of sight. "I will tell you when the bird has come and gone."

The tracker disappeared and Kinzi imagined Diamondback hiding in the brush, patiently watching the bird. On the other side of the boulder, the wait was much more difficult for Kinzi. It was getting late in the day, and he wanted to get to Tia before they made it very far into the mountains.

Minutes felt like hours as Kinzi waited for Diamondback to return from his makeshift blind. Eventually, the old Navajo appeared from around the boulder and grabbed his horse. "We must go now. Quickly," he said. "The bird is resting."

Kinzi knew that the high ground and distance would make it impossible for Logan and Tia to hear or see their progress along the ridge, so they moved quickly into position. The horses rode across the top of the canyon until they were ahead of Logan and Tia. Once in position, they began the descent to find a hiding place from which they could launch their ambush below.

At the suggestion of the veteran tracker, the group split up. Diamondback quickly found a hiding place for him and his horse. Kinzi and the remaining guard waited behind a rock outcropping further ahead in the canyon. By the time Logan and Tia saw Kinzi, it would be too late. They would be trapped between Diamondback and the other two guards.

After crouching silently behind a boulder, Kinzi felt relief when he finally heard horses coming towards him in the canyon. Logan and Tia passed Diamondback's hiding spot, and seconds later, Kinzi and the young guard walked their horses into view.

"Tia. Your father wants you to come home. You should not be out here," said Kinzi firmly.

Tia was visibly overcome with joy at the sight of the guards. "Kinzi, I am so glad you found us. We need your help. Erica was taken last night, and we are going to rescue her."

"It was skin …," shouted Logan.

Tia instantly shot him a mean look, cutting him off from saying the name of the supernatural enemy they feared was waiting at Hovenweep.

Kinzi and the other guard slowly made their way towards Tia and Kinzi's tone hardened. "Tia, we can talk about this back at Anasazi, but you are coming with me now."

"But what about Logan and Erica? They need our help."

"Logan is going to Hovenweep, but you won't be going with him."

\*\*\*

Tia's mind was racing. Kinzi knew where they were going, so he had discovered her clue. If he shared that information with Zuma, there was no way her father would have instructed Kinzi to let Logan go to Hovenweep alone. Her instincts were screaming that Kinzi couldn't be trusted.

"Turn around," she whispered to Logan. "Something is wrong."

The two turned their horses around and Jini took flight from Tia's shoulder with a loud shriek. As soon as they turned, however, Diamondback appeared on the trail behind them with his arm outstretched.

"Tia, you need to come on home," said Diamondback gently.

Kinzi pulled out his pistol and aimed it up in the air in Jini's direction. "Don't make me shoot your bird, Tia. Leave Logan and come home with us."

Tia looked at Diamondback and desperately pleaded with him in his native Navajo language. "I cannot let Logan go to Hovenweep alone. Help us find his friend."

Diamondback seemed torn between Kinzi's order and Tia's plea. He had known Tia since she was a little girl and came out here to keep her safe, not see her harmed. The older man turned to Kinzi and yelled, "Put that gun away. There's no need for that."

Kinzi, however, was not swayed by Diamondback's reasoning. "I disagree," he said loudly.

Kinzi aimed the gun at Jini, who was swooping and circling above his head, and pulled the trigger. The bullet shot up into the sky, narrowly missing Jini, but the sound caused Tia's horse to rear up onto its hind legs, throwing her hard to the ground. Tia's head barely missed the rocks that lined the canyon floor as she twisted and landed on her stomach with a thud. Logan almost lost control of his own horse as it jolted and panicked in response to the deafening noise of the gunshot.

In the chaos, Diamondback charged forward past a screaming Tia towards Kinzi. After closing the gap, he leapt from his horse and grabbed Kinzi's torso, knocking them both to the ground. Once he had Kinzi on his back, Diamondback drove his knee into Kinzi's stomach, and wrestled with him to keep Kinzi's hands away from his gun. "Go!" he shouted to Tia and Logan.

The remaining Anasazi guard behind Kinzi dislodged a spear on the side of the saddle and was now looking to get into the fight to help his captain. Tia saw the movement and yelled at Logan, "Do something. Use the knife I gave you!"

Logan pulled the knife given to him from Tia and quickly admired the shape and feel of the antique weapon in his hand. Then, without thought, Logan threw the knife at his attacker and watched in disbelief as it plunged deep into the chest of the charging Anasazi guard. The attacker's arm went limp and dropped the spear as the horse ran away into the canyon with its slumped rider in tow.

Back on the ground, Diamondback had successfully knocked away the pistol, but Kinzi was younger and stronger. Kinzi had now managed to pin Diamondback and was reaching for a rock to use as a weapon. Suddenly, Jini dropped out of the sky and scratched Kinzi's face with her talons, leaving a deep cut near his left eye. Taking advantage of the distraction, Diamondback pushed out from under Kinzi with a quick jerk, freeing up his arms. He picked up a rock of his own and struck Kinzi in the head, knocking him unconscious.

Logan was still staring in the direction of the runaway horse, shocked at the prospect that he had just killed one of the Anasazi guard. Tia grabbed the reins of Diamondback's horse and brought it over to the old man. "Thank you," she said.

Diamondback was dirty and had a bruise on his face from wrestling on the ground with Kinzi but seemed unfazed by the fight. "Kinzi isn't dead, but he won't hurt you now. We need to go before he wakes up." He quickly mounted his own horse and grabbed the reins of Kinzi's mount to prevent him from following.

"I will go with you to Hovenweep and then you will come back with me to Anasazi. Agreed?"

Tia nodded. They desperately needed the help and Diamondback seemed to be trustworthy. There really was no other choice but to follow him at this point.

"Logan! Let's go," Tia shouted.

Logan looked dejectedly at Tia. "I am … sorry for losing your father's knife. I didn't know what to do, so I threw it."

Tia smiled slyly at Logan as if she knew something he did not. "Concentrate on the knife. Remember how it felt in your hand."

Logan was surprised by the strange request but closed his eyes and did what he was told.

"If you want the knife back, put out your hand and imagine it has returned."

As Tia was talking, the knife suddenly appeared in Logan's hand as if it had never left. He waved it around with a confused look on his face as he felt the familiar weight and power of having it back in his hand. "How is this possible?"

The girl just smiled and shook her head as Logan figured out the secret of the special knife she had taken from Zuma's private collection.

Diamondback barked, "We must go now!" and the three rode quickly out of the canyon towards Hovenweep. Kinzi remained behind, face down in the dirt, blood pouring out of a deep wound on the side of his head.

# Chapter Twenty-Five

L ogan looked up into the sky as the sun went behind a cloud. *Finally*, he thought, *some relief from the heat*. After the run-in with Kinzi, they had left the canyons for the mountains, but the ground was still rocky and the small brushy trees offered little shade. Diamondback had set a fast pace on horseback after the deadly skirmish, which was now hours behind them. After releasing Kinzi's horse, they had quickened the pace even further, making sure they would arrive before dark.

Using the knife to kill the guard was still gnawing at Logan's mind. The knife felt good in his hand, and he was excited about the newfound ability to recall it after it was thrown. At the same time, he wondered if the man he stabbed was dead. He didn't mean to kill him. He was just trying to protect Tia, and it happened before he knew what he was doing. *Maybe the guard survived?*

Logan looked over at Tia and noticed she was nodding off as the horse followed in line behind Diamondback's lead. Tia had already shared the story of Erica's kidnapping and their urgent rescue mission to Hovenweep. Diamondback had listened intently but did not say much during the conversation. When Tia told him about Erica being seen following the coyotes at night, he appeared shaken as if he had been delivered some really bad news. Tia made a point of not mentioning skinwalkers, but Logan got the sense Diamondback had already made the connection.

Diamondback suddenly pointed to a small pool ahead at the foot of a steep rock wall. "We can rest here and let the horses get some water. Hovenweep is not far."

The pool was fed by a stream of cold water from higher in the mountains that collected near the bottom of the cliff via a small waterfall before continuing down the mountain to the canyons below. It wasn't big enough for a swim, but it was a good place to stop and rest—as they all were exhausted, including the horses.

Logan eagerly leapt down from his horse and splashed cold water on his face. He watched as Tia cupped her hands and reached them into the water. Instead of drinking the water herself, Tia offered the water to Jini, who hopped down from her shoulder and drank from Tia's hands like a dog drinking from a dish. Diamondback filled up his canteen and sat down in the shade of a small grove of cedar trees, before motioning for the two to join him.

Diamondback pointed to the ground near the pool of water. "Coyote tracks. Two of them were here. And a girl."

"Erica!" said Logan.

Diamondback nodded then looked straight at Logan. "She is under the spell of the *yee naaldlooshi*. She won't even recognize you. You must kill or weaken the skinwalker who has bewitched her to break the spell. That is the only way to get her back."

Tia muttered softly, "You know they can't be killed."

"I have run into the *yee naaldlooshi* once before," Diamondback replied. As he talked, a faraway look passed over his face and tears welled up in his eyes.

"One night when I was a young man, I was sleeping in my house and I heard the cry of a coyote. I jumped out of my bed and saw my twelve-year-old daughter walking from her room with a blank expression in her eyes. I grabbed her, but she kept trying to wrestle free and go to the howling coyotes. I held her tight until the wailing stopped, and she eventually fell asleep in my arms. I did not let go of her that entire night.

The next morning, I took my daughter by the hand, and we went back to the bedroom to tell my wife Rose what had happened. It was then that I noticed the bed was empty. She was gone. I never saw her again after the night of the *yee naaldlooshi*."

Diamondback looked up grimly towards Logan and Tia and his voice cracked with the emotion of retelling the story. "I don't know if we can kill the *yee naaldlooshi*, but tomorrow morning I will either have my revenge or I will be with my beloved Rose in the next life. That I know."

The two teenagers sat quietly, not knowing how to respond. Finally, Logan spoke up. "You both think we have no chance against these things, but we have to try."

Logan angrily pulled the knife out of the sheath on his belt and threw it at a nearby tree. The knife made a clanking noise as the handle struck the bottom of the trunk near the ground. Logan focused, and the knife immediately reappeared in his right hand. He repeated the process four or five times, throwing the knife at different trees. Each time, he got faster and more accurate.

Diamondback sat and watched with interest as Logan practiced his newly discovered knife throwing skills, before finally rising to his feet. "Can I see that knife?" he asked as he approached Logan.

"Sure," replied Logan.

Diamondback turned over the blade in his hands and carefully inspected the knife. It had a polished bone handle, and the blade was made of silver with tiny pictographs molded into the steel. Diamondback balanced the knife on one finger, then ran his finger along the edge that flared out in the middle and narrowed to a sharp point at the end.

"This is a very special knife. I am sure Zuma would approve of you taking it into battle against the *yee naaldlooshi*."

Diamondback smiled as he turned to see the reaction on Tia's face. Her face was beet red and she looked down at the ground, embarrassed Diamondback had discovered her theft.

"Your knife is part of a set called the Twins. They have been passed between the tribes as trophies of war, and no one knows who made them originally. One is believed to have been lost, and the other was most recently used in World War II by a Cherokee soldier to fight Nazis. You should wear it proudly into battle... but you are wearing it wrong."

Logan looked at the old Navajo with confusion. "I don't understand."

Diamondback asked Logan for the sheath and Logan removed it from his belt and handed it to him. The old warrior pulled out a leather strap from a saddle bag on his horse and fashioned a harness to hold the weapon. "I see you are left handed?"

Logan nodded affirmatively.

Diamondback slipped the strap over Logan's head and under his arm, then tied it tight, creating a secure resting place for the knife on the side of his chest, near his right shoulder.

"This knife is special. Wear it here. You can get to it quicker than down on your hip."

Logan looked confused as he reached for the knife awkwardly with his left hand. "No. You grab it like this," said Diamondback, as he demonstrated a swift motion with the wrist.

Logan tried it a few times, quickly realizing that the new location made the knife more accessible, and the slight angle caused the knife to fly out quickly into his hand. Tia watched the lesson from Diamondback with interest before finally commenting, "Looks like that knife is getting a lot more use out here than sitting in my father's collection."

"I appreciate the gift," said Logan to Tia as he paused with his practicing, "but I know I have to give it back. I will return it to Zuma one day."

"I know you will," replied Tia confidently.

Diamondback gathered the horses and took one last look at the position of the sun in the sky. "It is time to go see what is waiting for us at Hovenweep. Remember that the coyote is the trickster. These *yee naaldlooshi* will not fight fair and you must be ready for anything."

Tia and Logan mounted their golden horses from Anasazi and Jini flew down and landed on Tia's shoulder. Diamondback adjusted the spear and bow strapped on the side of his horse and placed a tomahawk into his belt that he removed from underneath his saddle. He moved with the precision and experience of someone who had used these instruments of war many times in the past.

The trio set off along the rocky path, climbing out of the desert upward into the mountains. Off in the distance, Logan got his first glimpse of what looked like the crumbling remnants of an ancient stone castle built on the top of one of the peaks. His heart sank into the pit of his stomach and he leaned forward a little bit more in his saddle. Logan reached into his shirt and tightly squeezed the necklace from his mother, hoping it would somehow keep him safe as it did his uncle.

# Chapter Twenty-Six

For thousands of years, Hovenweep had stood watch in the mountains near the Colorado and Utah border. No one knew why the fortress was built, or why it was eventually abandoned. The mysterious building that resembled a castle was clearly intended as a defensive structure—to protect the ancient people who occupied it from something they feared. Now, the guard towers and formidable walls had all been breached by time and weather, leaving only the ruins from which to imagine the original grandeur.

Logan followed Diamondback up a dirt road marking the end of their journey, leading directly to the ruins of the castle, now only about one hundred yards ahead. Diamondback hopped off his horse first and tied it to a tree. "We go on foot from here," he said.

Before leaving his horse, Diamondback removed a spear from the side of his horse and grabbed his bow. "Take this," he said, handing the bow and a quiver of arrows to Tia. "I know Zuma taught you how to use it and with that bird of yours, you will be able to see better than us in the dark. Send up Jini and tell us what she sees."

Tia slipped the quiver onto her shoulder and knelt down to pick up the bow. Jini leaped off her shoulder and flew up into the sky to provide surveillance on what was waiting at the end of the dirt road. As the falcon circled hundreds of feet above Hovenweep Castle, Tia closed her own eyes to focus intently on Jini's field of vision, leaving herself temporarily blind to her current surroundings. The few minutes that passed seemed like an eternity, but soon a familiar shriek signaled Jini's return when the bird landed safely on Tia's shoulder.

Tia opened her eyes quickly and a look of fear crossed her face. "They saw me!"

"What did you see?" hissed Diamondback. "How many of them?"

"I can't be sure, but I believe there were three or four—all in the main part of the castle by the big tower. They had animal skulls on their heads and pelts on their backs so I couldn't tell if they were men or women. I saw Erica. She was tied up and laying on the ground near one of the towers."

Tia continued. "While Jini was circling, one of the skinwalkers pointed up and said something to the other ones. I don't think I will be able to send her up again. It is too dangerous. They may try to shoot her down."

Diamondback processed the information in his mind and nodded his head. "Thank you, Tia."

He turned to Logan. "When the fighting starts, I want you to get Erica while Tia stays back to support me with the bow. After you get Erica, the three of you run back to the horses and go as fast as you can away from here. Follow the road and find people. It doesn't matter who they are, or where you go. Just get away from here. Do you understand?"

Logan nodded. Diamondback looked at Tia and she also nodded.

With agreement on the plan, Logan and Tia followed Diamondback in a single file up the dirt road towards Hovenweep as the sun began to set behind the mountains. The dying light created shadows on the crumbling walls up ahead, making the castle seem even more foreboding than what Logan had imagined based on Tia's stories.

Now close enough to make out the details of the structure, Logan saw that the skinwalkers had gathered in a part of the Hovenweep ruins that were largely intact on three sides, with soaring stone walls over twenty feet tall punctuated by sections that had crumbled down to the ground. The ceiling had long fallen away, and the building was open to the sky above. A tower rose from one side that still had an intact stairway leading up into the darkness. On the back side of the structure, the wall was crumbled almost completely away, leaving an unobstructed view of the mountains in the distance. On that side, a steep cliff awaited one wrong step outside the foundations of the castle.

Diamondback was the first to enter the ruins through a doorway on a partially intact wall, followed quickly by Logan and Tia. In the middle of the hollowed-out fortress, Logan finally got a close-up view of the *yee naaldlooshi*, and it sent a chill through his body.

There was a tall man who wore the skin of a mountain lion, with the preserved head of the beast sitting on top of his head like a hat. The beast's gaping mouth was open, baring its teeth as a warning to its prey. The remainder of the yellow and brown skin draped over his shoulders and fell down his back like a cape. The front legs of the lion covered either side of the man's face, but could not completely obscure the long black hair that also hung down and peeked out from behind the lion's paws.

The man crouched down to watch Logan and his companions enter Hovenweep. In this position, his human face was obscured by the lion head and the hanging front paws. To Logan, it looked like a real-life mountain lion was in front of him sitting on all fours on the stone floor.

In contrast to the large savage looking male skinwalker, the woman next to him was smaller and more elegant. Instead of a lion, she wore the head of a giant owl, with silver wings spread out across her shoulders. While the man seemed rough and animal-like, her appearance was clean and aristocratic. The owl woman wore a gray robe decorated with regal white lines, that resembled the trappings of royalty.

There was no doubt they were *yee naaldlooshi* because they were wearing the skins of predators. Tia had explained that, although Navajo routinely wore the skins from deer, sheep, and other animals, it was forbidden to wear the skins of an animal that killed its prey. It was a sure sign of a practitioner of witchcraft.

Any doubts Logan may have had about stepping into the world of the supernatural were now fading away. The two central figures stood in a large circle made up of skulls of all shapes and sizes. The skulls were all positioned to be facing the trio as they entered the ruins.

Behind the pair was Erica, lying unconscious within the circle of skulls with her hands bound behind her back. No one else was in sight.

The female skinwalker held up one hand to signal for them to stop in their approach. "We are glad to see Logan accepted our invitation to come tonight. If he stays, the rest of you are free to take the girl and leave with your lives. There is no need for Navajo blood to be shed here in this place."

Diamondback looked directly at the pair of skinwalkers and responded forcefully, "We will not bargain with you *yee naaldlooshi*. I know what you are. You are followers of the Witchery Way. We will take the girl and we will all leave here tonight."

As Diamondback was talking, Logan scanned the castle ruins, which were getting increasingly darker by the minute. Night was falling on Hovenweep, and Logan was deeply worried about what that would mean. As he searched every corner of the fortress, he thought he saw a pair of red eyes peering out from the entrance to the tower. Clearly, there were more than these two skinwalkers creeping around the castle. *But how many?*

The owl woman laughed coldly at Diamondback's threat. "You are an old man. Go enjoy the few days you have remaining. You don't have to die for this boy you barely know. Take the girls and return safely to Anasazi so you can rest by the fire like you deserve."

"You witches took someone from me long ago, and today I will have my revenge," said Diamondback. He briefly looked at Logan and Tia as if to remind them of the plan and let out a battle cry as he ran forward with his spear towards the man cloaked with the lion skin.

# Chapter Twenty-Seven

Diamondback's charge unleashed chaos inside Hovenweep Castle. The owl woman began muttering words in Navajo and the skulls ignited in an eerie blue flame that started on one side of the circle and quickly spread around the other skulls within seconds, encircling the two skinwalkers and Erica's unconscious body. The flames rose only a few feet off the ground, but generated a barrier of smoke that drifted high into the sky. Ghostly human and animal skeletons materialized in and out of sight within the white smoke. Logan watched in fear as the outline of a hollow-eyed human skeleton holding a tomahawk faded into the skeleton of a wolf with a snarling set of teeth.

The sudden ignition of the fire halted Diamondback's advance, and in the brief moment of hesitation, two large coyotes darted out from the darkness of the tower. Each of the coyotes had dirty gray fur and eyes that glowed like red embers in the darkness. The coyotes closed the distance across the castle floor within seconds and Diamondback barely had time to turn his spear in their direction before the two animals pounced.

One of the coyotes landed on the tip of Diamondback's spear, piercing its belly and running it through as its weight pushed the shaft out the other side of its torso. The other coyote snapped its jaws towards Diamondback's neck and the weight of the two animals knocked him to the floor.

Logan watched the scene unfold in front of him in horror and pulled out the knife given to him by Tia. The speed of the coyotes made it impossible to aim as they ran from their hiding place, but once they pounced on

Diamondback, Logan knew he had to act quickly. He threw the knife at the second coyote, held back from Diamondback's throat only by his forearm, which was taking vicious damage from the beast's teeth and claws. The knife landed with a thunk sound and stuck deep into the side of the coyote's neck, causing it to immediately jump back and let out a painful howl.

As practiced, Logan immediately thought about the knife and it disappeared from the coyote's neck and reappeared in Logan's hand. Diamondback, bloodied from the attack, pulled his spear from the now lifeless body of the other coyote and stepped back beside Logan to prepare for whatever came next. The seasoned warrior gave his young partner a nod of his head in appreciation for his help, and Logan felt a confidence building in his gut. For the first time, he began to think he might actually be able to save Erica.

The coyote pierced by Diamondback's spear suddenly opened its eyes and began transforming from a coyote to a man while it remained lying on the ground. The man stood up, now draped in the pelt of a coyote. The bloody gash on the side of his stomach slowly began to heal as the skin closed up around the wound. The skinwalker let out a horrible guttural howl that was like no sound a human would make, and a smile could be seen through the coyote's front legs hanging in front of his face.

The coyote struck by Logan's knife attempted the same healing trick by turning back into human form, but seemed surprised when his wound did not heal and blood continued to pour out of the side of his neck. The other coyote skinwalker ran to his partner's side and glared at Logan as he realized the knife that made this wound could accomplish something that most weapons could not—kill a *yee naaldlooshi*. He let out another loud noise, and this time he was not smiling. The sound was an angry scream that changed into the growl of a coyote as he transformed back into animal form.

The coyotes retreated towards the protection of the circle of flames, and a giant snarling mountain lion emerged into view as it stepped across the fiery skulls and through the smoky curtain. Logan looked at Diamondback, whose arm was still bleeding, and his momentary confidence immediately turned back into fear. Logan looked towards Tia, and he could tell she knew by his worried expression that it was time for her to do whatever she could to help.

Tia climbed up on the ruins of one of the castle walls and pulled out her bow. She laid down the arrows beside her and nocked her first one as Jini leapt into the air to take flight out of harm's way. Tia let the first arrow fly and it found its target, hitting the lion squarely on the side of its body. The lion roared and swatted the arrow, breaking it off, unfazed by the injury.

Logan threw his knife as hard as he could towards the remaining coyote, but it now knew the danger posed by the blade and easily dodged the projectile. Logan willed the knife back into his throwing hand and prepared to throw again when a gun shot rang out.

"No!" screamed Logan as he tried to catch Diamondback's body before it crumpled to the ground. The warrior looked confused, and his eyes scanned the darkness wildly for the identity of the gunman before he fell into unconsciousness. Logan looked down at his hands, now covered in blood from the gunshot wound that had pierced Diamondback's side. He felt the will to fight leave his body and realized in that instant that his belief he could rescue Erica was foolish. His friends were going to die.

A familiar man stepped out of the darkness behind Tia and pointed a pistol at her head. It was Kinzi, still bloodied from the rock used by Diamondback in the canyon. Standing next to him was the runaway Anasazi horse from the guard Logan thought he had killed at the canyon ambush. Even with Jini flying up in the sky, between the darkness and chaos, Tia had not seen Kinzi sneak up behind them at the castle.

Kinzi yelled out to Logan, "Give up the fight now or I will shoot her. This ends now!"

The leader of the Anasazi Guard glared angrily at the boy, then shot off another round right next to Tia's head to make clear he was serious. Tia's ears immediately started ringing with the noise from the gunshot and she crouched down in pain.

Logan laid down his knife next to Diamondback's body and put his hands up to surrender. Kinzi pushed Tia forward to join Logan in the castle. She begrudgingly complied, and tears were running down her face as she looked at Kinzi with disgust.

"How could you betray my father? You were supposed to protect our people."

"You can't possibly understand," said Kinzi. "You aren't a real Navajo. This is *all about* the future of our people."

Tia walked over to join Logan and grabbed his hand. The circle of flames subsided, and the robed woman walked over to join the lion who had now transformed back into a man. He removed the remaining piece of the arrow from his side and glared at Tia before throwing it to the ground.

"You are late, Kinzi," said the female skinwalker.

"I had an unexpected complication," he replied, pointing at the body of Diamondback still lying on the stone floor.

"Bring them into the circle, so they can join their friend."

The male lion grabbed Logan with one arm and Tia with the other and pushed them roughly into the circle of skulls. They were now both standing next to Erica, and Logan immediately bent over and shook her in an attempt to wake her up. Erica didn't move and Logan remembered Diamondback's warning. The only thing that could wake her from her sleep would be killing or weakening the skinwalker who had her under its spell. *But which one?*

Kinzi looked at Tia sadly. "I wanted to bring you back home to your father, but now you have to go, too."

"Go where? Where are we going?" she screamed angrily.

The female *yee naaldlooshi* smiled. "You are going to the Crow Keeper. He is waiting for you."

The robed skinwalker started chanting and swayed as she waved her arms. Inside the circle, the stony ground of the castle became hazy and then black as the night sky. Suddenly, the ruins of Hovenweep disappeared and Logan saw a cave with an identical circle of skulls. An old man was looking at him with a black wide brimmed hat. It was dark in the cave, but Logan could make out a crooked smile on his face.

At that moment, the loud rumbling of an engine pierced the quiet of the night and headlights lit up the castle through the jagged ruins of the wall. The tires of a large vehicle skidded in the dirt road and kicked up a dust storm as a pickup truck came to a screeching halt at the edge of Hovenweep's walls.

The female stopped her chanting to turn and face the new arrivals. Logan, Tia and Erica were instantly transported back into the now illuminated castle.

Chapa and Resnick threw open the doors to the truck and peered around them with their pistols drawn, aimed into the castle. "Logan, you OK?" shouted Chapa.

"We're good," replied Logan. "Kinzi is with them. Don't trust him!"

Logan bent down to pick up Erica and make a run towards the police officers, but the female skinwalker chanted a few words and the skulls reignited into flames. The three teenagers were trapped inside the circle and could only watch the action through the smoky haze.

Resnick was the first to open fire, and he shot three carefully aimed rounds in Kinzi's direction. One of the bullets found its mark, and pierced Kinzi's leg before he could find cover. Kinzi kept moving and scurried to the back edge of the castle where he could hide behind the rocky ruins of a wall. Kinzi angrily returned fire from his own pistol, landing several rounds in the armor plated car door protecting Resnick.

Sensing that they had the superior firepower advantage, Chapa and Resnick left the protection of the plated doors of the pickup truck and advanced to closer positions, ducking behind the cover of the jagged castle walls. "We are coming in, Logan," yelled Resnick.

Resnick jumped through an opening in the perimeter wall, only to be immediately met by a growling coyote that came up to his chest. The beast attacked Resnick, biting his arm with its giant fangs, causing Resnick to drop his gun. The FBI agent started wildly punching the coyote with his free hand, desperately trying to pull his other arm from the vice grip of the coyote's jaws.

Chapa followed when he heard Resnick's scream and shot one round point blank into the attacking coyote's head, and another into its flank as it struggled with his partner. The coyote let out a howl and immediately let go of Resnick and bounded back towards the middle of the castle where it was joined by the other two skinwalkers. The coyote shifted back into its human form and Chapa and Resnick watched as the bloody gunshot wounds slowly healed in the glow of the truck's headlights.

Resnick turned to Chapa, with a newly worried look on his face. "I hope you have some silver bullets. I'm fresh out."

The three skinwalkers could now be clearly seen in the center of the castle ruins, dressed in the skins of their predator alter egos. Kinzi came out from behind his hiding place, smirking but being careful to keep the skinwalkers between himself and the two armed agents. "I told you not to come here, Chapa. You can't stop us."

While Kinzi was taunting Chapa, the two male skinwalkers changed back into their animal form. They dropped down onto all fours and the skins on their backs merged seamlessly into their bodies. Logan watched the horrible metamorphosis and wondered how Chapa and Resnick would be able to stop the *yee naaldlooshi*. If bullets weren't effective on these monsters, the agents wouldn't stand a chance.

# Chapter Twenty-Eight

Logan paced anxiously around the skeletal prison circle looking for a way to help Chapa and Resnick. He tried running through the smoky barrier, but he was knocked back roughly onto his backside by a ghostly figure in the haze. He tried focusing on his knife lying on the ground next to Diamondback, but he could not retrieve it for some reason.

He grabbed Tia and looked directly into her unseeing dark eyes. "We have to do something, or they are going to die!"

"There is something I can try. When the *yee naaldlooshi* are transformed, they are animals. I choose to only bond with animals for their sight, but I have the power to do more. I can feel them and control them."

"Try the coyote."

Tia closed her eyes and concentrated. She broke the bond with Jini who was flying above the castle, and searched for the coyote on the other side of the circular prison. She had never bonded with such a large animal before and certainly not one that was inhabited by a skinwalker. She reached out with her mind and felt both the lion and the coyote. Tia felt rage and fear from both of the animals.

She focused on the coyote and opened the door to its mind. The blind girl felt the wild spirit of the coyote along with something else, something dark and evil. Beads of sweat ran down Tia's forehead as she wrestled control of the coyote's consciousness away from the *yee naaldlooshi*. Tia opened her eyes and she was now looking through the eyes of the coyote, with the lion to her side and Chapa and Resnick straight ahead.

The agents watched dumbfounded as the coyote suddenly lunged onto the mountain lion's back and grabbed hold of its neck with its jaws. The claws of the coyote dug deep into the lion's skin as it tried desperately to shake off its attacker. The attack surprised Kinzi and the female who both stepped back away from the dueling beasts.

Kinzi pulled his pistol and tried to aim at the coyote, which was now flailing around like a bull rider on top of the lion. Before Kinzi could get a clean shot on the coyote, Chapa opened fire at Kinzi and hit him twice, right in the chest. Kinzi looked shocked as he fell backward into a part of the crumbling wall, dropping his gun. Defiantly, Kinzi made one last effort to get back to his knees, but he could not muster the strength as the life quickly drained from his body. The Head of the Anasazi Guard fell backwards again, and remained still.

The mountain lion and coyote fought viciously in the center of Hovenweep while the robed female skinwalker looked on, unsure whether to run or fight. The lion finally managed to shake off the coyote and threw the beast across the stone floor. The lion turned its attention back to Chapa and Resnick, but failed to notice that Diamondback had awakened from his resting place on the ground and picked up Logan's knife. As the lion advanced, Diamondback sprang up behind it and plunged the knife deep into the side of its belly. The old warrior used the last of his strength to twist the blade for good measure as he cursed the *yee naaldlooshi* in his native tongue.

The lion roared in pain and responded to the unexpected attack with a deadly slash of its razor-sharp claws, knocking Diamondback to the ground. This time, Diamondback did not move, and the side of his face was bleeding profusely—badly damaged by the cat's deadly claws. The old warrior's eyes closed for the last time and a contented look crossed his face as he finally found his beloved Rose.

Tia saw the bravery of Diamondback, and the resulting fatal blow through the eyes of the coyote. Inside the circle of skulls she screamed and started to cry uncontrollably, and her loss of focus allowed the skinwalker to resume control of the coyote. Tia was exhausted and knew she would not be able to repeat the trick. In her panic, she longed for the comfort of her bond with Jini and instinctively reached up into the sky to ensure her friend was still flying and regain her sight.

When Tia next opened her eyes, she saw the full view of the castle below through Jini's vantage point. The coyote and lion were now closing ranks around the robed skinwalker and headed back towards the circle. Chapa and Resnick were unloading rounds into both animals, but the bullets seemed to be a mere distraction. The real damage had been done by Diamondback as the knife wound on the mountain lion's belly left an increasingly large trail of blood.

The female *yee naaldlooshi* began chanting and swaying again and the wall of smoke and flames stopped with a "whoosh" sound as it extinguished. Logan shouted out, "Chapa!" as he could now see him and Resnick advancing with guns aimed at the skinwalkers.

"Hang in there, kid," shouted Resnick as he quickly reloaded the clip in his Ruger.

As fast as the smoky barrier came down, the floor beneath the circle began to give way again to darkness. The robed female chanted and those inside knew what was about to happen. "They are sending us to the Crow Keeper," Logan yelled. "I don't know where. A cave, I think."

Logan focused one more time on his knife, and this time, now that the wall of smoke was gone, it materialized in his hand. Jini dove from the sky and landed on Tia's shoulder just as the three prisoners disappeared from the confines of Hovenweep, mysteriously transported to an unknown destination.

Satisfied that her work was done, the female skinwalker transformed into a great grey owl, and flapped up and away from the castle, fleeing out the back side into the mountains. The coyote and lion turned to follow, jumping off the cliff's edge into the darkness beyond the reach of the headlights of Chapa's pickup.

\*\*\*

Chapa and Resnick waited a few seconds to speak, scanning the shadows of the castle ruins to make sure there were no more threats. "What the hell just happened?" asked Resnick.

"I don't know," replied Chapa slowly as he looked around at the bizarre scene. "I don't know."

Resnick immediately got back to business and checked Diamondback, then Kinzi, for signs of life. Both were dead.

Chapa walked over to Diamondback and looked closely at the man. He could tell he was an older Navajo, but he had never met him before and had no idea what he was doing at Hovenweep fighting by their side. He picked up the spear nearby and laid it on his chest, then placed his arms over the weapon. Chapa paused and said a few words softly by the body.

"What did you say?" asked Resnick.

"It is a prayer my grandmother used to say when someone died. The prayer says, 'I give you this one thought to keep, I'm with you still, I do not sleep. I am a thousand winds that blow. I am the diamond glints on the snow. I am the sunlight on ripened grain. I am the gentle autumn rain'." Chapa continued. "I don't know who this man is, but he saved our life."

Resnick nodded in agreement. "I don't know about you, but I thought we were done."

Chapa walked with Resnick over to his pickup truck and started thinking out loud about their next move. "Did you hear what Logan said before they disappeared? He said they were being sent to the Crow Keeper, and something about a cave."

"Yep. That's what I heard, too. What does it mean?"

"All of the earlier kidnappings were in South Dakota, which makes sense because of the ties to Sitting Bull. I don't understand how they did it, but I think those things somehow transported Logan and the others to a cave in South Dakota tonight. That's where we will find Logan and the rest of the kidnapped people."

"Well, a few days ago, I would have said that was impossible, but I have given up on that front. Frankly, magical transportation would not even be at the top of the list of things in the last forty-eight hours I can't explain," said Resnick. "I just have one question," he added.

"What?"

"If what you say is true, how do you plan to stop them and rescue Logan and the others? You saw those things eat our bullets like they were dinner. We barely escaped from that gang at Logan's home. We are lucky to not be dead already, and now you want to go right up to their front door and knock? Look, man, we need some help," argued Resnick.

Chapa thought back to his call with Dawes and the politics of their situation. "I don't think we are going to get any more help from the BIA. I don't even think that is the kind of help we need. I know someone who might be willing to help us, and who has a better idea of what we are up against."

"Who?" asked Resnick.

"Zuma," said Chapa. "Logan wasn't the only one they took. Tia was with him, and I am willing to bet Zuma will help us get her back. Don't call in anything yet. I think we have a stop to make first."

# Chapter Twenty-Nine

I t was almost midnight by the time Chapa and Resnick made it back to Chimney Top. They entered the Kiva and were met by two guards on the floor level entrance to the city.

"Zuma is expecting you," one said and waved at the agents to follow him quickly.

Chapa followed the guard through the familiar passageway back into the golden city of Anasazi, which was now dark and lit only by torches along the city streets. The guard navigated through several twists and turns in the city before the street opened into a wide plaza with a fountain in the middle. He pointed to a building with a large bronze dome on top and hustled up a stone staircase. Chapa moved quickly behind the guard with Resnick on his heels.

The three men were greeted at the door by Zuma who thanked the guard and invited the agents into his home. It was built like most of the other structures within Anasazi, in that it was carved straight into the rocky innards of the mountain, but inside it looked more like a museum. The home was decorated with an incredible collection of Native American art on the walls. Large cabinets dotted the room, containing artifacts of all shapes and sizes, including knives, pottery, and traditional clothing.

"Sit down," said Zuma, offering the two men a seat in his living room. Although the furniture was by no means modern, it was very contemporary, including a red camelback sofa and two leather chairs. The sofas and chairs were flanked by mahogany tables with kerosene lamps burning oil to light up the room. A beautiful handmade rug covered the floor, emblazoned with a red Navajo pattern.

Hatani was already sitting on the sofa and Zuma sat down next to him. Chapa took a seat in one of the leather chairs, and immediately realized he was exhausted. "Look," said Chapa, "you should know that Tia was taken along with Logan and Erica. Kinzi was working with them, and we had to kill him. We did everything we could."

Zuma sighed. "I know," he replied softly. "I sent another group of guards a few hours after Kinzi's team left, just to be safe in case they got into trouble. They found Kinzi and Diamondback at Hovenweep and reported it to me. I hoped the two of you would come back here, and I am glad you did."

Hatani was aching to speak up and get more information about Logan. "Is Logan alright? Was he hurt?"

"Logan looked fine," said Resnick. "All three of them looked fine, but keep in mind they were in the middle of a fight with werewolves."

"Skinwalkers, *yee naaldlooshi*," said Zuma, correcting Resnick. "You should call them by their proper name."

"Whatever they were, they couldn't be killed by bullets, which is why we are here. We need help."

Zuma leaned back into the sofa and sat quietly for a few moments. "This is more serious than I thought. I knew there were those in Anasazi who sympathized with the Ghost Dance, but I didn't think they would go this far. This Crow Keeper and the *yee naaldlooshi* are working together, and Kinzi was part of it as well."

Zuma paused again. "There will be more bloodshed in Anasazi if we don't stop this now."

He leaned forward and suddenly became focused. "You must go to the Lakota Nation. You must stop whatever the Crow Keeper has planned for Logan and rescue Tia."

"I am glad you agree," said Chapa slowly. "But... we need some help. That's why we are here."

"Unfortunately, I will not be able to send Navajo into the Lakota Nation to assist you, but I have a better idea." Zuma then raised his voice. "Magaskawee, come join us please."

The distinguished middle-aged woman from the Blessing Way ceremony entered the living room from an adjoining space where she had been waiting and listening to the conversation. She was now dressed in casual clothes and boots. She had a backpack over one shoulder and a duffle bag on the ground by her feet. She appeared ready for a trip.

The woman spoke up. "If you are going up to the Lakota Nation, you will need a Lakota. No one is going to talk to outsiders, especially law enforcement types like you two."

Chapa looked at Resnick and he shrugged his shoulders, but Chapa seemed unconvinced. "Do you even have a gun?" Chapa asked.

Magaskawee shook her head in disgust and Zuma just smiled. "She won't need a gun," he replied. "I think you will find her to be exactly the kind of help that you need."

"I am leaving in the morning for Rapid City. You guys coming with me or what?" said Magaskawee.

Chapa thought for a moment. "Well, I guess we have a plan. You are welcome to ride with us in my truck in the morning."

Magaskawee laughed. "You are driving? I will have Logan and Tia located before you get out of Colorado." She pulled out her iPhone and showed her ticket. "Eight thirty flight out of Durango, landing before noon."

Chapa's face blushed in embarrassment, but he quickly gained his composure and turned to Resnick. "We have a long drive. We better hit the road now." The still red-faced agent turned back to Magaskawee. "If you need a ride from the airport, here is a card with my phone number. We will already be there."

"Dammit," said Resnick. "I was not looking forward to sleeping in a car again. Look on the bright side—at least she is not a werewolf. I don't think they carry iPhones and fly American Airlines."

Chapa thanked Zuma and Magaskawee for their help and then said his goodbyes to Hatani. Resnick was already doing the math in his head on the distance to South Dakota and was complaining all the way back to Chapa's pickup. "That's, like, a twelve-hour trip. We are going to be so exhausted."

"I do it all the time," replied Chapa. "Just don't ask for a bathroom break until we are out of the state. No way she is beating us to South Dakota."

# Chapter Thirty

Resnick offered to take a turn behind the wheel on the long drive to Rapid City, but there was no way Chapa was going to let anyone else drive his truck. Even though the aged vehicle had seen better days, it had served Chapa well, and had been his home away from home too many times to count.

As the vehicle sped down the Interstate in the middle of the night, Chapa found himself embroiled in a bitter verbal tug of war with his passenger. Chapa preferred to listen to classic rock, while Resnick desperately wanted to bide the time with conversation. After an hour of poking and prodding Chapa with questions and efforts at small talk, Chapa eventually capitulated.

"Has anyone ever told you that you talk too much?" asked Chapa.

"Let's see, my ex-wife, every partner I have ever had, and now you," Resnick replied with his usual smirk as he pretended to count on his fingers. "How are you so damn calm after all the craziness we saw back there? I don't know about you, but I don't normally deal with lost cities and werewolves in my job. It is mainly narcotics and human trafficking."

"I have seen some things I couldn't explain in the past, but nothing like this," replied Chapa. "We are definitely in uncharted territory."

"But you're an Indian, right? You understand this stuff."

Chapa bristled at yet another inappropriate comment from his partner, and decided it was time to try to educate him. "I'm part-Cherokee, but I grew up watching television and reading comic books. We didn't hunt buffalo or do rain dances. I was just a regular kid raised by a single mom who bought me frozen pizzas for dinner. My grandmother was the last generation who spoke the language fluently and maintained the traditions. I remember her teaching me words in Cherokee and telling me stories. She died from cancer when I was in high school.

Have you ever been on a reservation?" Chapa asked Resnick, changing the subject.

"Nope," he replied.

"Most people haven't," said Chapa. "I remember visiting the Cherokee reservation near Tahlequa in Oklahoma when I was a kid and thinking it was just like the movies. All the horses and teepees. Now I have grown up and realize that part of the reservation is all just for show, an echo of the past. The real life on reservations is pain and poverty. Pine Ridge in South Dakota—where we are headed—is one of the poorest places in the country. We won't get much help there. They're not fans of cops. Trust me I know from experience."

"So why do it if it's a lost cause?" asked Resnick. "Why did you work for the BIA instead of doing something else?"

"I don't know exactly. Seemed like the right thing to do when I got out of the Marines. I thought about my grandmother and how someone needed to protect people like her still living on the reservations. Too many good people have turned their back. I didn't want to be one of them."

Chapa was surprised at how much he had shared with Resnick about his personal life, but decided to continue, hoping it would help Resnick gain some perspective. "I never got married or had kids. Just couldn't bring myself to do it. Every day I see people losing family. People missing or shot. I always think about what if that was my wife or my kid. How do you live with something like that?"

"Wow, you really don't get it," said Resnick, before pulling out his phone. "We all worry about losing family. It's about enjoying the time you have together. Look here."

Resnick scrolled through photographs on his phone before settling on one with himself crouched down holding two blonde haired girls that looked to be around ten years old. "I have twin daughters!" said Resnick with a smile on his face. "I can't spend five minutes around their mother, but those girls are incredible. I can't wait to see the look on my ex-wife's face when I tell them their dad fought off werewolves."

Chapa just shook his head. "Those are some good-looking kids. My advice is to love on them every chance you get."

The sun was now coming up and the Rocky Mountains were fading out of sight behind the racing pickup. The sign alongside the highway had a colorful state flag with the words "Leaving Colorado—Come Back Soon!"

"You know what that means," said Resnick. "You owe me a bathroom break."

Chapa was a man of his word and pulled over at the next truck stop for gasoline. While Chapa filled the truck's nearly empty tank, Resnick emptied his bladder and bought snacks, bottled water and Red Bulls. By the time Resnick finished his shopping trip, Chapa had already finished his job and was waiting impatiently in the truck looking at his phone.

Resnick hopped into the passenger side and immediately took out a candy bar and started peeling back the wrapper. "You are like a little kid," said Chapa.

"Hey, man, I gotta eat," Resnick replied. "You want something?"

Chapa looked over the cornucopia of snack and drink options that was now available for selection, thanks to Resnick, and opted for a bottle of water and beef jerky.

"Thanks for breakfast," said Chapa.

Chapa took his time with the jerky, slowly chewing on the pieces as the sun rose higher in the sky. The miles rolled away, and the pair finally crossed over into South Dakota by mid-morning. The sign up ahead said eighty miles to Rapid City.

"I think we might actually beat her there," said Resnick, looking down at his watch. "By the way, what do you think about Magaskawee? Can we trust her?"

Chapa thought about the question for a while. "Not sure what to make of her or even Zuma, for that matter. I think Zuma *thinks* she can help us, and we really do need a Lakota up here to get anyone to talk."

"Well, she can get me to talk anytime," said Resnick before laughing at his own joke.

"You are an idiot," Chapa replied. Before Resnick could snap off a witty retort, Chapa's phone rang. It was Magaskawee asking for a ride from the airport. Her flight had landed early.

Chapa silently cursed his luck, then calmly informed Magaskawee that he was about an hour out and would swing by the airport to get her shortly. Chapa put down the phone and Resnick was happily waiting to twist the knife into Chapa's wounded pride.

"Magaskawee one, Chapa zero," Resnick announced with a smile.

# Chapter Thirty-One

Logan looked around the cave that was now a prison for him and his friends. They were held captive in a makeshift jail cell made of rusted steel bars affixed to the stone walls. Logan sat on the floor, surrounded by not only Tia and Erica, but six other people he didn't know.

The last few hours had literally been a blur. After disappearing from Hovenweep, Logan and his friends found themselves transported to a dark cave. Logan didn't understand how the magical skull circles worked, but the journey made all of them weak and dizzy. They were no match for the *ozuye* who greeted them after the transportation, and the men immediately took away Logan's knife and Tia's falcon. The good news was that Erica woke up after being jostled into the homemade jail cell, although she had no idea where she was, or how she got there.

Logan stared at the lone *ozuye* who stood guard a few feet away from the cell. He was wearing a black vest with the symbol of the soaring bird just like the men who had attacked his uncle back in Cortez. It was the same symbol as the one on the necklace still hanging around Logan's neck.

Although it was hard to tell time inside the darkness of the cave, Logan believed it was night because the other men and women in the cell were sleeping. He was exhausted and hadn't felt like having a conversation with Tia and Erica in front of their captors. The two girls had already nodded off and he was the last one left awake.

It was hard to see the details of the room by the dim light that permeated the space, but his eyes had adjusted. Logan wasn't sure where the light came from, but the room appeared to be connected to a larger complex of caves, and there were several passages leading in different directions. He could hear faint voices and other noise beyond his sight, signaling that more *ozuye* were close by in case there was trouble. *Getting out of here is going to be tough*, he thought to himself.

Logan squinted through the darkness for any clues as to his whereabouts. He assumed he was in South Dakota, but he wasn't very familiar with the local geography. All he knew about South Dakota was that it had Mount Rushmore and was below North Dakota on the map. Erica was going to be much better at figuring this out. She knew everything.

In the middle of the cave floor, Logan could make out the familiar profile of a small circle of skulls. There was also a place for a fire, and desks and shelves on the other side of the cave, lined with books and jars filled with animal parts. Old maps were hanging on the walls of the cavernous space near the desk, and a giant stuffed brown bear stood guard over the area. The ceiling was completely filled with ancient petroglyphs depicting buffalo hunts or dancing around a fire. But other scenes were much more frightening. Peeking out from behind the shadows on the ceiling were scenes of armed warriors killing women and children with tomahawks, and ghostly spirits rising out of the ground. At the head of the victorious army was a striking figure on a horse holding a spear. Logan stared at the ceiling and thought about his dream at the Blessing Way ceremony as he fell asleep. *Was the vision of Sitting Bull really a dream? Could this all just be a bad dream?*

The next morning Logan woke up to the surprising smell of breakfast. He suddenly realized he was starving and noticed that one of the guards was shoving plates of potatoes and eggs under the bars. Erica was already wolfing down a plate full of food, but Tia was sitting on the floor looking off into the distance with a blank stare. Without Jini, she had no sight, and the others in the cell didn't realize she was blind.

Unlike the darkness of the previous night, the cave was now dimly lit by natural light seeping into the space. *At least one of those passages was the way up to above ground and sunlight*, thought Logan.

He gathered two plates and took one back to Tia. Erica sat down next to him. "Looks like we will be eating well in this jail, but can someone explain how we got here?"

"More like fattening us up for the slaughter," Logan replied grimly as he ate the bacon with his hands.

Tia pushed away the food. "You go ahead and eat it. I'm not hungry," she said. "I can't feel Jini, and I don't know if she is dead or alive."

Erica looked confused and Logan explained that Tia was blind and used Jini to see. Seeing the look on her face after that revelation made him pause, but he decided to continue. "We are not in Anasazi anymore," he said.

"What do you mean? Where are we?" Erica asked.

"Do you remember anything after you went to sleep after the ceremony?" asked Tia.

"No," Erica replied. "I went to sleep and woke up here with you guys."

Logan looked at Tia for guidance but realized she was waiting for him to decide what to say next. Logan decided to share everything with Erica. "You were kidnapped by skinwalkers and taken to a castle called Hovenweep. Tia and I came to rescue you and there was a huge fight with the werewolf things and Kinzi was on their side. Chapa and Resnick came to save us, but the skinwalkers trapped the three of us in that skull circle over there and somehow used magic to transport us to this cave, which we think belongs to the Crow Keeper."

After he heard the words come out of his mouth, Logan realized how ridiculous the story sounded. He frowned, unsure of what to say next.

After letting Logan's words sit for a few seconds, Tia spoke up sullenly. "It's true. It's all true. Do you remember any dreams, Erica? Maybe a coyote or mountain lion?"

"Yes!" said Erica. "I remember that in my dream I was chasing a big dog through Anasazi. He was so fast and I couldn't catch him."

"Yeah... that really happened," said Logan. "That big dog kidnapped you to get to me. Looks like it worked."

"I'm... so sorry. I can't believe you risked your life to save me. That's so brave!" As she handed out the compliment, Erica gave Logan a long hug, resting her head on his shoulder.

Logan was uncomfortable with the attention and broke off the hug. "Tia helped, too. She deserves more credit than me."

Erica gave Tia a much faster hug before turning back to Logan. "So, who are all of these people?" she said, pointing at the other end of the cell.

There were six other men and women congregating on the other side of the cell, eating their breakfast and studying the new occupants. One older man came up to the three and offered his hand in greeting. "Good morning, I am Samuel White Elk."

Logan and the others shook his hand and offered their names. "Where are we?" asked Logan.

"Hard to tell," replied White Elk. "We all went to sleep in our beds and woke up in this cave. They won't let us leave and keep us locked up."

Logan knew the answer to his next question but asked it anyway. "Who is the old man with the hat? Has he said anything?"

"He comes and goes. The young men call him the *Khanji Kipa*. The Crow Keeper. He asks a lot of questions and sometimes spends time talking with us. He likes to sing songs while he works at his desk."

White Elk paused before speaking again. This time his words were softer. "He thinks we don't know, but we know what he is. He is a medicine man who calls upon the spirits of the dead."

Almost as if he was listening to their conversation, the Crow Keeper walked from behind a corner entrance and into the cave. He had on a wide brimmed black hat and was carrying a black pot cradled on one side of his body.

The Crow Keeper walked slowly into the room from feeding his crows and put down the pot full of peanuts and chopped up apples on his desk. He walked over to the jail cell and his eyes focused quickly on Logan. The Crow Keeper's mouth parted into a crooked smile, and his yellow decaying teeth betrayed his age.

The next words that came out of the Crow Keeper's decrepit mouth were not what Logan was expecting to hear. "Welcome home, boy. Now show me that necklace."

# Chapter Thirty-Two

Chapa sat in the pickup truck waiting impatiently for Magaskawee to exit the airport. She eventually came into view, sprinting across the lanes of traffic with her large duffle bag hanging over her shoulder. The woman was wearing sunglasses and dressed in khakis and a white blouse. Even though she was middle-aged, she was athletic and moved quickly towards the truck.

"You need to get into the back seat," ordered Chapa. "You know, chivalry and all."

"Yeah, yeah," Resnick replied. "I'm going."

Magaskawee threw her bag into the bed of the truck and sat down in the passenger seat. "How long have you had this piece of junk? It's a miracle you made it here in one piece."

Chapa bristled with the criticism of his treasured pickup. "She is fast enough and gets the job done."

Resnick chuckled in the back seat, so Chapa immediately changed the subject. "Where do you suggest we start?"

"I think we should start in Standing Rock. There is somebody there you both should meet," said Magaskawee.

Resnick suddenly got interested in the conversation and leaned forward from the back seat. "Who?" he asked.

"She is hard to describe, but I will try. Her name is Ina Blue Sky, which means Mother Blue Sky. People go to see her for advice, and she will know about any cult operating up here."

Resnick started laughing, and Chapa shot him a dirty look. "We have an investigation to do, and you want us to go see a fortune teller? Are you serious?"

Chapa was also dubious but a little more respectful. "Magaskawee, I trust you know what you are doing, but we don't have a lot of time. Are you sure she can help us?"

Magaskawee shook her head and frowned in frustration. "You can't win every fight with bullets. I would have hoped you would have figured that out by now. If you want to rescue those kids and defeat the Crow Keeper, we have to understand his plans and find a weakness. You are going up against a power that you don't understand."

Chapa knew when to admit defeat. "You're right," he said. "Standing Rock it is."

"Good," she replied. "And by the way, you can call me Mags."

Within minutes of hitting the highway, Resnick quickly dozed off and could be heard snoring over the rhythmic sounds of the engine. Standing Rock, the reservation that was once the home of Sitting Bull, was only a few hours away. The time flew quickly as Chapa and Mags discussed Blue Sky's background and the few clues they had on the missing teenagers' current whereabouts. Although Logan had mentioned a cave before disappearing at Hovenweep, Mags explained that South Dakota was littered with caves, any one of which could be a hiding place. This clue wasn't very helpful without more.

The entrance to Standing Rock reservation was set up to funnel traffic to the casino and the surrounding small city of hotels, restaurants, and modern accommodations. Chapa drove past the flashing lights and billboards, and within a few miles the landscape became very different. The buildings were old, and the homes were run down and spread out.

Mags pointed the way down a small farm road that led towards the Missouri River. The homes were now even further apart, and the road was lined with beautiful green grasslands. The next turn was onto a dirt road that seemed to be made for horses, not motorized vehicles. Chapa's truck bounced up and down on the uneven road and Resnick was finally wakened from his slumber.

"Where the hell are we?" Resnick asked as he looked around at the rising and falling landscape. "Are those buffalo?" he said, pointing out the window to his right where several groups of large brown animals were grazing in the fields.

"Yes," said Mags casually. "We have a number of herds on the reservation."

Up ahead was an old farmhouse with a wraparound porch that spanned the perimeter of the home. The home sat at the top of a small hill and looked out over a bend in the Missouri River and the field where the bison were grazing.

"We're here," said Mags. As they got closer to the house, Mags' eyes were darting around as if she was looking for something or someone.

Chapa navigated up the dirt driveway and parked on the side of the modest one-story ranch house. The home was surrounded by giant elms and cypress trees, which formed a row lining the river below. On the side facing the road was a fenced-in field with brown and white horses grazing on the tall grass. A small barn with stables sat back on the property away from the house and the river. There were two men who could be seen tending to horses by the barn in the distance.

After stepping out of his truck, Chapa paused to admire the beautiful farm. Resnick seemed unimpressed. The FBI agent stretched his arms above his head in an exaggerated motion then let out a big yawn. "That back seat was getting cramped," he remarked. "So, where's the fortune teller?"

Mags turned to Chapa. "I think we may need to leave him in the truck."

"He will be good, I promise," Chapa replied.

The three walked up the steps to the front porch and Mags opened the screen door. She was about to knock when an old woman suddenly appeared at the front door and waved them inside.

Mags smiled. "Ina, it has been a long time."

The old woman embraced Mags then stepped back into view. She was a small woman in stature, but her face reflected an aura of strength and intensity. Chapa guessed that Blue Sky was in her seventies, but her hair was still jet black and beautifully braided into two tails that dropped down on either side of her face. She was wrapped in a multi-colored shawl that she wore like a cape around her body as she led them into the living room.

There were photographs everywhere, hanging on the walls and in frames sitting on furniture. Many of the photos were old. Some were even in black and white. Others were modern color photos, including scores of pictures of children taken with horses in front of the barn that was visible on the property outside.

Mags and the old woman immediately fell into a conversation in Lakota, which Chapa couldn't understand. It went on for a few minutes, and eventually Mags mentioned their names and pointed in their direction. They both waved back to Blue Sky and said hello.

Blue Sky turned to Chapa and Resnick and smiled. "Go sit on the back porch. I will get some tea." She turned back to Mags. "I have been working on my English with my children. They come here to ride horses and learn Lakota, and they teach me about the internet and iPhones."

After a few minutes waiting for Blue Sky to bring out the tea, the group eventually all sat down together at a table on the back porch.

The old woman meticulously poured everyone's tea before nodding her head up towards the sky. "A storm is coming. The boys are putting the horses up and you should think about staying here to wait it out. It's going to be a bad one."

Chapa looked up in surprise at the sky that had been clear on the long drive from the airport. It was now filled with storm clouds moving rapidly across an eerie green background. Gray clouds were rolling in from the north and the wind was picking up speed. The birds were getting louder in the trees surrounding the home, and a lone crow landed on a fence only a few yards away from the back porch. There was a feeling in the air like the weather was about to change.

Mags drank a little of her tea and then got directly to the point. "These agents are looking for some people that were taken, and I am helping them. We think there is a medicine man up here called the Crow Keeper who is trying to bring back the Ghost Dance, and we need your help."

Blue Sky listened patiently to Mags' plea and then looked out across the grasslands. She seemed to be staring right at the crow sitting on the fence.

Chapa noticed Mags was now on the edge of her seat waiting to hear what Blue Sky would say. During the ride, Mags shared that she had grown up in Standing Rock and was one of Ina's "children" to whom she taught Lakota. She was truly like a mother to Magaskawee. The trips to Blue Sky's ranch were some of the fondest memories of her childhood—learning to ride horses and hearing stories about the history of the Lakota people. Those stories, of course, included tales of Sitting Bull, and the Ghost Dance. Mags believed those tales were not just made up stories, and Blue Sky was not just an old woman. Chapa wanted to believe, too, and now they would both find out together.

Finally, Blue Sky began to speak, and she aimed her words directly at Chapa and Resnick. "Over a hundred years ago, police officers like you murdered Sitting Bull. It happened right here in Standing Rock when they pulled him out of bed and murdered him on his front porch."

Blue Sky paused again and calmly took a drink from her glass of tea. "He didn't have to die, but they were afraid of him. They were afraid of the strength that our people would have if they banded together—not just the Lakota people—but all of the tribal nations. That was the dream of Sitting Bull and Wovoka."

Mags was now slumped back in her chair, stunned by Blue Sky's confrontation of the agents.

"They not only killed Sitting Bull, but they murdered everyone who followed him—men, women and children. That is the sad legacy of this reservation," said the old woman.

"What happened to Wovoka?" asked Chapa.

"He survived. But it was never the same. He lived in exile, and the secrets of the Ghost Dance died with him."

"Are you sure the Ghost Dance died with him?" asked Mags.

Blue Sky focused her gaze on Mags as if she was reading her mind. "I have heard of the one they call the Crow Keeper and I know his plans to resurrect the power of the Ghost Dance."

"Then *help* us."

"I will not help him fight his war. But I will also not help you defeat him."

Mags' heart sank when she heard the blunt words from Mother Blue Sky. The betrayal quickly turned to anger and frustration.

"I don't understand. How can you side with a gang of murderers and kidnappers?" exclaimed Mags.

"Child, did you not hear me? There are murderers on both sides. Ask this BIA agent how much Lakota blood is on the BIA's hands. The man who killed Sitting Bull—McLaughlin—was BIA and they named a town in our reservation after him. One man's murderer is another man's hero."

Resnick had heard enough. He finished off his tea and placed it on the table. "Ma'am, I appreciate the iced tea, but I think it's time for us to go." Resnick looked at Chapa as if to say, "I told you so."

*** 

Mags could not believe the cruelty of the words she was hearing. Blue Sky was the closest thing she knew to a purely good person in the world. Her mind raced as to her next move. She was sure Blue Sky would help them find the Crow Keeper. Without her aid, it would be impossible to stop him.

The old woman sat up as if to accept Resnick's cue that it was time to leave. She looked at Mags and then her eyes moved over to a lone black bird sitting on the fence across from the porch. Ina's apparent hostility suddenly began to make sense.

Blue Sky smiled at Mags. "Thank you, child, for coming to see me. I always enjoy company. Mags, will you walk with me inside? It has been so long since I have seen you and I would love to show you a picture before you go. Brings back so many memories."

Mags looked at Chapa, her confidence beginning to return. "It's OK. I will meet you outside. Just give us a minute."

As soon as the pair were inside the house, Blue Sky turned to Mags. "Child, you need to leave now. The Crow Keeper and his *ozuye* know you are here. They are already coming."

"We will go. I am sorry I dragged you into this."

"You were always my best student, and I am so proud of you. You are too much like me when I was young," said Blue Sky. "Always looking for trouble."

The old woman searched around her living room and found the one she was looking for amongst the many photographs of children. Blue Sky picked it up and handed it to Mags. She pointed to a young Lakota boy with green eyes standing at the edge of a line of children posing for a group picture. "Find this boy and you will find the Crow Keeper. His name is Red Moon from Pine Ridge and he is the key to your search."

Mags folded the picture and put it in her pocket then gave Ina a big hug. "Thank you. I knew I could count on you, and I will be back to see you when this is done."

The hug was cut short by the sounds of motorcycles approaching in the distance. "The *ozuye* are here," said Blue Sky, matter-of-factly. Then she smiled, "And so is my storm."

# Chapter Thirty-Three

Logan was finally face to face with the Crow Keeper, albeit separated by the bars of his subterranean prison. The man was a walking paradox. He appeared old and weak, but almost glowed with exuberance and passion. One minute he would move slowly, then another he would dart quickly around the cave. Logan knew the Crow Keeper was evil, yet he could not help but be drawn in by the smile.

The old shaman seemed disinterested in Tia and Erica. He focused his attention on Logan, and was especially interested in his family tree. Logan tried to avoid the interrogation, but his resolve weakened once the Crow Keeper brought up his mother.

"I understand you not wanting to talk to me. After all, you are being kept in a cage. It is a necessary step, however, and it will be temporary—I promise you."

"I have seen that necklace before," the Crow Keeper continued. "A student of mine fashioned it herself from one of the sacred stones from the birthplace of our people deep in these caves and emblazoned upon it the symbol of our movement. Her name was Tolulah—your mother. Oh, did you not know your mother was a follower of the Ghost Dance?"

The Crow Keeper paused and peered intently at Logan who was now paying close attention. "Of course you didn't. Why would she tell you that? She was ashamed of her past, but she was strong and would have been even stronger if not pulled away from us by your father."

Logan didn't know how to respond to the Crow Keeper's revelations, or even whether to believe the things he was saying about his mother. He just sat on the floor and remained silent.

"Now, I ask you again—show me the necklace." This time the Crow Keeper raised his voice, and he was not smiling. Logan, however, remained glued to his spot and avoided the gaze of the old medicine man.

After waiting a few moments, the Crow Keeper turned his attention to Tia. "And you must be that girl who belongs to Zuma. The blind one who uses a bird to see. Like you, I have an affinity for birds. I use them as tools to see things and do things that I cannot. We are not that different, you and I."

Tia could hear the Crow Keeper's voice, but avoided looking at him directly. She looked down instead and tried to ignore the taunting.

"I find it interesting that you have chosen a falcon to be your guide."

The Crow Keeper began pacing in front of the jail cell, and exclaimed in a mocking tone, "A bird of royalty! How fitting for Zuma's daughter."

He lowered his voice and took on a serious look as he pointed at his chest with his finger before slowly enunciating each word for emphasis. "I prefer the lowly crow. A bird for the common man."

The old man cackled as if he was privy to an inside joke. "Something else about crows. Crows don't mind being kept in a cage as long as they are well fed. They will literally eat anything—including other birds."

The medicine man looked directly at Tia, ignoring her blindness. "Did you know that?"

Tia shook her head and put her face into her hands to mask the tears that were now forming in her eyes.

"No, I guess Zuma didn't teach you that. How about your falcon—does it like being kept in a cage? I have it locked in a tiny one right now outside these cave walls. Poor thing may never see the sky again."

She tried to hide them, but tears were now running down Tia's face as she listened to the Crow Keeper's words. Logan's anger bubbled over, and he couldn't stay silent any longer.

"Enough!" he yelled as he finally rose off the floor of the cave and walked towards the bars of the prison. "Leave her alone."

"Leave her alone? I am just getting started," replied the Crow Keeper. "I will throw that bird into the cages with my lowly crows, and they will lick every bit of meat from its royal bones. The next time I ask any of you to do something, I expect you to be courteous and cooperative. If not, the girl's bird will be ripped apart as a snack."

The Crow Keeper's anger was now evident, but the cold smile remained, as if he enjoyed making threats. "Don't worry, Logan, you and I will get plenty close in the short time you have on this Earth. You will beg me to take your mother's trinket from you. But I won't. I want you to keep it for him. Sitting Bull is coming and you can't stop him. I will have my war chief."

The Crow Keeper continued, "The Ghost Dance has given me a powerful vision. Tomorrow, there will be a solar eclipse, and on that day, I will bring back Sitting Bull. You and the rest of his bloodline descendants will make it possible."

He watched Logan as he talked and Logan unsuccessfully tried to hide the fear in his own eyes. Not just blind fear, but a fear of something else, something that was familiar to Logan.

"Ha! You have seen him, haven't you!"

Logan looked away and ignored the question. He was disgusted with himself for betraying his vision from the Blessing Way.

"This is a sign," the Crow Keeper said excitedly. "I knew it."

The shaman turned and walked briskly out of the cave, and two *ozuye* immediately took his place to watch the prisoners. After the Crow Keeper had gone, Tia finally let out the emotion she had held back and began sobbing. Erica gave her a hug and White Elk and the others came over to console their new companions in the jail.

"Jini will be okay," said Erica.

Logan was unable to get past his anger and whispered urgently to the group, "Has anyone tried to escape?"

White Elk shook his head. "No. It's not possible. The bars are built into the cave walls and are too strong to break. Even if we could escape the jail, there are too many guards right outside. They would kill us before we could get away."

Erica was listening to the conversation, frustrated by the negativity she was hearing. "But why would they kill you? He brought you all here for a reason, and if he wanted it, you would be dead already."

Logan nodded his head in agreement. He knew Erica was right. Erica was always right.

Erica saw the nod and seemed to gain confidence. She pointed to the passage where the *ozuye* had just entered. "I see everyone leave that way out of the cave towards the light and the noise, but there is another way out of the cave on the other side—through the darkness. Can we get out that way?"

The three teenagers turned to White Elk as the senior statesman in the group, who appeared to know the most about their surroundings. Everyone waited to hear his answer to the question of what was lurking in the deepest part of the caverns.

"I would not go that way," he said. "There are many caves in the Lakota lands, and our people are said to have sprung from the earth through one of the caverns we call the Wind Cave. I do not know this cave, but I know there are many spirits who never followed the Lakota to come and live on the surface. They chose to remain in the dark. If the Crow Keeper has chosen this place, it is almost certainly a place of evil."

Erica was not deterred. "It's our only chance." She looked Logan directly in the eyes. "We have to try. It is our only way out."

Logan turned to Tia who was still fighting back tears. "What do you think?"

Tia exploded in anger. "What do I think? What do I think? I think I made a mistake in leaving Anasazi. I think I will never see Jini again. I think we will all die in this cursed place."

The *ozuye* guards turned towards the shouting and stared at the blind girl, who briefly stopped shouting. After a few moments, they returned to talking and seemed disinterested in the activity.

Logan tried to give Tia a hug, but she pushed him away. "Logan, I am blind. I am not going anywhere without being able to see. It's over. We are just kids. We can't defeat the Crow Keeper and his army."

Erica kept pressing. "Tia, you're so wrong. You're not blind." She approached Tia and grabbed one of her hands tightly.

"Don't you see? You are the *only* one who could guide us through a dark cave. We just need to find you an animal that can help you see in the dark."

Tia finally stopped crying and looked up at Erica. This time she had the same determined look on her face. "You're right."

"She's always right," said Logan. "Get used to it." He grabbed Tia's other hand and whispered to the two girls. "I'm ready to get out of here. How about you?"

# Chapter Thirty-Four

Mags ran out the front door of Blue Sky's home and was immediately hit with the competing sounds of the approaching motorcycles, Chapa's truck roaring to life, and claps of thunder. A bolt of lightning flashed in the not-so-distant sky.

Chapa waved at Mags to get in the truck, but she had different plans. "Go!" she yelled. "I will catch up." Mags ignored the look of confusion from Resnick and raced off in a full sprint towards the barn at the back of the house. The rain was now coming down in sheets, making it difficult to see.

Behind her, Mags could hear the sound of Chapa pulling out of the driveway and bullets hitting the metal of the truck's frame. She threw open the door to the barn and breathed a sigh of relief when she realized nothing had changed since the last time she had visited Blue Sky's ranch. The innocent looking school taught Lakota children more than just traditions and language. It taught them how to ride and shoot a bow, using the techniques passed down for hundreds of years. Mags was one of Blue Sky's best students and was deadly at anything less than thirty yards. She grabbed a familiar looking bow and a handful of arrows before running back out into the rain to find a horse.

Outside the barn was a row of stables, filled with horses that Blue Sky's ranch bred for rodeos. Mags knew she didn't need to be picky, and opened the first stall, which was occupied by a dark brown quarter horse. The constant waves of thunder had spooked the animal and it was pacing nervously around its small shelter. Mags stroked the side of its head and talked to it in a gentle voice while she quickly connected the bridle and reins. She led the horse out of the stable and leapt into a bareback position before nudging the horse into a gallop across the fields.

Mags sped across the field towards the dirt road leading to Blue Sky's farm, battered by the wind and the rain. In the distance, she saw a game of chicken playing out on the road as four motorcycles were speeding straight for Chapa's truck.

She leaned her head down onto the neck of the horse and barked out commands in Lakota that she knew would be familiar. Mags was more comfortable on a horse than behind the wheel of a car, and she knew every inch of these fields. Her horse accelerated while Mags held on tightly to the reins, hoping she could make it back to Chapa and Resnick in time.

*** 

Resnick leaned out the passenger window and fired at the four motorcycles speeding towards Chapa's truck. Notwithstanding the difficult conditions, Resnick's marksmanship prevailed, and he hit one of the riders, causing him to veer off the road and crash into the ditch.

Chapa gunned the accelerator, and the truck lurched straight into the remaining three motorcycles. Chapa and Resnick ducked down as more bullets hit the front windshield, but Chapa never relented. At the last minute, the riders veered off the road and the truck passed between them, kicking up mud from behind its wheels.

"Apparently, the *ozuye* have guns now too," Resnick shouted.

The remaining riders quickly turned their bikes around and resumed their pursuit of Chapa's truck. The rain had intensified, and a lightning bolt struck a tree next to the road. The accompanying clap of thunder was deafening, even in the pickup. The storm was right on top of them, and the lightning strikes were getting closer.

As the caravan of vehicles exchanged gunfire through the blinding storm, no one noticed a figure on horseback charging across the grassy field lining the road.

Mags pulled an arrow from the quiver hanging around her shoulder and notched it in the bow. Even in the wind and rain, she was able to hold onto the horse with her legs and pull back the bowstring. She carefully aimed at the rider closest to the road and let the arrow fly.

The impact of the strike knocked the surprised *ozuye* off the bike as the tip buried itself deep in his side. The now riderless motorcycle slowed down behind the other two before dropping over into the muddy road.

One of the pursuers looked back to see what had happened to his partner but couldn't see anything in the rain. As he turned back towards Chapa and Resnick, a brown quarter horse jumped the fence separating the road from the field and kicked the *ozuye* in the head as it knocked him off his motorcycle.

Chapa watched the amazing episode play out in his rearview mirror and immediately turned to Resnick. "Stop shooting," he yelled over the wind. "Mags is back there."

The lone remaining *ozuye* was now focused exclusively on Mags and moved into formation, driving parallel to her horse on the road. The man glared at Mags and pointed his gun in her direction, squeezing off a couple of shots at close range.

Mags instinctively slid around the opposite side of the horse while the bullets sailed through the space where her body had been sitting only seconds earlier. As she rotated back up onto her mount, she leaned her back down on the horse and laid on it while she aimed her bow sideways at the *ozuye*. In the pouring rain, her body blended in with the horse making her almost invisible to the rider who was sharing his attention between the road and the horse galloping beside him.

Mags shot the arrow and it landed in the man's thigh on the side of the motorcycle. He howled in pain as the arrow had completely penetrated his leg and lodged partly into the fuselage. Every bump on the road caused the arrow to shift in his leg, causing new waves of pain. He was stuck to the bike.

The *ozuye* screamed in rage and fired his gun in Mags' direction but she was gone. Mags had dropped back behind the motorcycle and notched another arrow. This time she aimed at the back tire and quickly hit her mark. The arrow blew out the tire, sending the motorcycle spinning out of control. Resnick watched through the back window as the last *ozuye's* bike careened off into the trees lining the opposite side of the road.

Chapa slowed down, allowing Mags to gallop up alongside and climb off the horse into the bed of the truck. She grabbed the roof of the cab and swung feet first through the sliding rear window before plopping down into the back seat. She smiled at the puzzled look on Resnick's face, then pointed up ahead through the windshield. "Look," she said. "The storm is over."

Resnick whistled. "This lady is full of surprises. I have never seen anything like that in my life."

Chapa seemed unimpressed. "Thanks for the help, but we had it under control. I am just glad you didn't get shot."

Mags smiled. "I am glad you didn't get shot, too. Wish I could say the same for your truck." She reached in her pocket and took out the photograph given to her by Blue Sky and showed it to the men in the front seat. "By the way, I picked this up from Ina back at the house. If we find this kid in the front row from Pine Ridge, Ina said he will lead us to the Crow Keeper."

"I think I know someone who can help us," said Chapa. "I know the police chief on the reservation, so that is probably a good place to start."

# Chapter Thirty-Five

Chapa's truck had a few new bullet holes as it pulled up at a plain looking one-story brick building with police cars lined up outside. The sign on the outside of the building said "Oglala Department of Public Safety."

The three exited the truck, only to be welcomed with stares from two tribal police officers who were talking in the parking lot. It was hard to tell if they were more put off by the sight of strangers or Chapa's truck, which was now missing a side window. Chapa noticed the stares, but it didn't bother him. He knew what he was doing.

Chapa showed his BIA badge to the clerk at the front desk and asked to see Chief Mesteth. "I called ahead so he knows we are coming," said Chapa confidently.

Chapa and Mags sat down in the small, uncomfortable chairs in the lobby to wait while Resnick walked around the office looking at the pictures on the wall. The FBI agent lingered in front of a bulletin board containing a series of "Most Wanted" suspects from the local area.

While Resnick was looking around, an older man in a black police uniform came through the door behind the front desk. He was middle-aged with thick Coke bottle glasses. The man looked like he had not missed too many meals and had a gut that extended out in every direction, giving him the shape of a bowling pin.

The chief immediately glared at Chapa and turned to the clerk at the front desk. "Who let this BIA dog in here?"

The clerk looked confused for a moment then shook his head and went back to work on his computer. Everyone else looked nervous except for Chapa who remained silent and just smirked.

After a few seconds, the chief broke into a smile and gave Chapa a warm hug. "So good to see you again, Chapa!"

Chapa returned the greeting and patted the chief on the back. "Chief Mesteth, I would like you to meet my friends. This is Agent Resnick with the FBI and Magaskawee. She is from Standing Rock and is helping us on a case."

"Nice to meet you," said the chief as he shook each one's hand.

"Can we speak in private about something?" said Chapa.

"Sure," replied the chief. "This way." He led them through a tight hallway into a small conference room. It was not filled with expensive furniture like those back in Washington D.C. The centerpiece was two smaller tables pulled together, and the chairs looked like they were at least twenty years old. Pine Ridge reservation was one of the poorest places in the country, and its public buildings reflected the lack of resources.

While everyone was getting situated, Chief Mesteth made a point of singing Chapa's praises. "You know, this one here is the only BIA agent I ever liked. He helped me on a really nasty case years ago. We had a home-grown serial killer, and we would never have been able to catch him without Chapa. I didn't think I would ever see Chapa again, and now here he is—back in Pine Ridge. I have a feeling you are not here on a social visit. Am I right?"

Mags pulled out the picture given to her by Blue Sky. She pointed to the young boy in the front row of the school children with green eyes. "Do you know this boy?" she asked.

Resnick jumped into the conversation without warning. "His name is Red Moon."

Chief Mesteth looked at the photograph and then turned calmly to Resnick. "Yes. That's right."

Chapa looked at Resnick with amazement. "How in the world did you know that?"

"That kid grew up to be the same guy who attacked us back in Cortez and his poster is hanging on the Most Wanted list outside. I recognized the eyes.

Something creepy about those green eyes."

Chapa shook his head and turned back to Chief Mesteth. "What can you tell us about Red Moon?"

The police chief's demeanor became serious. "His name is Joe Janis and that one is a stone cold killer. You know how it is, Chapa. These kids on the reservation grow up in broken homes without a future. They drop out of school and by the time they are sixteen they are in a gang. I remember when Joe was just a young kid and he was in and out of jail for theft and all sorts of small stuff. He grew up and the crimes just kept getting bigger and more violent. The saddest part was that his father was a police officer. Between the job and alcohol, his family was a mess."

"So, where is the father? Is he still a cop?" asked Resnick.

"No. When Joe was a teenager, the boy disappeared for a while and when he came back he was a different person. His father was killed with his own gun and everyone thought Joe did it. His dad was a mean drunk and had a ton of enemies, so there never was a prosecution. After that, the boy started calling himself Red Moon. He has been a suspect in a number of murders, and always seems to be around when people go missing. Him and his gang come in and out of the reservation, but everyone is afraid of them, including most of my own officers. If you are looking for him, good luck. He is like a ghost."

Mags had been so quiet that everyone almost forgot she was still in the room. "Does he still have any family in the reservation?"

"Sure. His older sister still lives here. I don't think she will be of much help, but you are welcome to speak to her. She hasn't seen him in years as far as I know, and she doesn't have anything to do with her brother anymore."

Mags looked at Chapa. "We need to go see her. It is important."

Chapa turned to the chief. "We will go ahead and pay her a visit and see what she knows. I would appreciate the address."

Chief Mesteth escorted them out of the conference room and back to the lobby. He turned to the clerk and asked him to look up the address for Leona Janis and write it down for his guests.

"I hope she can help you," said the chief. "And one more thing. If you find

Red Moon, be careful. I've heard some strange stories about him and... I don't believe them... but... just be careful, that's all."

"Yeah, we know," said Resnick, as he took the piece of paper out of the clerk's hand with the address for Red Moon's sister. "Time to go."

Chapa thanked Chief Mesteth for his help and the chief would not let Chapa leave without promising to have a steak dinner with him before he left town. Chapa happily agreed but knew he would never keep the commitment. If he somehow managed to make it through this alive, he would not stick around. He never stuck around.

The three piled back into Chapa's truck and it roared out of the parking lot towards the address on the paper provided by the clerk. Chapa's mood brightened as he finally had a real lead and a trail to follow in the investigation. Up until now, he had been out of his element, facing supernatural forces that he didn't understand. He suddenly felt like himself again, and that brought him confidence. Even so, he couldn't help but wonder whether that trail would lead them to Logan and the others before it was too late.

# Chapter Thirty-Six

It wasn't far from the police station to the home of Leona Janis, and the route took Chapa straight through the heart of the Pine Ridge Reservation. Mags was intimately familiar with the poverty inside the reservation, but each time she visited it broke her heart. The fifteen-minute drive was a culture shock for Resnick, who had never visited Pine Ridge. The FBI agent remained glued to the window, staring at what he was seeing.

The streets were lined with dilapidated trailer homes, many with roofs or parts of the structures covered with blue tarps to keep out the rain. Empty fields were filled with garbage and abandoned commercial buildings outnumbered businesses that were open along the drive. Young men and women walked the streets and many of the homes had abandoned vehicles in the yards. Those that appeared to be operational were old, and rusted from the harsh winters.

Chapa drove slowly past an old woman walking alongside the road, pulling a children's wagon filled with bags of groceries. Beside her walked two elementary aged boys with no shoes, playing catch with a ball.

"Wow," said Resnick. "This place is so poor your truck might actually be the nicest vehicle in this place."

Mags muttered something to herself under her breath in Lakota and Chapa groaned. "You really are an ass, Resnick."

"Look, we are here," said Resnick as he pointed to a small home up ahead on the right. The home was part of a small neighborhood of cookie cutter one-story homes. There were several blocks of what started out decades ago as identical public housing that were now almost unrecognizable from each other. Many of the homes were in bad need of repair, while others were abandoned shells or missing entirely, leaving a gap where the concrete foundation had been overgrown by vegetation.

The Janis home, however, was in good condition and had none of the clutter that was prevalent in nearby yards. A small nondescript mailbox lined the road with the address painted neatly on the side.

After getting out of the truck, Mags turned to Chapa and Resnick. "Look, with all due respect, I don't think you should do the talking. I am from around here, and she will listen to me. Let me handle this my way."

Resnick was about to say something, but Chapa spoke up quickly. "Agreed."

Mags had earned Chapa's confidence by the way she handled the *ozuye*. Chapa also knew that law enforcement officers from outside the reservation were not going to be welcome. Flashing a BIA or FBI badge would likely do more harm than good, and the soft touch was the smart move. Mags was the best one to play that role.

Chapa and Resnick hung back to watch by the truck, while Mags walked straight up to the door and knocked. After a few minutes, the curtains in the nearby window moved and Chapa saw a woman's face. Another minute passed, and the woman finally opened the door.

Leona looked past Mags straight towards Chapa and Resnick and it was obvious she was nervous. "I didn't do anything. You are at the wrong house."

Mags smiled and immediately went to work putting Leona at ease. "You are not in any trouble. They are looking for some missing kids and I am helping them on behalf of our community. Can we talk to you for a few minutes?"

Leona opened the door reluctantly and the three followed her inside. She welcomed them into the small, cramped living room where Mags and Leona shared a couch.

Since he wasn't doing the talking, Chapa tried to size up Leona. She appeared to be in her forties and was overweight. She had on a blouse and skirt that looked like something to be worn to work, not around the house.

There were no photographs on the walls, so he presumed the woman had never been married. The home was remarkably clean and organized. There were no dishes in the sink and not a speck of dirt on the windows.

Above all, however, a sense of sadness permeated Leona's home. It was not just clean—it was surgical. The walls were painted gray, and there was not a bright color or decoration to be seen in the home. The surroundings were simply and purposefully plain by design, devoid of anything memorable.

Mags started the conversation with small talk about how she grew up not far away from Leona, and they quickly discovered they knew some of the same members of the tribe. After a few minutes, Mags dutifully turned the discussion to Joseph, and it was clear she hit a sore spot.

"You aren't the first ones to come here looking for my brother. I haven't seen Joe in almost ten years and have no idea where to find him. Last time I saw him was at Mom's funeral and we barely spoke."

"Were you close to Joe growing up?" asked Mags.

"I am a lot older than him. After the divorce, Dad moved out and Mom was never around so I helped when I could. I went away to college to become a teacher, and when I came back, it was not the same. Joe had moved out and I moved back here with Mom and took care of her until she died."

"Did your mom keep any of Joe's things?"

"I have some stuff in the garage. I boxed up everything and moved it out of the house when she died. I have some stuff from my father, too. Why would you want to see a bunch of old pictures and stuff?"

"We want to know everything we can about Joe, and there may be a clue here to help us find him."

"So, are you like a profiler or something?"

Mags smiled. "Something like that. I won't be long, I promise."

***

Leona got up from the table and led Mags into the garage where there were boxes stacked neatly along one of the walls. Each of the boxes had a label on the side with descriptions like "Mom Bedroom" or "Pictures." Leona pointed at two of the boxes that had "Joe" written in Sharpie on the side of the box.

Mags carefully opened the first box and saw it was full of baseball trophies and an old glove. She looked up at Chapa and nodded her head towards Leona as if to suggest she wanted some time alone to sift through the items.

Chapa cleared his throat. "Any chance we could get a bottle of water, ma'am?"

"Sure."

Leona led the two agents back to the kitchen, and Mags went to work. She had a gift to see the imprints left behind by people on objects and places. Some things had memories that could be recalled, especially if the experiences were traumatic or emotional. As someone had explained to Mags when she was a little girl, everyone leaves bits and pieces of their spirit behind them as they go. Some are small pieces, almost invisible. But sometimes people leave behind big pieces, and those are easy to see if you know how to look. Mags knew how to look.

Mags picked up a baseball glove from one of the boxes labeled "Joe" and closed her eyes. She was immediately bombarded with memories of Joseph's childhood. She saw a young boy hitting a baseball. She felt the bitter disappointment when the boy's mother and father were not there to see him play. Just Leona—she was always there to watch his games and walk him home.

The memories faded in and out until Mags saw vivid memories of Joseph's mother who had a drug problem. In her mind, Mags saw Joseph trying to wake his mother up to take him to a game. A younger Leona came into the room and took the keys. "I will take you."

Mags put the glove down and moved on to the next box. This one was filled with Joseph's clothes. Jackpot, thought Mags. She sifted through the clothes on top and settled on a belt, something the boy would have worn every day. Now, she saw Joseph and he was older. He was running and was very afraid. A police officer pulled up in a parking lot as Joseph ran out the front door of a grocery store on the reservation. More images flashed through Mags' mind and she saw Joseph getting arrested for stealing cigarettes.

The next vision was the teenage Joseph sitting in a jail cell, and a feeling of embarrassment for his father to find out he was arrested. He started crying and looked away into the corner as he pounded his fist into the wall until it bled. Mags could feel the deep sadness and shame as if she was there with the boy in the jail.

A few minutes later, one of the police officers for the reservation opened the door to the cell and asked the boy to come with him. He led Joseph to the office and the teenager saw a man in a coat and tie he had never seen in his life. The man flashed a BIA badge and put out his hand, "I am here to take you home." Joseph looked to the police officer, unsure of what to do next, wondering whether this man was sent by his dad who was a local police officer.

Joseph went with the man but he did not take him home. Instead, Mags saw a place in the mountains with cages full of crows. Standing to greet Joseph was an old man with a black wide brimmed hat, surrounded by men and women moving and working behind him amongst a group of wooden buildings. Mags felt excitement and fear welling up from within the boy, then nothing. The memories faded.

Mags hastily sifted through the other items in the boxes with Joseph's name written on the side but found nothing that would shed any clues on what happened after Joseph was older. All of the items had childhood memories or nothing at all. *There must be something here. I need to know more.*

Her thoughts next turned to the boy's father. Everyone thought he was killed by Joseph when he got older. *Maybe there would be something in the garage that would provide a clue as to what happened?* Mags systematically rotated the boxes to see the labels. Luckily, Leona was meticulous in labeling every single one of them with great detail. Finally, Mags saw what she was looking for—"Dad Stuff".

The cardboard lid folded back easily, and Mags gasped at what she saw lying tucked against one of the sides of the box. Near the bottom of the box was a large clear baggie with a logo from the Oglala Department of Public Safety. On the side was printed "Officer Joseph Janis Sr." *Interesting*, thought Mags. The father had the same name.

She opened the bag carefully, which she suspected was the contents recovered from the man's body after the murder. Typically, any items on the victim would be inventoried at a crime scene and returned to the family. In this case, inside the bag were a number of items that were unsurprising, including a set of car keys, a lighter, and a wallet. But one item was a surprise. A Glock handgun. Not just any handgun, but almost certainly the handgun that took the life of Janis' father.

Mags went immediately for the pistol, wrapping her fingers around the grip tightly and closing her eyes. She saw Joseph Sr. driving a car into a parking lot at night. His son was already waiting in the lot, next to a motorcycle. He was now older, at least in his twenties.

The lot was in a wooded area, but there were lots of signs. Up ahead was a mountain, and on the side was a familiar profile carved into the rock. The events happened quickly and Mags watched the death unfold as if she was there with Joseph Jr. Watching a death is hard, and it leaves a mark on a human being. But for someone like Mags, *feeling* a death was indescribably more difficult. She had never used her ability like this in the past, and it was almost too much for her to bear. She dropped the unloaded gun into the box, and quickly tidied up to leave no trace of her activity. She had seen enough and knew where they needed to go next.

Mags hustled back into the house to find Chapa and Resnick now sitting at the kitchen table next to Leona. Chapa was drinking a bottle of water, but Resnick was drinking a cup of coffee that Leona had been kind enough to make at his request.

"Leona, thanks for talking to us and letting me look at the boxes. You have helped us more than you know."

Mags next turned to Chapa and Resnick. "We need to go. I got what we needed."

The two agents expressed their appreciation to Leona as well and followed Mags out to Chapa's waiting pickup truck. Chapa started the engine and waited for Leona to re-enter the house before interrogating Mags. "So, what did you find?"

"I will tell you later. Right now, we need to get out to the Crazy Horse Memorial. That's where Red Moon and the Crow Keeper will be. It will be nightfall soon, and I have a feeling we are running out of time."

Mags couldn't help but think about the importance of the place where they were headed. Crazy Horse was a friend of Sitting Bull and was the leader of the surprisingly victorious Lakota army at the infamous Battle of Little Big Horn. The Crow Keeper would no doubt appreciate the symbolism of launching a war from the shadow of a larger than life sculpture of the Lakota hero.

# Chapter Thirty-Seven

Logan sat down on the floor of the cave, watching the two *ozuye* who were on guard duty. It appeared to be nighttime, and it was now quiet outside the main passage that Logan assumed led to the surface. Most of the men and women in the jail cell were asleep. Logan and his companions, however, were wide awake.

He pulled out his knife and started scratching it along the cave walls, making an annoying screeching noise that echoed around the chamber.

The guards looked up and one noticed that Logan had a knife. "How did you get that? We took that away from you."

Logan smiled, "Not this one. I had another one."

He continued to scratch the blade along the walls of the cave, carving the first few letters of his name into the stone. "I wonder what the Crow Keeper would think if I wrote my name in his cave."

The two guards exchanged worried glances and one got up and went over to the jail. "Stop that now. Give me the knife."

"Sure, here you go." Logan casually handed his knife to the guard through the bars of the jail cell and sat back down on the cave floor.

The *ozuye* smiled at how easily he solved the problem and took the knife over to the Crow Keeper's desk, where he put it back onto the shelf where it had been placed when Logan arrived. As he turned and walked over to his chair, he heard the screeching sound start again. He turned to see Logan continuing to carve his name into the cave wall.

The guard's face turned beet red, and he ran over to the shelf where he had just placed the knife. It was gone.

The *ozuye* was now enraged, thinking this was some sort of trick. "Stop playing games. Give me that knife!"

"This one?" asked Logan, waving the knife. "No, I think I will keep this one. I already gave you my other knives. What did you do with them? Did you lose them?"

The more Logan talked, the more the *ozuye* guard became angry. His face was getting flushed, and he was approaching a breaking point. "Give me that knife!"

"I don't think so," replied Logan calmly as he kept carving on the rocks. "If you want this knife, you are just going to have to come in here and take it."

The guard quickly located the key to the jail and was headed back to open the door when he was stopped by the other *ozuye*. "You know we are not allowed to open that door. The Crow Keeper will be furious."

"Would you rather that he comes back in the morning and sees the boy with a knife and his name carved on the wall? Watch my back and don't let anyone get past you."

The guard with the key yelled at Logan. "I am coming in there and getting that knife." He grabbed a spear from one of the walls and approached the entrance to the cell.

The guard put the key into the lock, and it clicked when it turned. The door closed behind him with a clank, and the other *ozuye* remained on the outside to prevent anyone from escaping.

Logan casually watched as the guard stepped around the sleeping men and women on the floor, making a beeline towards him. After closing the distance quickly, the *ozuye* pointed the spear at Logan's chest and demanded that he drop the knife on the floor. Instead of dropping it, however, Logan threw the knife through the bars of the jail cell. This act of defiance set off the guard even more and he slammed the back end of the spear into Logan's stomach, causing him drop onto one knee. While bent over and facing away from the guard, Logan recalled the knife into his hand and tossed it over to White Elk who was pretending to be asleep on the ground. White Elk caught the knife and plunged it into the guard's foot with both hands. Blood poured out of the boot and the guard dropped the spear as he fell to the floor and rolled around, desperately trying to remove his shoe.

White Elk had quickly removed the blade from the bloody boot and pressed it to the guard's throat once he was on the ground. "You are no *ozuye*. You are a disgrace to your people, beating up on women and children. I should kill you now."

The guard was taken by surprise and Logan could see that the young man was fearful White Elk would carry out his threat.

Tia and Erica leaped up from their simulated sleeping and Logan grabbed the spear off the floor. "Let us pass," Logan shouted to the remaining guard blocking the door, "or White Elk will kill your friend. He will do it!"

The guard blocking the exit looked nervously to the other *ozuye* who was now on his back bleeding profusely from his foot. The wounded *ozuye* gasped, "Let them go. They won't get far."

That signal was all the three companions needed to push their way past the remaining guard, who reluctantly followed the advice of his partner. Tia and Erica ran out of the jail cell, but Logan first paused to thank White Elk. "Sam, we will come back for all of you. I won't forget you."

The teenagers fled quickly into the dark passageway leading away from their subterranean prison. Logan recalled the knife to his hand and put it back in his sheath, while Tia unrolled her shirt to reveal a new companion—a small gray rat. The rodent was now Tia's eyes and would serve as their guide through the pitch black darkness, which hit them almost immediately after leaving the prison chamber. The darkness of the cave was so deep that it was disorienting, bringing them to a dead stop.

"Hold my hand and don't let go," whispered Tia to Logan. The three created a chain with Logan in the middle holding Tia's hand, while his other hand held Erica.

Logan could now hear yelling back in the jail cell as the guards called for help. Logan knew that the Crow Keeper would send someone or something to follow them. Their only hope was to put as much distance as possible between them and their pursuers and find a way out of the dark underground maze before they were caught.

Tia's newfound guide scurried ahead of the trio across the rocky floor of the cavern, leading a slow but steady march through the dark passage.

"Did you name the rat?" asked Erica.

"Of course," replied Tia. "He's Jerry."

Logan groaned. "Well, that's original, let's hope there's not a cat down here named Tom."

"Tell me, what are you seeing?" begged Erica. "It is so creepy not being able to see where we are going." Erica had taken the spear from the jail cell and was using it as a walking stick to feel the ground ahead of her before taking a step.

*** 

Tia's eyes glowed red like the rat as she took in the surroundings. The passage was clearly headed down, and the walls were slick and marked with the lines of water flow. Pools of water collected the occasional drops that fell from the ceiling, which were so loud they sounded like heavy rocks being dropped in a lake. "It's just a cavern. Nothing special. We need to keep moving."

The three moved quickly through the rocky passageway, with Tia leading the human chain. Besides the occasional drops of water, the only noises were the clip clop of Erica's spear hitting the ground, and the heavy breathing caused by the increasingly cold air. Finally, Tia stopped.

"What is it?" whispered Erica.

"Why are you whispering?" asked Logan. "It's a cave, not a library."

Tia ignored Logan and replied in a hushed voice, "We are now in a bigger cave. It's... filled with statues and all kinds of old things. Someone has been in this part of the cavern."

As she described the room for her friends, Tia looked around at stone statues of Native American men and women that were at least ten feet tall. The figures were on one side of the large cavern fixed to the ground atop a mound of rock. They were carved directly into stalagmite formations rising out of the stony floor. The figures on the stone dais were positioned so they could watch over everything that occurred in the cavern.

Strewn across the cave floor in front of the dais were piles of clothes. As the rat ran across the floor and afforded a better view, Tia saw that the piles of clothes were filled with skeletons. Many were so old they were falling apart.

It was like a morbid fashion time capsule as skeletons in tattered U.S. Army uniforms from the 1800s, and decaying bodies in bright colored female dresses from the 1950s could be seen only a few feet apart. Some of the piles of clothes were small. Children.

There was a horrible smell in the air that Tia could only imagine was the smell of rotting corpses. The pungent odor assaulted her senses as they entered what she now knew was a place of death.

"Tell me what you see!" said Erica, no longer worried about whispering.

"Guys, I think we are in some sort of tomb. I see skeletons everywhere. We need to leave now."

Suddenly, Jerry ran back to Tia and climbed up her leg into her waiting arms, causing Tia to immediately stop talking. For a long tense moment the trio sat in the dark, hearing only the thump of their racing heart beats resonating in their heads. The quiet was eventually broken by the sounds of rustling in the darkness. They were no longer alone.

# Chapter Thirty-Eight

It was a few hours before Chapa finally pulled into the parking lot of the Crazy Horse Memorial. Even in the dark, the giant sculpted face of Crazy Horse was easy to spot in the distance jutting out of the side of the mountain. Although Mount Rushmore was more well known, the life-like profiles of Presidents Washington, Jefferson, Lincoln, and Teddy Roosevelt were not the only sculptures carved into the rock of the Black Hills. After the completion of Rushmore, the Lakota hired one of the sculptors on the project to carve an even bigger profile of a native hero into the same mountain range only a few miles away. That work began in 1948, but the project was never completed. Although the slow work continued, only the human face was now visible of what was planned to be a massive sculpture of Crazy Horse riding into battle with his hand outstretched pointing the way.

Chapa had to flash his BIA badge to get through the guard shack for the Memorial, and it was now around midnight. The restaurant, gift shop and the surrounding buildings were all closed, but past that point they spotted a small picnic area next to a dirt road leading up to the sculpted mountain face. On the way to the Memorial, the group had already decided that wandering around in the middle of the night looking for the Crow Keeper was not the smartest move. Resnick was insistent on getting some sleep, and Chapa had reluctantly agreed. The hunt for Red Moon would start in the morning at first light.

As they piled out of Chapa's pickup, Chapa told Resnick to find a place to start a fire. "If we are going to be out here all night, we need to stay warm. We can't all sleep in the truck."

Chapa found two camping chairs in the bed of his truck and pulled them out. He rummaged through the storage area under his back seat and also found a couple of blankets and a jacket. Chapa was used to living out of his truck while on the road, and knew there were a lot worse things than sleeping under the stars with a warm fire and a comfortable blanket. He didn't know about Mags and Resnick, but he was planning to sleep well.

Mags helped Chapa carry their makeshift camping gear over to the picnic area and discovered that Resnick already had a small blaze going in one of the fire rings.

"That's a good-looking fire, Resnick. You must be part Lakota," said Mags.

"Nope. Eagle Scout."

"Okay, Eagle Scout. I got two chairs and the lady gets one of them. You want a chair or the ground?" asked Chapa.

"I'll take the ground if you give me one of those blankets. Anything is better than another night sleeping in a car."

"Done," said Chapa, tossing Resnick one blanket and giving the other one to Mags. Resnick wasted no time kicking off his shoes and making a bed on the ground next to the fire.

"Can't wait for some eggs and bacon from that restaurant back there," said Resnick, pointing to the welcome center on the edge of the parking lot. He then pulled the blanket up to his shoulders and turned over on his side away from Chapa and Mags.

Chapa sat down in a camp chair on the other side of the fire ring. Mags set up her chair a few feet away and wrapped herself in the remaining blanket. Even though it was summer, the mountain air was crisp and the warmth from the fire was making it hard to stay awake.

The BIA agent, however, was determined not to sleep until he had some answers from Mags. "What did you do in the garage back there? How did you know to come to this place?"

"This probably won't make any sense to you, Chapa, but I see things that others don't see. I don't even fully understand how it works, but I believe that people leave bits and pieces of their spirits in places they have been, and things that they touch. Some people, like me, have the ability to pick up on those pieces left behind."

After hearing the strange explanation, Chapa instinctively looked over at Resnick and noticed he was already snoring. *Good*, he thought, turning back to Mags. The last thing he wanted to deal with right now was Resnick's corny jokes.

Mags watched Chapa's face as if trying to gauge his reaction. He simply shook his head, slowly processing the meaning of what he heard. The BIA agent knew how to read people, and he knew that Mags sharing this information with him was a calculated decision. She believed she could trust him, and he hoped she chose wisely.

"So, let's assume what you are saying is true. How does it work?"

"I touch something that belongs to a person, and I can sometimes see their memories. I don't see everything, and usually I don't get much. I can only see memories that touched that person deeply while they were around that object or place. Wonderful memories or traumatic events—the types of things that cause their spirit to flash brightly and leave a trace of it behind."

Chapa thought about the implications of such an ability. Mags could be seeing memories of other people right now from this place. She could have touched his things in the truck and seen his own memories. He suddenly felt violated and fearful that such a power could be used to manipulate people.

"So, what are you reading off the blanket I gave you?"

Mags seemed prepared for this question. "It's not like that. I learned long ago to block my ability unless I really need it. It is like noise in the background unless I focus hard to hear it. I know part of you is thinking I am delusional, and the other part is wondering how terrible a person I would be if I really had the power to peek into everyone's memories without them knowing. Believe me, I would rather shut it off and never use it again. And to answer your question, no, I haven't read any of your things, and I give you my word that I won't—unless you give me your permission."

Chapa seemed satisfied for the moment with Mags' answer, but he knew the implications of Mags' newly revealed power would continue to gnaw at him. *How could anyone ever trust another human being so completely that you would knowingly allow that person to see and know everything about you, to share all your most intimate and private memories?*

He turned back to the matter at hand. "Fair enough. So, what did you see in the garage at Leona's house?"

"I saw Joseph's childhood and it was as tough as you might expect. The sister was the only bright spot for him. The mother was an addict and the dad was always gone. I didn't see anything that you didn't already know. Then I found a box with some things Leona kept from her father. Lucky for us, she was so organized and kept *everything*. She even kept the contents from her dad's body that were given back to the family by the police department after he was murdered."

Mags pointed to the Memorial. "Chapa, I grabbed his gun and saw what happened through the dad's eyes. Joseph killed his father right here in this place."

Chapa exhaled slowly, wondering if Mags really was right.

Mags looked down at the fire, and continued talking, this time in a softer tone. "Did you know he had the same name as his father? That's why he never used his real name again after that night."

Chapa shook his head but was too stunned to respond. Her story was obviously difficult to believe, but he felt deep down that Mags was telling the truth. At least *she* believed it to be true, and that was enough for Chapa. For now.

Mags had brought them to this place and everything she had said and done to this point told Chapa that she could be trusted. If Mags thought the night Joseph shot his father was important, then he needed to know what happened as well. As a trained investigator, he knew that every detail was important, and one of them might be the key to finding Logan.

Chapa got out of his chair and walked over to Mags. He crouched down and looked her in the eye. "Mags. I believe you. I don't think you are crazy, and I don't think you are a bad person because you have this gift. But I need you to tell me everything that you saw. I need to know everything you know about what happened here that night. Everything."

Mags let go of his hand and looked back into the fire. Her gaze never left the flames as she allowed herself to relive the memory that she saw from Joseph Sr's last moments, in the same place where they were now sitting.

# Chapter Thirty-Nine

Joseph Sr. drove his police car along the dirt road looking for signs of life. It was dark, and he had followed his son Joe's motorcycle off the highway onto an old mining road that wound around the hills behind the Crazy Horse Monument. The white stone with the carved face of the Lakota hero shone in the moonlight in the distance.

His son had dropped by the house to see Leona but hadn't stayed. He never stayed. He always ran off to wherever it was that he went.

Joseph was angry. Angry at Joe for quitting school and not having a job. Angry at his dead wife for allowing the boy to turn into such a punk when she knew it would be an embarrassment to him as a local police officer.

Up ahead, the headlights illuminated a clearing with a number of cars and motorcycles parked beside the road. There were simple wooden buildings forming a compound around the entrance to an old mining cave. In front of the cave entrance were wooden cages of all shapes and sizes filled with black birds.

The police officer pulled up behind the motorcycles and turned off the engine. He took a long drink from the cup beside his seat and removed the Glock handgun from his side holster to make sure it was loaded. The drunken man tucked the gun back into the holster and left the car, ready to confront his son. He didn't care who was around to see it.

Joseph walked up to the buildings and started yelling his son's name. "Joe! Joe!"

He paced in front of the compound, waiting for a sign of his son, getting

181

angrier by the minute. "Get your ass out here!"

By now people were starting to gather from around the compound, drawn outside by the noise. A few men and women left the buildings while others streamed out of the cave to see who was yelling outside. It was dark, but there were floodlights outside the cave, and a number of light poles strategically placed outside the buildings.

Joseph scanned the mostly Lakota faces in the crowd, looking for his son. He kept yelling, undeterred by the gathering crowd. He was a police officer, and he could do what he wanted.

"I know you are here!"

After a few minutes, his son walked out from the cave, calmly wearing his now well-worn black vest bearing the mark of the Ghost Dance cult. "Go back home. You are a drunk and a disgrace to our family. I do not call you my father any longer. Do not call me your son."

Joseph was surprised at not only the words his son spoke, but the confidence with which he spoke them.

"You don't talk to me like that. Like it or not, I am your father. You bear *my* name."

The police officer looked around at the people staring at him as he argued with his son. He should have been ashamed, but he was too drunk to think straight. All he could feel was wave after wave of anger, each one bigger and more powerful than the last one.

At the pinnacle of his rage, an old man in a black wide brimmed hat walked out from the crowd and stood beside his son. Time seemed to stop as he spoke.

"This is no longer your son. He is now a son of the Lakota people. He honors them. He fights for them. What do you do? You drink your alcohol and sleep it off in the captivity of a reservation. You hide behind that uniform and imprison your own people for petty crimes. Your life wastes away and no one will speak of your deeds when you are gone. This man beside me is a warrior and he has found his home. He has found his true family. You should leave this place before you bring more dishonor to yourself."

No one had ever spoken to Joseph that way in his life. *Who was this old man?* The alcohol and the anger pushed Joseph into action. He had to show his son that he was not a man to be disrespected.

Joseph pulled out his Glock and aimed it at the old man's chest. He didn't even stop to think before he pulled the trigger. He was beyond thinking. There was only rage, and a momentum towards action that was too powerful for the drunken police officer to stop, once it was put into motion.

The bullet, however, never reached its intended target. Instead, the projectile struck Joe as he pushed the old man to the side and took the bullet in his chest. The anger in Joseph's mind instantly turned to fear and regret. His intoxicated brain tried desperately to process what had just happened, and tears streamed down his face as he stared at his son's body lying face down on the ground.

Snapping out of the momentary paralysis, Joseph ran forward to Joe's motionless figure. Terrifying thoughts flew through his mind. *He didn't mean to shoot his son. It was an accident. Joe can't be dead.*

Joseph lifted a shoulder to turn over Joe's body and was relieved to see movement. *His son was alive! But where was the wound?* He had seen the bullet hit his son and expected to see blood. Joseph was no stranger to treating gunshot wounds as a police officer.

His son slowly stood up off the ground and his father saw a small hole in the front of the black vest where the bullet hit his body. Strangely, there was no blood, just a bruise.

The father was hysterical. "Joe. You're alive! How is this possible? I saw the bullet hit you."

The old man spoke again, this time loud enough for everyone to hear. "I told you. This man is a warrior. He has been reborn with the strength of the Ghost Dance. You can't stop him with your bullets."

Joe coldly walked over to the handgun that was lying on the ground. He picked it up and returned to stand by the man in the black hat.

The man in the black hat spoke again, this time raising his voice so everyone who was assembled could hear: "I am a prophet of Wovoka. I have walked on this earth since the buffalo ran free and the Lakota people ruled these mountains. You have come here to bring death, and now death will come to you."

The shaman turned to Joe. "This is not your father, and you will never again have to use his name. You are now Red Moon. You are destined to make the moon turn red with the blood of those who try to kill the followers of the Ghost Dance."

The man's finger pointed towards the gun, now held firmly by Red Moon. "Use his own weapon and end his life."

Joseph was paralyzed with fear, not only of the mysterious medicine man but of what his own son might do in response to his words. The weakness took over and he thought of pleading with his son to spare his life, to tell him he loved him. But soon the fear was again replaced by anger. Even faced with what could be his last moments with his son, Joseph could not bring himself to show compassion. It just wasn't in him.

"You think you're special? You're nothing but a punk kid caught up in a crazy cult. I am a police officer. If you kill me, you will all go to jail."

Joseph looked around to the staring crowd and shouted, "You're all crazy. All of you."

As soon as Joseph broke eye contact, his son pulled the trigger, firing three rapid shots into his father's body from only a few yards away. Joseph fell to the ground and no one came to his aid as the last seconds of his life unfolded in slow motion. His son stoically turned and walked back to the cave entrance, throwing the gun to the ground. He knew the deed was done, and had no desire to linger in the aftermath.

Joseph watched his son walk away from him while he bled out onto the ground. The father's last memory was looking up into the dark night sky and noticing that the moon had a strange red hue, before it all gave way to a deep and never-ending darkness.

***

Mags took a deep breath and noticed that the flames on the fire were close to going out as she finished her story. She had told Chapa everything she knew about the murder, down to every last detail and emotion that she saw and felt back at the garage in Leona's home.

Chapa had not interrupted her the entire time, and now looked deep in thought. He finally got up from his chair and spoke, "So, the Crow Keeper knew Wovoka? That's just not possible. He would be over a hundred and fifty years old. This guy is just some fraud using a famous medicine man's name because it makes a good story."

Mags looked perplexed. "Maybe. I am afraid we are dealing with something that none of us yet understand."

Chapa remained unconvinced. "Time to throw some more wood on the fire. We need to get some sleep."

# Chapter Forty

After hearing the sounds, Tia led Logan and Erica by the hand to a hiding place behind a rock formation that jutted out from the cavern floor. "Quiet. Someone is coming."

All three crouched down out of sight as Tia placed Jerry gently down on the ground with both hands. The rat boldly scurried out into the cavern and found its own hiding place behind a skeleton of a man who was wearing blue jeans and boots. The rat peered over the boots, which were still remarkably preserved, waiting to see the source of the noise.

Through Jerry's eyes, Tia scanned the large antechamber and realized this was a place of significance. She knew that the Wind Cave was nearby, a holy place the Lakota believed was the birthplace of their people. There were literally hundreds of miles of caves in the Black Hills, most of which remained unexplored.

In addition to the giant statues on the dais presiding over the large cavern, there was a stone altar in the middle of the chamber that resembled a table. It was at least four feet off the ground and long enough to hold an adult's body.

There were multiple passageways providing access to the chamber. Tia counted the one passage that led back to their jail cell, but there appeared to be at least two other ways to exit the cavern. One passage near their hiding place led downward, while another passage on the far side of the chamber near the dais appeared to slope upwards. The noise was coming from that direction, and it was getting louder. Something was being dragged across the cave floor.

An old man slowly came into view. He was hunched over under the weight of what he was dragging behind him, and was moving slowly. In the back of her mind Tia knew who it was the moment she saw him, but waited until he got closer to accept the reality of their situation. It was the Crow Keeper, and he was dragging a body into the chamber to share the fate of the countless other people lying on the floor. They were trapped in the dark, and had no choice but to wait until the Crow Keeper finished whatever he was planning to do.

Tia felt helpless because she knew Logan and Erica could hear the noise and would be wondering what was happening. She had no way to tell them it was the Crow Keeper or warn them of the danger without risking being heard in the dead quiet of the cavern. All she could do was squeeze their hands tight and somehow hope they followed her lead and remained quiet. Their lives depended on it.

The old medicine man dragged the body into the chamber and heaved it up onto the rock table. Lifting the body was remarkably easy for someone his age, and he accomplished the task as if he had done it a hundred times. The limbs of the body hung off the altar so the Crow Keeper picked up the arms and placed them neatly on the table. Through the darkness, Tia could see that the person was a female, likely in her twenties or thirties. It was not one of the captives from the jail, but was someone different. The woman looked like she was dressed for work in an office, and Tia thought to herself that she might be a secretary. Maybe even a teacher.

The Crow Keeper stood by the side of the woman and held her hands tightly. Jerry's view of the woman lying on the table was blocked by the Crow Keeper, so the rat scurried from its hiding place, and advanced closer to the action to find a better vantage point for Tia. She desperately wanted to observe what was happening through the rodent's night vision.

Jerry scrambled over the wet and dirty cavern floor until Tia spotted a rock formation that was high enough to afford a view of the table. Jerry hopped from one rock to another, but, after a few successful jumps, he slipped. His tiny feet clawed into the soft limestone to catch his fall, causing a piece to break off and hit the floor. The impact of the rock fragment hitting the ground was unmistakable in the dead quiet of the cavern, and the sound echoed through the chamber. Tia froze, squeezing the hands of Logan and Erica even more tightly as a warning to remain silent.

The Crow Keeper whipped around and peered through the darkness in the direction of the noise. The medicine man's eyes quickly locked onto Jerry who was still perched on the rock, and Tia saw that the Crow Keeper's eyes glowed like a distant animal in the forest at night. She was fearful the Crow Keeper could see right through the rat's eyes, and somehow discover their presence.

After what seemed like an eternity, the Crow Keeper turned back to his work and Tia let out the breath that she did not notice she had been holding in her chest. Jerry continued his journey to the higher ground of the nearby rock and Tia could finally see what was happening.

The woman's arms were crossed on top of her chest and the Crow Keeper was still holding her hands in his own. Tia could hear soft guttural chanting from the Crow Keeper, as if he was singing an unintelligible melody to himself. The chant was unfamiliar to Tia, but she instantly recognized the language—it was Lakota.

Because Anasazi received visitors from all of the Native American tribes, Zuma had worked to teach Tia most of the prominent languages, including Lakota. Tia was far from fluent, but she could make small talk in the Kiva. Now, concentrating in the dark, she could understand bits and pieces of the Crow Keeper's chant, and there was no doubt as to his purpose. He was offering a human sacrifice to the ancient spirits—and, in exchange, he wanted "*Wakhan*," which meant energy or life.

Tia watched as the stone altar was bathed in a soft green light that seemed to emanate from the table itself. At the same time, the eyes on the stone statues carved into the dais looming over the altar began to glow with the same eerie green light. Something was happening and the only word Tia could think of to describe it was feeding. The Crow Keeper was feeding on the woman lying on the table using some terrible magic derived from the statues. The woman's face began to shrivel and the skin on her hands became tight. Without warning, her eyes opened and she let out a terrible scream that shook the silence of the chamber. Almost as soon as the scream started, it stopped—the last gasp of a dying woman—now reduced to a lifeless husk.

The only thing going through Tia's head as she watched this horrible sight was that this was someone's daughter. Someone's mother. And, now the woman's family would never see her again.

For a change it was Logan and Erica now squeezing Tia's hand after they heard the scream. She squeezed back as if to say, "Just hang on. Stay quiet a little while longer."

Before the Crow Keeper was finished with his feeding, a crow flew into the chamber from the same passageway used to transport the body. The bird circled the room before flapping its wings and landing on the altar near the dead woman's body. The Crow Keeper moved his head close to the bird, listening to a message that was being conveyed in a language that only the Crow Keeper could understand.

After a few seconds of conversing with the bird, the Crow Keeper lost focus on his feeding and turned abruptly towards the passage leading back to the jail cell. He shooed away the crow and set off at a fast pace through the rocky passage from which the trio had arrived in the large chamber. Tia didn't understand how, but she somehow knew the crow had told the Crow Keeper of their escape.

After waiting a few minutes to ensure he was gone, Tia stood up and led Logan and Erica over to the other route used by the crow to fly away. If the Crow Keeper and the crow could get into the chamber, they could use the same path to get out.

"This way," Tia whispered, pulling their hands in an urgent dash to get out of the cavern before the Crow Keeper returned. Jerry led the way for Tia, scampering ahead across the cavern floors. The terrain became more solid, and Tia's pace quickened as she hurried to get to what she hoped would be the surface and an exit from the caves.

After several minutes had passed without any signs of being followed, Tia did her best to describe for Logan and Erica the gruesome events in the chamber. She described the Crow Keeper's feeding on a woman and revealed that the scream they heard was her dying in his grasp. Tia recalled the chamber filled with skeletons and shared her suspicion that the Crow Keeper had been feeding in the depths of the caves for decades.

Erica's mind was racing as she remembered the book she read back in Anasazi. "Guys, what if Wovoka never died? What if he went into hiding when Sitting Bull was killed and has been waiting to return all this time?"

"I don't think so," said Tia. "The words were in Lakota and Wovoka was a Paiute."

Erica hated to be wrong. "Wovoka could have learned Lakota... especially if he figured out a way to live for hundreds of years."

No one responded. "Look," said Logan suddenly. "Up ahead."

The absence of light in the cave had been so absolute that even the darkness of the nighttime sky now seemed bright by comparison. Up ahead were stairs carved into the rock that led up to an opening, and the welcome light of the moon and stars. Tia took a deep breath and smelled the fresh air that she had been longing to enjoy again. All three picked up their speed even further since Logan and Erica could now see well enough to guide their own movements without Tia's help.

Logan was the first to peek out the cave entrance to see if there were any *ozuye* nearby that would pose a threat. The cave entrance was at the rocky base of a mountain and there were no other people in sight. Logan quickly waved up Tia and Erica, who followed him out of the cave and into the rocky terrain. From their vantage point on the rocks, the teenagers could see they were surrounded by a thick forest of trees.

Tia scanned the forest through Jerry's eyes, desperately looking for signs of anyone who could help. In the distance, along the edge of the mountain to their left, were lights suggesting the presence of a camp or parking lot. Based on the distance, she knew that was likely the location of their captors and they should instead go in the opposite direction. But she also knew there was someone still imprisoned who she couldn't bear to leave behind.

Tia grabbed Logan and Erica's hands again. "We have to go get Jini. I know she is there. I can feel it. I just can't leave her behind."

"No way am I going back there," said Erica sharply. "Logan, they will be looking for us. We have to get help first."

Logan looked at Tia and then at Erica, unsure of what to do next. "Tia, if we get help, we can come back to get Jini."

Tia shook off any suggestion of leaving without her bird. "She is like a part of me. I can't leave her behind and risk that she is killed by the Crow Keeper. I am going back for Jini, with or without you. I have to try."

Logan knew that they only had a short amount of time before the sun came up. "OK. Let's circle and see if we can find Jini. If we don't find her before dawn, or we run into the *ozuye*, we turn around and head for the nearest highway to get help. Deal?"

Tia nodded her head in acceptance, but she was already moving into the woods with Jerry now in a familiar position on her shoulder, using his vision to scout ahead in the night. Jerry's claws dug through Tia's shirt so he could stay in place as she moved quickly over underbrush and between the trees. Logan and Erica followed them silently into the forest, heading in the direction of the lights, back towards the danger they had just escaped.

# Chapter Forty-One

Word of the teenagers' escape had spread through the Ghost Dance compound quickly, generating a buzz of activity even though it was the middle of the night. After screams for help from the wounded *ozuye* stabbed in the foot by White Elk, other nearby guards had run into the cave and easily secured the remaining prisoners without any further conflict.

Red Moon and the team from the failed Cortez raid had only recently returned to the compound hours earlier, and the *ozuye* leader was sleeping in one of the dormitory buildings when he was awakened with the news of the escape. In his mind, it seemed the bad news would never end.

Making matters worse, Red Moon soon discovered that the leader of the compound was nowhere to be found. During the night, it was typical for the Crow Keeper to disappear into the depths of the caves, and this night was no different, leaving Red Moon temporarily in charge of the search efforts. After scolding the guards responsible for the prison break, Red Moon quickly gathered the remaining guards who could be found, and divided up search assignments. The most challenging assignment proved to be finding someone willing to follow the escaped prisoners, as the passage into the mountain was thought to be haunted by evil spirits.

Although Red Moon did not believe in such superstitions, he also knew that the Crow Keeper's power was somehow connected to the caves, and there were things about them he would never understand. The leader turned to his friend Adriel for help, as he often did, hoping he would lead the search party into the caves.

"Adriel, I know we just got back, and you are exhausted, but I need you to lead a group of men into the caves to search for the kids. The *ozuye* trust you."

Red Moon's friend looked uncomfortable at the request, and folded his arms across his chest in defiance as he shook his head slowly from side to side. "I will follow you into battle against a hundred men, but I will not go into the Crow Keeper's caves. Those kids went into the dark without a light, and are either dead or already captured by the Crow Keeper. This is a fool's errand."

Surprised at the public rebuke in front of the other *ozuye*, Red Moon held his tongue, not sure how to respond. The awkward silence was finally broken up by Mato who stepped forward and began laughing with his deep voice.

"I am not afraid of the dark. Give me a lantern and I will find those children. I bet they didn't get far, and are huddled on the ground somewhere, too afraid to move in the darkness. Who will come with me?"

After Mato broke the ice by volunteering, a few other *ozuye* agreed to accompany the giant man into the caves. After the search party set out from the prison room with lanterns and flashlights lighting the way, Red Moon finally felt comfortable enough to consider returning to his bed to finish his sleep. Hopefully, Mato would indeed bring back the prisoners, but if not, Red Moon would lead the search himself once the sun came up in the morning. Right now, all he could think about was his exhaustion, but something else was nagging at the back of his mind—Adriel's refusal to follow his directions.

Red Moon walked past the raised wooden temporary building that doubled as his dormitory and continued to the back side of the compound. In the distance, he saw a metal building that everyone called Adriel's Garage, and he noticed the lights were still on inside. His friend was still awake.

The rolling door on the side of the building was partially open, and Red Moon ducked underneath it and entered the familiar space. The giant garage had a concrete slab for a floor, and one side was filled with parked motorcycles, some of which were missing tires and were obviously under repair. Adriel was the compound's resident mechanic, but he was also much more. The garage contained a welding shop and high tech machining equipment on the other side away from the motorcycles. It was there Red Moon saw Adriel, standing at a workbench, tinkering with a piece of metal that Red Moon knew would ultimately be fashioned into one of the *ozuye's* weapons.

Adriel's skills had proven useful because Red Moon hated guns and believed that all of the *ozuye* should use traditional weapons. As usual, Adriel had a better idea, and used his fabricating skills to incorporate new technology and building materials. The result was a powerful array of spears, bows and other weapons made of lightweight metal that could be easily hidden under casual clothing when they traveled outside the compound.

Red Moon wasn't sure Adriel heard him enter the building, so he pounded on the side of a piece of sheet metal with his fist to get his friend's attention. "You should be asleep," he shouted.

"So should you," replied Adriel without looking up from his worktable.

"What was that about back there? Why wouldn't you go into the caves?"

"Red Moon, you know I will always help you, but I don't like this plan to bring back Sitting Bull. Kidnapping these people brought us too much attention, and now the FBI is after us. Even if the Crow Keeper could do what he says, what does it even mean? Do you really want to suddenly take orders from an old war chief from the 1800s?"

The *ozuye* leader listened intently and gathered his thoughts. He chose Mato and Adriel as his lieutenants intentionally because they complemented each other's strengths. Mato was brave and headstrong, while Adriel was cautious and meticulous. Unlike Mato, however, Adriel couldn't just be ordered around. He had to be convinced, and if he had a better idea, he didn't hesitate to share it.

"So, what do you propose, Adriel?"

Finally, Adriel stopped working and looked up at Red Moon. "I will help you find the boy, but let the girls live. There will already be enough killing tomorrow."

"I can't promise that," said Red Moon. "They know where we live, and will bring back the FBI and BIA."

"They are already coming. You know that. The Crow Keeper wants a war, and he will get it one way or another."

Red Moon had never heard Adriel talk this way. It was disturbing and began to make him angry. He approached the workstation and raised his voice at Adriel. "You knew what you signed up for when you started. You went through the Ghost Dance so that you could protect our people. You can't turn your back on them now!"

Adriel slammed the wrench in his hand down on the wooden workstation. "Did you protect the men shot in Cortez? Did you even know that one of them died an hour ago? You have forgotten what it is like to care about death. Most of the people in this camp don't have the gift like you and I. If they get shot, they will die, and, unlike us, they are not strong enough to endure the Crow Keeper's magic to gain protection."

Red Moon was now fuming and beginning to regret ever being asked to get this boy.

Adriel sensed the frustration building and decided to end the argument. "Look, it's late and you are exhausted. I think I know how to find the boy and let's see if the *kunja kipa* can really bring back Sitting Bull tomorrow. If so, none of us will have any choice but to fight."

Red Moon wasn't satisfied, but the desire to sleep was too powerful to resist. He left the garage hoping the new dawn would somehow bring an end to the trouble that had entered his life in the last few days.

# Chapter Forty-Two

Moving steadily and carefully through the dense woods, Logan and the girls made their way towards the lights that marked the edge of the Ghost Dance compound. They crouched at the edge of a clearing that revealed a small network of buildings lining a central plaza leading to a giant opening in the mountain. Presumably, this cave opening was the source of the lights and noise they heard while trapped in their subterranean jail cell.

Off to the side of the cave's opening was a network of bird cages of all shapes and sizes. Some of the larger cages were built around and into the trees, almost like tree houses. The cages were filled with crows, who appeared to be sleeping on anything they could find, including tree limbs and man-made roosts.

One of the small cages housed a beautiful falcon that was noticeably out of place in the Crow Keeper's menagerie. Jini was wide awake and staring in their direction, eagerly awaiting her chance for freedom. Luckily, Tia's bond with the bird was strong enough to keep the falcon quiet to avoid waking up the sleeping crows.

The challenge now was figuring out a way to free Jini without waking the crows and setting off an alarm throughout the compound. Unfortunately, Jini's cage was not close to the trees, but was instead out in the open. Like the others, the cage had a door secured by a rope with a simple knot. The rope would take too long for Jerry to gnaw with his teeth, leaving the only viable options to be cutting it with Logan's knife or someone untying it with their hands. Either option meant one of them going out in the open, and risking being seen.

"I will go," said Logan. "It is almost morning anyway, so the crows making noise won't raise suspicions. I will make a run for it, cut the rope, and open the door. The rest is up to you, Tia. Once you get Jini up in the sky, we will follow you out of here."

Logan scanned the dark and sleepy compound one more time before making his move. He had seen a few guards occasionally walking around, but the vast majority appeared to be still asleep or concentrated in the cave. It was now or never, and there was not a person within sight.

Before making his mad dash, Logan crept silently through the trees until he found himself surrounded by cages and hundreds of black birds sleeping on limbs above him. He could hear a few of the birds rustling around and knew that dawn was getting close. Soon, these trees would be filled with a deafening racket of caws and tweets.

Once he was as close as he could get to Jini's cage without revealing himself, Logan ran out from the cover of the trees, twisting and turning through the maze of cages until he found Jini's prison. Logan pulled his knife and cut the rope in mere seconds, allowing the cage door to fly open. He took one more look in the dark to confirm he had not been seen before running back towards the cover of the forest. As he turned, he heard Jini crash her way out of the tight quarters and flap her wings as she climbed up into the sky. Logan never turned back, instead keeping his eyes focused on the safety of the tree line. The rest was up to Tia.

Unfortunately, it soon became clear that the crows were awake. Logan was surrounded by a deafening cascade of clicks, coos and caws that would no doubt alert the men and women sleeping in the compound. But there was something else catching the crows' attention, and Logan immediately sensed he was not alone.

Logan saw Tia and Erica waiting for him in the forest and decided it was time to put some distance between himself and the crows by breaking into a full run. Against the noisy racket, however, Logan heard a new noise. Something was following him through the brush in the forest. It was big, and it was getting closer in the darkness.

Weighing this new risk, Logan decided he was no longer worried about staying quiet. He waved at Tia and Erica. "Go get help! They are coming. Don't wait for me."

The girls were hesitant to leave Logan, but they followed his advice and ran off ahead. Jini was now in the air and Logan knew Tia would be able to see anyone following them as they ran through the forest away from the cult compound.

Logan saw Erica look back over her shoulder and she suddenly stopped in her tracks. She screamed out Logan's name in a desperate attempt to warn him of the approaching danger, but it was too late.

He didn't see the beast until it was right on top of him. The wolf leapt from his side and tackled Logan, rolling around until the shadowy beast ended up on top. Logan struggled to free his right arm so he could reach his knife, but the paws of the canine were too heavy.

Tia and Erica saw the attack, and Logan knew there was nothing they could do to combat the wolf and whoever was controlling it. As they disappeared into the darkness of the forest, Logan was both relieved they would not suffer his fate, but also afraid he would never see them again.

Logan fought to push the wolf off his body as it pinned him down and gnashed its teeth near his throat. The wolf was black as the night and ethereal, only a ghostly outline of an animal. It was real enough, however, and Logan felt its weight on his chest and heard the gnashing of its teeth. But he knew this wolf was not an ordinary wolf. This was some kind of medicine man trick from the Crow Keeper, just like what happened at Hovenweep.

After straining against the wolf's weight unsuccessfully, Logan next heard the sounds of someone else approaching in the darkness. He suspected it would be whomever unleashed the wolf to track him down, and realized his situation was increasingly becoming urgent. The boy kicked his feet and twisted his body in a desperate attempt to throw the wolf off his torso, but nothing he tried was successful. Logan felt like he had a cow sitting on him. He couldn't move and the futility of the situation was maddening.

Adriel casually walked out from the trees and admired his successful capture. He knew the prize was the boy, and the rest of the *ozuye* could easily capture the girls. While the others spread out to search the mountains and the caves, Adriel had made the decision to stake out the girl's bird.

"I knew the girl with the bird would come back. I am an animal lover myself, so I understand."

Once Logan saw the familiar face of the *ozuye* that had attacked him in Cortez, he knew his situation was dire. He pounded on the side of the animal with his hands, hoping to force it to change position, but all he accomplished was making the wolf angry. Logan focused on his knife, and it materialized in the hand that was trapped by the paws of the wolf.

The wolf dug its claws deep into Logan's chest, and he could feel the saliva dripping out if its mouth onto his face. Adriel walked calmly over to Logan's side and stepped on the hand that held the knife. He calmly stroked the back of his pet. "Morning will be here soon. I think it is time for you to get some rest so you can get ready for your big day."

Adriel leaned down on his knees beside Logan and blew a finely powdered dust from his hand into Logan's face. Logan wasn't expecting the move and inhaled a full breath of the dust before he realized what was happening. Slowly, the world went dark to Logan, and the weight of not only the wolf but his entire body melted away.

# Chapter Forty-Three

Tia ran full speed through the canopy of trees, desperately trying to get as far away as possible from the cult compound. Jini was flying low to stay out of sight, which limited Tia's ability to see if anyone was following. Erica was constantly looking over her shoulder, but she had not heard or seen anything since Logan was captured.

After running themselves to exhaustion, the pair stopped and leaned on a tree. "I can't keep running," said Erica, her chest heaving with every breath.

Tia decided to risk exposing Jini and sent the falcon high into the air to scout for a source of help. "I will find some place for us to go."

Through Jini's eyes, Tia saw that the mountain they had been circling had the face of a man carved into the white stone face on the front side of a ridge. She then spotted a parking lot and cluster of small buildings on the other side of the mountain. *I know this place*, Tia thought. *We are in South Dakota and this must be the sculpture of Crazy Horse.* She could not believe they had been held prisoner underneath a tourist attraction and no one had noticed.

She calculated that if they could just get up on the rocks by the sculpture carved into the mountain, someone would see them, and they would be able to signal for help. Of course, that would also require them to leave the cover of the trees, which could give away their position to anyone searching for them.

"I think we should go up," Tia said to Erica. "No time to explain but we are in a tourist area. There are people on the other side of this mountain. If we get up on that ridge, we can signal for help. Otherwise, we have to hike all the way around through the forest, and there is a chance we don't make it to civilization before they catch up to us."

Erica nodded her head in agreement. They both knew they had to get help fast if they wanted to save Logan. Tia took the lead, hiking up the steep mountain trail, leaning forward to fight the difficulty of the incline. Each step brought the girls closer to the sculpted profile of Crazy Horse, but also higher above the tree canopy and increasingly out into the open. They would not only be visible to those who could help them, but also to those who were no doubt hunting them at this very moment. It was a gamble, but one they were willing to take.

*** 

On the other side of the Crazy Horse Memorial, Chapa and Mags were packing up their camping chairs that had doubled as beds for the night. Chapa walked over to Resnick who was still lying on the ground by the long-exhausted fire, wrapped in a blanket.

Chapa kicked Resnick in his side with the point of his boot. "Wake up, sleepyhead. Daylight is wasting."

"I'm up. I'm up... And that hurt," said Resnick.

The sleepy-eyed FBI agent folded up his blanket and walked back to Chapa's truck. Mags was already standing by the open door going through her backpack, pulling out items and laying them in the seat. Chapa was looking at a map of the area on his phone to find the road to the Ghost Dance compound described by Mags.

Resnick threw the blanket into the back seat storage compartment and peeked over Mags' shoulder to see what she was doing. Laid out on the seat were two tomahawks with shiny silver blades and leather wrapped handles dyed a deep blue. Resnick saw a six-inch knife next to its sheath and something he had never seen in his life—two metal spheres the size of tennis balls tied together with a thin metal fiber.

"What are those?"

"Bolas," replied Mags calmly without looking up at Resnick. "They come in handy to get someone big on the ground."

Resnick pulled his Ruger out from his holster. "This puts people on the ground, and they don't get up. You should try one."

Chapa heard the exchange and decided to weigh into the conversation. "Based on the way she handled herself yesterday, I don't think she needs your help. At least some of these guys can survive gunshot wounds, so be ready to hit them with everything you got. And by the way, Resnick, Mags figured out that Red Moon shot his father here at the monument and the Crow Keeper has apparently been waiting a hundred and fifty years to restart the Ghost Dance. Anything I left out, Mags?"

Mags just glared at Chapa and continued her work placing weapons on her belt and into several leather compartments that she tied around her leg.

Resnick reached into the truck and lifted up Chapa's back seat, revealing the rifle he had used back in Cortez. "Whatever you say, Chapa. At this point, nothing sounds crazy anymore. Good thing you have an arsenal back here." He picked up the rifle and made sure it was loaded. "Now, I'm ready."

Chapa went back to searching for the road to the compound on his phone, when a screech caught his attention. A large falcon flapped its wings as it landed roughly on the black brush guard on the front of Chapa's pickup. It let out another screech, this one louder than the first.

"That's Tia's falcon," Mags said. "They're here!"

Everyone dropped what they were doing and scanned the area for Tia and the other teenagers. Resnick finally spotted two figures on the mountain ridge standing next to construction scaffolds near the carving of Crazy Horse's face. He picked up the rifle and looked through the scope to get a better look.

"Up there on the landing by Crazy Horse's face. It's Tia and Erica."

Chapa looked up at the mountain and saw two distant figures jumping up and down, waving furiously to get their attention. Mags shouted to the bird, making sure that Tia could read her lips, "We are coming. Don't move."

Mags quickly locked her tomahawk blades into place onto a belt tied around her waist that contained powerful magnets. Like Resnick, Chapa chose to grab extra firepower from the truck, selecting a shotgun in case they ran into the *ozuye* again. Mags was the first one to hit the trail, and the two agents struggled to keep up with her speed and agility as she easily scaled the rocky incline leading up the path to the top of the Monument.

Resnick fell behind while Chapa pushed himself to match Mags' pace, wheezing as he followed only a few yards behind. Resnick instinctively scanned the mountain every few minutes with the scope to see if anyone else was looking for the girls.

"Chapa! Four *ozuye* coming at you from the other side. One of them is Red Moon."

Chapa briefly turned around and nodded affirmatively to Resnick, then focused his attention back to the steep path. He had already fallen behind Mags, and she wasn't waiting for him to catch up. Chapa knew she heard Resnick's warning, but nothing was going to slow her down. She was determined to get to the girls first, and Chapa knew Mags was likely the best chance those kids had of surviving a run-in with Red Moon.

# Chapter Forty-Four

L ogan slowly opened his eyes and then closed them again quickly. The sunlight was bright and he had a splitting headache. All he wanted to do was close his eyes and go back to sleep, but he instinctively knew that would be a terrible idea. The last thing he remembered, it was dark and there was a giant wolf sitting on his chest. Now, the sun was up, and he knew he had been unconscious for at least a few hours.

Fighting back a wave of nausea in his stomach, Logan finally opened his eyes for good and surveyed his surroundings. He was sitting in the dirt with his back leaning against a wooden pole. His body was lashed to the pole with rope to keep him from falling over, and his hands were tied separately behind his back. He struggled against the rope to test its strength but quickly determined he was not going anywhere.

His field of vision was limited to what was in front of him and to his side as far as he could turn his head. Logan had no ability to see behind him, and it was an unnerving feeling of vulnerability. In front of Logan was one of the small wooden buildings he had seen in the dark when he rescued Jini. To his right was the entrance to the cave and to his left was a row of buildings leading to a parking lot and dirt road. Based on his limited view of the area earlier in the dark, he surmised he was sitting in the common area at the center of the Crow Keeper's compound.

To both his left and right were people he recognized from his short stay in the jail cell, and they were in the same predicament as Logan—bound to wooden poles. One was an older woman and the other was a boy younger than Logan. Both were still unconscious. Approximately ten feet in front of Logan was a sight that caused his heart to sink—a line of skulls that were organized in the shape of a circle. *Just like Hovenweep*, Logan thought to himself.

The Crow Keeper had said that, on the day of the solar eclipse, he would sacrifice Sitting Bull's living descendants to bring back the war chief from the dead. Now, all the kidnapped descendants were sitting in a circle for some sort of ceremony, and Logan knew he had run out of time. He needed to find help quickly.

"Sam, are you out here?"

A muffled voice from behind Logan responded to his cry. "I'm here, but I can't see you."

"I can't see you either, but we have to get out of here or we are all going to die."

"Logan, I am sorry to hear your voice as I hoped you would have escaped our fate. The *ozuye* are standing behind you and can hear everything we say."

Logan feared they were not alone, but was handicapped by his inability to turn his head. Now, he knew there was no point in trying to talk to White Elk or anyone else. His mind raced as he tried to think of a way out of his desperate situation, and his emotions finally exploded in a primal scream. It was the one thing Logan hadn't tried—a desperate cry for help, hoping that someone would come to his aid.

Logan shouted and shouted until a young-looking *ozuye* walked over and slammed the back of his head roughly against the post.

"Shut up, idiot" he ordered, glaring menacingly at Logan.

Instead of complying, Logan screamed again at the top of his lungs. This time, the man shoved a wooden stick in Logan's mouth. The *ozuye* tied the ends of the stick to the back of Logan's head to form a gag, then laughed at his efforts to spit it out.

"Save those screams for the Crow Keeper. No one is coming to help you."

Logan struggled against the gag in his mouth, first pushing it with his tongue and then rubbing the rope on the back of his head against the post. After using all of his energy, the best he was able to accomplish was to loosen the knot and release some of the pressure. The laughter behind him signaled that the *ozuye* were enjoying the show, and he knew that even if he was somehow successful, it would only earn him a new and improved form of restraint.

The reality was finally setting in that his prospects for escape rested entirely in the hands of Tia and Erica. He had not heard anything about their capture, and he was optimistic they had found a way to escape. Logan knew they would find help and return for him, but didn't know if it would be too late. All he could do now was wait, and every minute seemed like it could be his last.

Logan watched as people slowly started to gather around the perimeter of the circle. There was murmuring in the crowd on all sides, speaking in both English and what he assumed to be Lakota. They seemed so normal—like a crowd getting ready to watch a soccer game or a movie. Logan wondered how the death of innocent men and women could be so normal to them. Surely, someone would object, or call the police? The more Logan watched the crowd, however, the more convinced he became that no one would object. That was the insidious nature of a cult. It slowly eroded an individual's moral compass and replaced it with the values of the group and its leader. The Ghost Dance cult *believed* in the resurrection of Sitting Bull and the retaking of the native people's rightful place of power in the world. Surely, this righteous mission was worth the deaths of a few innocents. Logan could hear the arguments of the Crow Keeper echoing in his mind. *No*, he thought sadly. *No one here will object.*

Suddenly, the crowd of onlookers became dead silent. Logan strained to turn his head to see what was happening as everyone looked towards the cave entrance. Through his peripheral vision, Logan saw the Crow Keeper exit the cave and walk slowly and purposefully towards his victims. The old medicine man was no longer dressed in his usual black attire with a bolo tie, but instead wore traditional native clothing. The Crow Keeper was wearing a special shirt made for the ceremony, which consisted of animal bones and antlers tied together with sinew and decorated with black crow feathers.

On his head, the Crow Keeper wore a headdress with an elaborate display of colorful feathers. The headdress was wrapped in leather at the base and the symbol from Logan's necklace was displayed prominently on the front—a circle with the wings of a bird reaching upwards to the sky. Logan recognized the headdress. It was the one from the photograph in the book at Anasazi. The one Sitting Bull wore on the night of his death.

The bones and antlers on the shirt clanked together in an ominous rhythm as the Crow Keeper entered the circle formed by the onlookers, eventually passing out of Logan's field of vision. He felt a sense of dread, as if his executioner was approaching. It was time for the Ghost Dance.

# Chapter Forty-Five

Chapa sprinted up the rocky steps, finally reaching the top of the ridge that leveled out in front of the chiseled face of Crazy Horse. There was a gravel clearing at the top of the ridge in front of the sculpted face. The trail continued around the back side of the head to another area at the top, which was lined with guard rails. About fifty feet away, he saw Tia and Erica, huddled at the base of the sculpted white rock near Crazy Horse's chin, with Jini perched on Tia's shoulder. When the two girls saw Mags, they jumped up and ran forward away from the sculpture to meet their rescuers in the middle of the ridge. They both gave Mags and Chapa a quick hug, overcome with the relief of knowing they were finally rescued.

Erica began talking quickly as tears ran down her face, hysterical with worry they would be too late to save Logan. "They have Logan and the others. We saw the Crow Keeper kill a woman in a cave. He said something about a ceremony during the eclipse today and they are going to kill Logan if you don't save him."

Chapa grabbed the girl's arms. "Right now, we need to get you two off this mountain and back to safety. Don't worry, we will get Logan."

Before Chapa could finish reassuring the girls, however, Red Moon, Mato and two other *ozuye* climbed up onto the ridge from the back side and the trail leading towards the compound. Erica screamed and pointed behind Chapa as the men ominously came into view.

Upon reaching the top of the ridge, Red Moon seemed surprised to discover the girls were not cornered and helpless as he expected. He silently motioned to the others and they fanned out around the ridge to cut off any downward avenue for escape. The only options for the two girls and their protectors were to climb to the top of Crazy Horse's head, or to stand and fight.

Mags leaned over to give quick instructions to the girls. "Go to the top and wave for help to any people you see down below in the parking lot. We will fight the *ozuye* here but if they make it up to you, that means we are dead. Listen to me—if they make it up there, you fight. You fight or you die. Do you understand me?"

Both girls nodded, in shock from the blunt warning from Mags. Jini took flight from Tia's shoulder and the two girls ran towards the steep path up the side of Crazy Horse's carved face. Mags did not have the luxury of watching them very long, but instead turned immediately back to the approaching gang led by Red Moon.

Chapa sensed Red Moon was surprised by their presence and decided to push that advantage. "I am Special Agent Chapa with the Bureau of Indian Affairs. More BIA agents are on the way as well as the Oglala police department. They are going to arrest the Crow Keeper and anyone who gets in our way. It's over and you don't need to die for him."

Mato and the others hesitated at the warning from Chapa and looked at Red Moon.

"You lie!" he said, loudly enough for all to hear. "Today *you* will die, and the Crow Keeper will bring back the spirit of our greatest ancestor to reunite and lead our people. Those who stand in our way are enemies."

Mags decided to support Chapa's tactic with a different, more personal distraction for Red Moon. "I am Magaskawee. I am a Lakota from Standing Rock. Killing these girls is not honorable and they are not your enemies. Your true enemy is your hate that has been flamed by the Crow Keeper to twist your mind. I know your birth name, Joseph. You have the name of your father, who you killed. Was he your enemy, too? Killing your own people is not going to make the world a better place. It will just make you a murderer."

Red Moon's face blazed red in anger at the words of Magaskawee. He pulled the black carbon fiber bow off his shoulder and unclipped an arrow from a storage compartment encircling his lower leg below his knee. Without saying a word, Red Moon notched the arrow and let it fly directly at Mags, who was standing no more than twenty yards away.

Mags dodged the arrow effortlessly, and as she tumbled to the side, she pulled out one of her tomahawks. In a single motion, Mags not only evaded the arrow but sliced the shaft into two pieces. After picking up the end of the shaft containing the arrowhead from the ground, Mags threw it back at Red Moon. In Lakota she said, "You are not *ozuye*. You are children playing with toys."

Mato was getting frustrated with all of the talking back and forth and wondered if Chapa and Mags were stalling. The giant scowled at Mags as he removed a metal rod from the strap across his back and clicked a button in the grip section. The pole extended into a staff and a blade clicked into place, forming a spear.

Red Moon followed Mato's lead, and the two charged Chapa and Mags. The other two *ozuye* remained at a distance and began firing arrows from metal bows like the one used by Red Moon.

Chapa got off one blast from his shotgun at the charging Mato before sprinting for cover behind rocks lining the side of Crazy Horse's face. Mags was right behind Chapa and now had both tomahawks loose, ready for close combat.

As Red Moon and Mato charged across the ridge towards Chapa, two rifle shots rang out, dropping both of the remaining *ozuye*. Resnick emerged onto the ridge from the path below where he had been hiding, waiting for his moment to catch Red Moon's gang in a crossfire. They were now exposed on the ridge with no cover between Chapa's shotgun and Resnick's rifle.

Taking advantage of Resnick's distraction, Chapa fired his shotgun again, this time aiming for Red Moon. Chapa felt a rush of adrenaline as Red Moon's shoulder flew backwards from the pellets impacting his torso. Chapa's excitement was short-lived, and he exhaled in frustration when Red Moon paused his charge for only a few seconds. Chapa had hit Red Moon at point blank range with a shotgun, and only managed to make him angry.

Mato stopped his charge and decided to turn his focus towards the newfound threat of Resnick's rifle. The giant man ran in a zig-zag pattern back across the gravel plateau towards Resnick while the FBI agent fired three more quick shots from the rifle. Two of the shots missed completely, but one shot grazed Mato's arm, drawing a howl of rage. Mato closed the distance in seconds and was almost on top of Resnick when he got off a final shot.

This time, Resnick's bullet hit Mato in the thigh, stopping his charge and dropping him to his knees.

While Mato had turned his attention to Resnick, Red Moon continued his charge towards Chapa, rapidly firing arrows from his bow as he sprinted across the ridge. Once the Lakota attacker got close to Chapa's hiding spot, he dropped the bow and removed a knife from a sheath in his belt. Red Moon pounced on Chapa with his knife raised in the air, but was blocked by Mags and one of her tomahawks.

"Go help Resnick. You can't do anything here," Mags shouted.

Chapa dropped the now empty shotgun and ran across the ridge towards Resnick. Behind him, Chapa could hear the sounds of Mags and Red Moon's metal weapons clanging, locked in furious hand to hand combat. Chapa ignored the fight behind him and pulled his Sig from the holster on his hip. Chapa raised the gun and aimed at Mato as he slowly approached the giant man from behind.

"Resnick, you alright?" Chapa asked as he approached.

"Just a little winded from climbing this damn mountain, but happy to be able to save your butts." By this time, Resnick had also pulled out his Ruger and turned his attention back to Mato. "You are under arrest, big boy. Drop the spear and lay face down on the ground with your hands behind your head."

Mato paused for a second and Chapa wondered if the man had heard Resnick's command. Mato finally looked up and Chapa saw by the look in the giant's eyes that the fight was far from over. Before Resnick could react, Mato jumped to his feet and tackled the FBI agent, which sent them both rolling on the ground towards the edge of the ridge. Resnick stopped his momentum before it carried him off the side of the cliff, but dropped his pistol in the process. Mato had also lost his spear, but it became instantly clear that his size and strength were formidable weapons by themselves.

Mato rolled on top of Resnick and dropped an elbow into his jaw. The crack of the impact of bone upon bone was followed by Resnick spitting out blood as he landed his own punch into the kidney of Mato. Chapa continued to approach, gun drawn, waiting for an opening.

"I need a clean shot, Resnick," Chapa yelled as he approached the rolling pile of fists and kicks. Resnick failed to respond and Chapa knew that if he didn't make a decision, the brute in front of him might do fatal damage to his partner. Mato was now on top of Resnick squeezing his throat with both hands.

Chapa took a long, controlled breath and aimed at Mato's moving torso before gently squeezing the trigger. The bullet struck Mato in his side and instantly achieved the desired result. The giant stopped choking Resnick and rolled off the agent, clutching the side of his body where he had been hit by the bullet.

Resnick caught his breath and slowly crawled away from Mato while Chapa continued shooting. Mato, however, was only dazed by the initial bullet and was able to avoid the next volley of shots from Chapa by rolling across the ground. Mato leaped to his feet with the mobility of a gymnast and reached around to pull another metal rod from the strap on his back. He extended the spear and leaned forward in preparation to charge towards Chapa.

Without warning, there was a noise that sounded like a tiny helicopter as two metal bolos flew by Chapa and wrapped around Mato's knees. The giant man tried desperately to keep his balance while stumbling around on the edge of the ridge clutching his spear. Resnick looked at Chapa and then at Mato. Chapa saw a look in Resnick's eyes that he had never seen before and his heart stop beating as he realized what was about to happen. Resnick launched himself across the ridge and grabbed Mato's waist with both arms, letting his momentum carry them both towards the edge of the cliff as he drove forward with his legs.

Mato tried to break the charge, but without the benefit of control over his legs, he had no stability and could only fall backwards, carried by the momentum from Resnick's tackle. They both went tumbling over the gravelly edge of the landing in a mass of flailing arms and legs, with each one desperately trying to hold on to something to avoid the fall onto the rocks hundreds of feet below.

Chapa immediately rushed to the edge and saw Resnick holding onto a protruding rock about fifteen feet below. The beaten and bloodied FBI agent was desperately clutching the rock with both hands while kicking at Mato who was wrapped around his legs.

"Hang on, Resnick," Chapa shouted as he tried to aim at the hulk pulling on his partner. The angle was terrible with rocks blocking his line of sight, but Chapa fired wildly at Mato until his gun was empty. None of them hit his target, and the bullets just whizzed by Mato or ricocheted off the rock wall of the cliff.

He saw the exhausted look in Resnick's eyes as Chapa loaded a new clip, and all he could say to his friend was, please don't do it. Don't let go. Resnick looked up at Chapa one final time and flashed his trademark smirk. The FBI agent's fingers slowly slipped off the rock and Chapa watched with horror as the partner he had only just gotten to know in the last few days, and the monster who tried to kill them, both plunged down the side of the mountain onto the rocks below.

Chapa paused for a brief moment then looked away from the edge. "Godspeed, Resnick," he said under his breath as he turned his attention back to Mags. He was surprised, however, when she walked up behind him and put her hand on his shoulder to let him know that the battle was over, at least for now. Chapa could not believe Mags had both fought off Red Moon and helped take down Mato. "What happened to Red Moon?"

"He ran away after Mato fell off the ridge. I didn't follow him."

Chapa looked down at the tomahawks in Mags' hands and was encouraged to see blood on the blades.

Mags followed his gaze down to her weapons. "Yes. He is wounded but he will be back. We need to get the girls to safety and rescue Logan before it is too late."

The reality of the situation was slowly sinking into Chapa. Somehow, Red

Moon was impervious to bullets but could be harmed by Mags' blades. He didn't understand any of it but was thankful that he had Mags watching his back. And now, Resnick's sacrifice had given them a chance to save Logan and the others.

Tia and Erica were already up on the ledge screaming and waving at tourists down below who were arriving at the Memorial to take pictures. Instead of the normally peaceful scene in the mountains, the tourists were greeted with a gunfight, men plunging off the side of the mountain, and screams for help from the girls. Several had their phones out recording the fighting while others were calling the police.

Chapa looked down at the crowd gathering below and felt relief. At least the cavalry would be on the way. The only question was, would it be quick enough to help stop whatever the Crow Keeper had planned for Logan?

# Chapter Forty-Six

Logan strained his neck to see what the Crow Keeper was doing behind him. The timing of the ceremony was tied to a solar eclipse, so Logan anxiously watched the sky for any sign of activity. So far, it was a normal sunny day, and Logan held out hope that he still had time for Tia and Erica to bring back help.

The shaman had purposefully moved into the middle of the circle, into the open space behind Logan and the others so that he was out of their line of sight. The old medicine man raised his hands to signal to the crowd that he had something to say. Instantly, the men and women surrounding the circle quieted down in anticipation of the words that were about to be spoken.

"Over a century ago, the great medicine man Wovoka performed the first Ghost Dance when the sun was dark in the sky. On that day, the spirits revealed a great secret. They told him it was our people's destiny to take back our lands, but we must first reunite with our ancestors. Only with the strength of the past *and* the present would we see a great victory. The sun will be dark in the sky again today, and the spirits will once again reveal our destiny. Through the blood of Sitting Bull's descendants, we will reunite the past and the present. We will bring back the murdered war chief from the afterlife to finish what he and Wovoka started."

The crowd in the plaza hung on every word and were transfixed by the Crow Keeper's message, which was delivered with the skill of both a religious leader and snake oil salesman rolled into one. His cadence would rise and fall, and the mechanics of his speech was almost song-like. In a slow and deliberate movement, the Crow Keeper removed the headdress and lifted it up towards the sky.

"This is the headdress of Sitting Bull, the great war chief of the Lakota people. He wore this sacred crown upon his head on the day when he was murdered. He will wear it again today when he returns from beyond the grave to lead our people. This time, Sitting Bull will be invincible and no one will be able to stop us from taking back what was stolen."

On this last note of the speech, the crowd began to whoop and holler as the excitement of what was promised started to take shape. Men and women around the circle pumped their fists in the air and yelled, "Tatanka Iyotake," the Lakota translation of Sitting Bull's name. The Crow Keeper pulled the headdress down to his chest, then thrust it back up quickly above his head. Each time, when he raised the headdress, the crowd repeated, "Tatanka Iyotake." The medicine man repeated this maneuver over and over, and each time the crowd got louder. Eventually, the crowd of cult members worked themselves into a frenzy, and began to move into a formation just outside the skull circle boundary.

The speech from the Crow Keeper was like a dagger through Logan's heart and he began to sweat with anxiety as he realized the ceremony was beginning. This was it. He squirmed furiously in a pointless effort to break the ropes that bound his hands and body to the post. His fear turned to anger as he thought about everything he had been through in the last few days and the sacrifices his friends had made to keep him safe. His life could not end like this—he was no sacrificial lamb.

By this time, the men and women of the compound had joined hands around the circle and were swaying to a melodic chant from the Crow Keeper. Logan had seen traditional Native American round dances before, but this one was like nothing he had ever experienced. The Ghost Dance performed by the Crow Keeper did not use a drum or any other instruments. The dance relied solely on the old medicine man's voice, which somehow projected the melodic chant above the noise of the cult members who were now lining the circle. Periodically, the Crow Keeper would break from his chant and raise the headdress above his head, prompting the crowd to all yell Sitting Bull's

Lakota name in unison as they looked to the sky.

Logan and the others were blinded to the Crow Keeper's actions as he remained out of sight in the no man's land behind their backs. The swaying masses circled the bound victims with a bloodthirsty look in their eyes, and Logan feared that at any moment the Crow Keeper may come up behind him and take his life. He looked to his right and left and saw that the others bound in the circle had similar looks of panic on their faces. They all had the same questions running through their heads. How long would this dance go on? What did the Crow Keeper have planned for their sacrifice?

Behind them, the Crow Keeper continued his chanting and the Ghost Dance seemed to be stalled. Finally, Logan detected something different in the sound of the shaman's voice. He was moving away towards something, or someone.

The bones on the old medicine man's shirt clanked as he approached a middle-aged Lakota woman bound to a wooden stake on the opposite end of the circle from Logan. Like all of the other descendants of Sitting Bull sitting in the circle, her hands were behind her back, tied with a rope. The Crow Keeper carefully removed a knife from a sheath hanging around his neck and raised it into the air so everyone could see it.

He yelled to the crowd, "Blood for blood!"

The Crow Keeper used the knife to slice one of the hands of the bound woman, then rubbed the knife into the bleeding wound. The gag in her mouth could not completely muffle the woman screaming in terror in response to the sudden painful attack and the fear of what was coming next. The old medicine man then took the bloody knife and rubbed the blood on the headdress, chanting "Blood for blood," a mantra that was echoed by the crowd still circling the victims.

After ensuring that the blood of the woman was effectively smeared on the headdress, the Crow Keeper raised Sitting Bull's relic high into the sky and then brought it down quickly onto the head of the unsuspecting woman. She screamed again and squirmed to resist the incredible downward force from the surprisingly strong old man, who was holding the headdress firmly in place. Crow Keeper's old weathered hands glowed hot with an unnatural heat and slowly the woman's resistance subsided as the life poured out of her body, captured in Sitting Bull's headdress. Her head dropped down, and the Crow Keeper removed the headdress in a sweeping motion, again holding it high above his head for the crowd to see.

The temporary lull from watching the Crow Keeper sacrifice one of Sitting Bull's descendants erupted again into raucous cheers and renewed chanting of, "Tatanka Iyotake, Tatanka Iyotake."

A chill went through Logan as he heard a muffled scream, followed by silence and then celebration. Without seeing what had happened, he knew the woman who screamed was dead and, unless he escaped, he was going to share the same fate.

One by one, the Crow Keeper approached the bound victims from behind, spilled their blood on the headdress, then placed the relic from Sitting Bull upon their heads. Each time, the result was the same. No matter how much the victim struggled or resisted, their screams eventually died out, along with their last living breath. The Crow Keeper's power drained their spirit from their bodies and trapped it in Sitting Bull's headdress. Blood for blood.

Each time one of the seven prisoners fell victim to the Ghost Dance, the terror grew in Logan's mind as he wondered what devilry was occurring behind his back. His heart sank as he heard the screams of White Elk, and knew that his friend was no more. Tears ran down Logan's face as he became angry knowing that White Elk's last moments were spent screaming out in pain begging for his life. Logan painfully recalled his promise that he would come back for White Elk after he helped Logan and his friends escape their jail cell. His friend deserved better. They all deserved better.

At long last, the Crow Keeper made his way around the circle to the younger boy tied next to Logan. Through his peripheral vision, Logan could see the Crow Keeper approach him from behind and slice his hand with his knife. Logan saw the tears running down the boy's face and his swollen red eyes as the headdress was placed on his head, igniting the same screams that had sealed the fate of each prior victim. This one was no different, and he fell silent within seconds, resulting in another round of triumphant celebration from the Crow Keeper and the crowd of frenzied cult members.

Logan tensed as the Crow Keeper walked behind him, bracing for his turn as a sacrifice in the Ghost Dance. Instead, the old medicine man leaned down behind Logan and whispered into his ear. "It is not your turn yet. The spirits have chosen you to be the vessel for the return of Sitting Bull. When the sun goes dark, your life will end and his life will begin anew."

Logan held his breath as the Crow Keeper passed him by and continued his work around the circle. His eyes scanned the sky for any sign of the solar eclipse that would mark the end of the ceremony. Logan's heart sank into his stomach as he noticed a slight decrease in the amount of sunlight, as if a cloud had passed in front of the sun. The bright blue sky betrayed the lack of clouds, and Logan knew that the eclipse was approaching, along with his death.

# Chapter Forty-Seven

Chapa and Mags ran up the steep switchbacks taking them from the base of Crazy Horse's sculpted face to the top of his head, the highest point on the mountain. Chapa reached into his pocket on the side of his pants and removed three shotgun shells, then turned back to the gravel path. He struggled to keep up with Mags while reloading his shotgun and periodically craning his neck to see if they were being followed.

The BIA agent cursed to himself about losing Resnick and hoped his friend had not died in vain. Surely, someone in the growing crowd below had called the police by now. He also knew there was a strong likelihood someone in the Monument's parking lot had recorded the fight and posted it on social media. This place should be covered up with law enforcement soon.

Chapa finally made it to the top of Crazy Horse's head and saw Erica and Tia clutching to Mags' side near the edge of one of the sides. They were all looking down on the ridge where they had just fought with Red Moon's gang. Chapa immediately joined them and scanned below for any sign of life.

"We need to get the girls off this mountain. Red Moon is still out there and will be coming back with reinforcements."

Mags shook her head in disagreement. "No. Chapa, we don't have time. Look up in the sky. The eclipse is coming, and the Crow Keeper is going to kill Logan along with all of those other people he kidnapped. You know Resnick would have wanted us to rescue them."

The last comment stung Chapa, and he could tell Mags regretted mentioning his partner's name so soon after his death. Nonetheless, he knew she was right and knelt down beside Erica and Tia. "Can you take us to Logan?"

"Yes," replied Erica. "The camp is on the back side of the mountain. It's not far."

"Fine," replied Chapa, turning back to Mags. "Lead the way, but if we hit trouble, I want the girls to run back to those cars down there in the parking lot as fast as they can. Red Moon is still out there, and we may not be able to stop him next time."

Mags looked at Tia. "I think we have a way to avoid anyone sneaking up on us. Right, Tia?"

Tia nodded her head as Jini leapt off her shoulder and launched into flight. The falcon circled the mountain and swooped down into the trees towards the Crow Keeper's compound, allowing Tia an aerial view of any *ozuye* blocking their path. Jini's flight did not reveal Red Moon or any *ozuye*, but Tia saw Logan tied up in the familiar circle of skulls, which she knew signaled the start of the Ghost Dance.

"We have to go now!" Tia said worriedly. "The ceremony has started, and the Crow Keeper is going to kill them all. He told us he would do it during the eclipse."

Chapa looked at her with confusion. "How do you know that?" he asked.

Mags replied matter-of-factly, "She is blind and uses the bird to see. I will explain later, but she is right. We need to go now."

The four ran down from the crest of the Crazy Horse sculpture to the ridge below, but did not stop. With the girls barking out directions, Mags led the group down the path on the back side of the mountain into the forest bordering the cult compound. The girls and Chapa struggled to keep up with Mags, but they ran as fast as they could, knowing time was running short. The sky was increasingly getting darker, leaving no doubt that the eclipse was about to begin, and they all knew that when it ended, so would Logan's life.

As they entered the woods, Jini flew from tree to tree keeping just ahead of the group. Occasionally, the shrieking falcon would soar above the tree canopy and circle the area looking for the *ozuye*. This pattern continued for half a mile as the group steadily closed the distance on the compound where

Logan was being held. Chapa was gaining confidence that they just might be able to get to Logan in time to save his life, when Tia froze.

"She sees something," whispered Erica.

Jini was perched in a tree above them, staring intently through the forest ahead. Tia was likewise frozen staring through Jini's eyes at something ahead that had caught her attention. It was movement. Definitely movement.

"What is it?" asked Chapa.

Tia remained quiet, staring straight ahead. Finally, the girl saw what had caught Jini's attention. Mags saw it, too, and immediately closed ranks around the girls.

Adriel and his shadow wolf stepped out from behind a large oak tree, followed by Red Moon. The *ozuye* leader now had a bloody wound on his arm, and bruises on his face from his earlier battle with Mags.

Red Moon notched an arrow to his bow, and it flew just over the heads of the girls as they dropped to the ground. The pair of *ozuye* moved quickly to a different position and Red Moon shot another arrow in their direction, again missing the mark.

"They are just trying to slow us down," Chapa shouted at Mags.

She nodded her head in agreement. "Follow the girls and go get Logan. It is our only chance."

"Are you crazy? I can't leave you here alone," Chapa replied.

"All I need to do is hold them off and give you a head start. I will be right behind you."

Chapa grabbed the girls and sprinted through the woods in the direction of the compound. Mags ran behind them, keeping a close eye on Red Moon.

Red Moon immediately took off in pursuit and Adriel sent his shadow wolf on an intercept course to block their path and turn them away from the compound. The wolf crashed through the thick underbrush and the nearly invisible beast let out a howl that caused Erica to scream in fear at the top of her lungs.

"Do not stop!" Mags shouted to the girls as she pulled out both tomahawks. She ran behind Chapa, splitting her attention between the wolf's advance and the path in front of her feet. The sounds of the breaking branches and the heavy breathing of the wolf was steadily getting closer. It was now only seconds away.

The wolf emerged from the forest floor and launched in the air towards the girls and Chapa. But it never touched them. Chapa heard a whooshing sound as the beast was met with a fierce upper cut from the silver head of Mags' tomahawk blade, passing only inches away from his head. The wolf fell to the ground and its shadowy form dissolved into thin air.

Without the wolf to block their path, Chapa kept the girls moving in the direction of the Ghost Dance ceremony. Behind him, he saw Mags standing defiantly with her tomahawks held tightly in a crossing pattern against her chest.

All she had to do was buy them some time, but Chapa knew Mags was not one to run away from a fight. He worried that Red Moon might be more than even Mags could handle.

# Chapter Forty-Eight

The chants from the Crow Keeper's voice filled the air, wafting through the compound in repetitive waves. The pitch of his melodic voice rose and fell in an almost hypnotic pattern. The medicine man's voice was accompanied by periodic humming and chanting from the crowd as they held hands and swayed around the circle. The old shaman's rhythmic song never stopped or even slowed as he methodically went about his work taking the life of every living descendant of Sitting Bull in the circle next to Logan.

Logan watched as the Crow Keeper made his way to the last remaining member of the group from the jail cell who was still alive—the older woman to his left. Logan had never got her name during the short time they were locked in the cave, and now he regretted it. She was old enough to be Logan's mother, with long black hair and dark weathered skin. The woman looked straight ahead, determined to meet her end with dignity and resolve. She was still wearing the same black scrubs from when Logan saw her in the cell. He imagined she had probably worn the same clothes for days since she was kidnapped by Red Moon and his gang on her way home from the hospital where she worked.

Even though the woman could not see what was happening behind her, she had seen enough through her peripheral vision, like Logan, to know her fate. She knew that her life was about to be over and she had made peace with her end. Just like the others, the Crow Keeper cut the woman's hand, wiped her blood on the headdress, and placed it firmly on her head. Unlike the others, however, the brave woman did not cry out or give any sign to the crowd that the Crow Keeper's ritual was successful. She simply closed her eyes and quietly drifted away into the next life. Nonetheless, the medicine man accomplished his goal and confidently raised Sitting Bull's crown in victory for a sixth time. The cult members responded with another round of chanting, "Tatanka Iyotake."

Logan felt a mixture of rage and despair as the brave woman lost her silent battle with the Crow Keeper. Other than following her example and meeting death with dignity in protest, what else could he do? What did the Crow Keeper mean when he said Logan would be his vessel for the return of Sitting Bull? He chose Logan's death to be last for a reason, but it seemed clear that this decision was a tactical delay and not a reprieve. Whatever the medicine man had planned for Logan could very well be worse than death, and he might soon envy the quiet passing of the woman he had just witnessed.

***

The medicine man's shirt clicked behind Logan as he walked around the middle of the circle. The shadows of the buildings slowly extended and merged together to darken the ground. The moon was drifting in front of the sun, causing the normally bright afternoon light to fade as if it were evening. The eclipse was getting close, and the Crow Keeper knew he wouldn't have much time once the heavenly event started. It would last only minutes, and the success of the ceremony hinged upon perfect timing.

The Crow Keeper knew the Ghost Dance could open a connection between the living and the spirit world populated by their ancestors. He had performed the ceremony thousands of times since discovering the secrets of the Ghost Dance. The ceremony was unpredictable, but each time he performed it he learned a little more. Each time, the Crow Keeper gained insight into the world beyond the living, as the two worlds temporarily touched. When those worlds touched, miracles could occur. The Crow Keeper had seen men and women receive great gifts from their ancestors through the Ghost Dance—gifts of strength, and power over the natural world. He now had almost a century of experience in performing the ceremony and he had gained a control that Wovoka never even imagined in the past.

He had waited patiently for decades, hiding in the shadows as he tended his crows, and now he was finally ready to use the secret first learned by his teacher—that an eclipse could temporarily break down the walls between the living and the spirit world completely. The bridge between the living and the dead would be wide open, and the entire bloodline of Sitting Bull would be in one place during the Ghost Dance, shining like a beacon in the night for his war chief to return to the world of the living. Logan and the others would be sacrificed, and in their place would be Sitting Bull, once again proudly wearing his headdress.

The old man purposefully walked behind Logan's back, in and out of his line of sight, teasing him with anticipation. The Crow Keeper suddenly stopped his melodic chant and raised his hand in the air to signal for the crowd to be silent. He took a deep breath and prepared to address those who had assembled to view his triumph—the resurrection of the greatest Lakota war chief who had ever lived.

"Today, the sun and the moon will come together as one, opening a bridge between our world and the world of our ancestors. I had a vision that Sitting Bull will cross over that bridge and return to lead his people. He will once again wear the headdress of a war chief and together we will take back what belongs to us."

The crowd cheered and chanted, "Tatanka Iyotake" as the Crow Keeper again raised Sitting Bull's headdress above his head. The horizon was almost completely black and stars were now becoming visible in the daylight sky. In the distance, a rooster crowed and the cicadas began their nighttime song. For a brief moment, it was both night and day. Sensing the need to move quickly, the Crow Keeper sliced the base of one of Logan's hands, which was tied to the post behind his back. The boy jerked in response to the sudden unseen assault from the Crow Keeper, and screamed in pain as blood ran from the deep cut. The medicine man rubbed his knife against the wound and, once it was fully covered in Logan's blood, spread the red substance along the already bloodstained leather band of the headdress. For the seventh and last time, the

Crow Keeper held his trophy above his head and yelled, "Blood for blood" to the frenzied cheers of his followers.

Next, the Crow Keeper placed the headdress on Logan's head, but unlike his practice with the others, his purpose was not to quickly drain Logan's life away. Instead, the medicine man stepped back and left the head piece in place, focusing instead on increasing the pace of his melodic chant. The Crow Keeper needed Logan alive, and this was the culmination of a century of planning. Logan was the last remaining descendant of Sitting Bull, and only someone from the war chief's bloodline could serve as the connection for the Ghost Dance. With the recently departed spirits of the remaining six members of the bloodline temporarily trapped in the headdress by the Crow Keeper, the item would serve as a bridge between the worlds. If Sitting Bull could cross that bridge, his spirit could take advantage of the eclipse to travel back into the world of the living and reclaim a living body. For the next four minutes, the barrier blocking the spirit world from that of the living would be down, and Sitting Bull was waiting, ready to cross over and live again.

*** 

Once the headdress was placed on Logan's head, the boy felt a rush of disorientation as if his entire consciousness was being pulled in every direction. He soon realized that it did not matter if his eyes were open or closed because his normal senses no longer worked. He saw without his eyes and felt without the use of touch.

Logan realized he was no longer bound to the post on the ground, but he nonetheless still could not move. He seemed to be floating in place above his body, which he saw below him tied to the pole. Logan could see the Crow Keeper and the others in the crowd, but they were moving slowly. It was as if time operated differently in this place.

As the boy acclimated to his new astral reality, Logan slowly began to realize he was not alone. There were other spirits floating with him in this different plane of existence. Translucent reflections of people, floating effortlessly around him as they stood and watched. In fact, a crowd of ethereal forms was closing in on him and the ones closest to him looked strangely familiar. He saw Samuel White Elk and the woman from his left who was the last to die. All of the other descendants killed by the Crow Keeper were now with him, closing ranks as if to form a line of protection. He looked further into the gathering crowd, and he saw someone else he recognized—his mother.

Logan desperately tried to reach her but he still could not make his body move in this uncomfortable form. His mother only smiled at him and placed her hand on a necklace around her neck—a necklace that was identical to the one Logan was still wearing. Logan noticed that his necklace was now glowing, just like it did during the Blessing Way ceremony. In the distance, Logan saw a sight he had also seen during that same ceremony. A stoic warrior charging toward him on a horse with a spear by his side. It was Sitting Bull, and he was coming to take Logan's life.

# Chapter Forty-Nine

Mags stood alone in the forest, staring at Red Moon and Adriel. This was the second time she would face Red Moon today and she knew her tomahawks could spill his blood. But Mags also knew Red Moon was dangerous, and she could see a flash of rage as their eyes met for a brief moment. The green eyes were haunting, and she sensed a primal anger that was now boiling over to the surface.

She braced for the charging Red Moon, gripping the handles of both tomahawks so tightly that her palms turned white. Red Moon pulled two knives out of his belt as he ran straight towards her, leaving Adriel behind to watch. Without breaking stride, Red Moon used one of his knives to slash at Mags' throat. She capably blocked the thrust with the back of her tomahawk and slammed the metal head into Red Moon's wrist. The move should have broken a bone, but only caused the leader of the *ozuye* to drop his knife.

Red Moon swung wildly with his other knife, and Mags kicked him in the chest, sending him flying to his back on the ground. As he hit the dirt, and was temporarily stationary, Mags took advantage of the opening and threw one of her tomahawks, hitting Red Moon squarely in the shoulder. The weapon dug deep into Red Moon's flesh, and Mags could tell that she had finally injured him.

While Mags was focused on finishing Red Moon, a dark shadowy bird swooped down from the sky and scratched at Mags' face with its claws. She thrashed wildly in the air with her arms to block the bird, but the unexpected aerial attacker opened a gash on Mags' forehead, narrowly missing her eye.

The distraction allowed Red Moon to remove the tomahawk from his shoulder and return to his feet. He threw Mags' tomahawk deep into the underbrush, leaving her with only the one weapon in her hand.

Red Moon pressed his advantage with a swift flurry of attacks with his remaining knife. This time, his anger seemed to give him strength and his frenzied attacks were increasingly difficult for Mags to avoid. Mags fought back the burning sensation in her eyes as the blood ran down her face from the gash in her forehead. Even a momentary blink could mean death. She somehow managed to block each one of Red Moon's attacks until Adriel's bird swooped down in another vicious attack on Mags' face. This time, Adriel's coordinated attack achieved its purpose, as Mags' split second move to block the bird allowed Red Moon an opening. He sprinted forward and, as he ran past Mags, he opened up a deep cut in the woman's side with a slice from his knife.

The instant heat of the blood running down Mags' side was overwhelming and Mags instinctively knew the cut was deep. She had been in plenty of knife fights and understood that if she did not get pressure on the wound, she would soon be unconscious due to blood loss. Mags dug her right hand deep into the dirt and gathered a fist full of debris as she remained on her knees feigning weakness. As Red Moon turned back to strike again, Mags threw the dirt into his face before leaping up and stumbling away through the underbrush. Mags applied pressure on the wound as she ran, desperately searching for a place where she could hide from Adriel's bird.

She settled on a large oak that had been blown over, leaving a giant root ball that was a perfect hiding spot. Mags ducked under the uprooted tree stump and used a small knife from her boot to cut a line of cloth from her shirt. She quickly tied the makeshift bandage around her waist, squeezing it tightly across the cut against her abdomen. Tears ran down her face as she applied the pressure, but she knew the tourniquet was necessary to stop the bleeding. She paused to catch her breath, and focused on slowing her heart rate and thinking about her next move. Mags looked up into the sky for a glimpse of Adriel's bird and noticed the sky was darkening. In an instant, day turned into night and the combination of the eclipse and the tree canopy blocked out the sunlight completely.

Mags felt both relief and fear as she knew at that moment, she had done her job. Logan's fate was out of her hands, and she could only hope that Chapa and the others made it to the boy before it was too late.

Red Moon also noticed the onset of the eclipse and stopped his attack to watch as darkness fell over the wooded battleground. The sounds of cicadas suddenly came to life and Red Moon shouted excitedly to Mags: "There is nothing you can do now. The Ghost Dance is over, and the boy is already dead."

From her hiding place, Mags ignored Red Moon's words and calmly scanned the sky for the dark form of Adriel's bird. It would be almost invisible in the darkness, but she could still hear the flap of its wings and knew it would spot her soon. Mags focused on the sound, and when it seemed the noise was almost on top of her location, she bolted from her hiding spot and sprinted across the forest floor.

As she expected, the shadow bird followed Mags, tracking her in the darkness and leading Red Moon and Adriel who followed. Mags looked over her shoulder to gauge the height of the bird above her head and slowed down until it was close. As she approached the next large tree, Mags jumped up onto the side and swung her tomahawk forcefully—landing it deep into the bark. With the newfound anchor, she turned and launched herself even higher into the air behind her, removing the tomahawk as she leapt from the tree. The maneuver allowed Mags to soar high enough into the air to reach Adriel's bird, and she destroyed it with a blow from the tomahawk as she had done with the wolf.

Mags' surprise maneuver left Red Moon and Adriel with no way to track Mags through the dense forest in the dark. Mags remained still, hiding in the underbrush, worried that she would be given away by her labored breathing. After a momentary pause, she quietly slinked away from the *ozuye*, staying low to avoid being seen. The eclipse would not last long, and Mags knew she needed to take full advantage of the darkness. As soon as she felt it was safe, she began to run in the direction of the cult compound. Each stride bringing a searing pain in her side, reminding her of the cut from Red Moon's blade.

"You can't stop us. No one can stop us," shouted Red Moon.

Mags heard Red Moon's words echo through the darkness. She desperately hoped he was wrong, but she had to know the truth. She had to get to the compound to find out if Chapa had been able to stop the Ghost Dance.

# Chapter Fifty

The Crow Keeper was drenched in sweat as he circled Logan, chanting the melodic song that he had learned from his teacher, Wovoka, and perfected during his unnaturally long life. The song formed the backbone of a secret so powerful that only a small number of shamans had ever dared attempt the incantation.

His long-dead teacher had warned the Crow Keeper in his youth that tampering with the connection between the living and the spirit world was unnatural and unpredictable. The Ghost Dance was too powerful and chaotic, and should be used sparingly, if at all. When Wovoka first set the Ghost Dance loose into the world in 1890, the medicine man thought it would be used for peaceful purposes. Instead, the threat it posed was instantly recognized and met with a crackdown that was swift and brutal. Wovoka's newfound power resulted in virtually all of his followers being killed. Sitting Bull and hundreds of others were murdered, including the Crow Keeper's Lakota parents.

The Crow Keeper was only a boy when the Ghost Dance was made illegal, but after luckily escaping death himself during the massacre at Wounded Knee, he devoted his life to rebuilding the movement and becoming a master of the power that instilled so much fear. Wovoka initially taught the young Lakota boy, but it became clear that Wovoka was not looking for a war, and only wanted peace for his people. The Crow Keeper, however, was looking for something more powerful, and he found it deep in the caves of the Black Hills.

Now, after decades of hiding, and honing his skills as a shaman, the Crow Keeper was finally ready to set his plan into action. The world had changed, and was ripe for the taking. With Sitting Bull by his side, and hundreds of witnesses to spread word of his miracle, their power would grow. Allies would flock to his movement and their enemies would be distracted and divided, too weak to stop them like before. The Crow Keeper had even taken on the persona of Wovoka, dressing like him and encouraging his followers to believe that the famous medicine man had returned from the dead.

The Crow Keeper was curious as he stopped chanting in front of Logan, looking anxiously at the boy's face, searching for signs of the transformation. In minutes, Logan would be no more, and Sitting Bull would be living in his place. The medicine man could only wonder what was occurring in the spirit world, but he remained confident that soon it would all be over. The Ghost Dance could not be stopped.

***

Logan was unfazed by the danger he faced in the spirit world and could not take his eyes off his mother. The boy gazed into her face and wished he could talk to her or touch her, but he found he could do neither. All he could do was observe as a watcher, helpless as a baby who had just come into the world of the living. Logan finally broke his gaze on his mother and noticed Sitting Bull coming closer on horseback. He was now only a few yards away, blocked by the crowd of spirits encircling Logan's floating astral form. Undeterred by the attention, the war chief dismounted and grabbed the spear from the side of his horse.

Sitting Bull walked straight towards Logan and the spirits of his descendants parted to make way for the war chief, lining up on either side and bowing their heads as he passed. The spirits made way for Sitting Bull, until he reached the ones closest to Logan who formed a protective barrier. Logan realized he was somehow connected to the other six men and women killed by the Crow Keeper because of the headdress. But there was also one more to whom he was connected—his mother. The necklace created a bond between Logan and her spirit. He didn't understand the rules in this world, but he knew from the expression of anger on Sitting Bull's face that this was an unexpected development. The boy now had help.

The spectral form of the war chief lunged at the spirit of Logan's friend Samuel White Elk and thrust his spear at the old man's ethereal form. He hit nothing. Instead, White Elk, then the others surrounding him, dissolved and merged into Logan's spirit form. Instantly, Logan's consciousness was assaulted by a flood of emotions, memories and thoughts that were not his own. At the same time, he felt invigorated and infused with a newfound strength. He realized he could now move his arms and legs, and had gained the knowledge and ability to function within the spirit world. He couldn't run, but he could at least will his spirit to move.

Logan looked at his mother who was the last spirit remaining between him and Sitting Bull. He reached for her using his recently discovered ability, desperately wanting to feel her touch one last time. Before he could reach her, she looked straight in his eyes, and he knew his effort would not be successful.

"I will be with you always, Logan," she said, before merging into his ethereal form like the others. This time, Logan was greeted with memories that he recognized. His mother's love washed over him in a powerful wave, and he felt a sense of calm as he prepared to face the approaching spirit of Sitting Bull.

The war chief wasted no time in savagely attacking Logan with his spear. Logan was now able to dodge the thrust, and quickly realized this was going to be a fight to the death. If Sitting Bull killed his spirit in this world, he would take over Logan's body in the real world. But the war chief had to do it quickly before the eclipse was over. He didn't need to defeat Sitting Bull. He just needed to survive long enough for the bridge between the worlds to collapse and his spirit to return to his body.

Through the corner of his eye, Logan saw something below him in the real world that gave him a burst of hope. Chapa, Tia and Erica had made it back to rescue him. Surely, they could find some way to help.

Logan had no time to think about a rescue, however, as Sitting Bull attacked him again. This time, the war chief rushed Logan and dipped his shoulder, knocking Logan backwards onto the ethereal ground of the spirit world. Before Logan could recover, Sitting Bull drove his spear downward in a forceful motion, aiming it directly at Logan's heart. Somehow, Logan mustered the strength to grab the spear with both hands and stop its momentum only inches away from piercing his spirit form. Even with his newfound strength, however, Logan realized he was no match for Sitting Bull. The old war chief pushed on the spear, using his body weight and leverage against Logan. The spear slowly pushed downward and Logan was only inches away from the grizzled and wrinkled face of his would-be executioner. There was no satisfaction or joy in the face of Sitting Bull, only determination as the tip of the spear pierced Logan's ethereal body. Logan again felt the assault on his consciousness, except this time he felt his spirit collapsing. Sitting Bull was in his head, and Logan was struggling to hold onto his own existence.

***

Chapa and the two girls emerged out of the forest and crouched behind one of the buildings surrounding the courtyard where the ceremony was taking place.

"Look, there," said Erica, as she pointed at Logan sitting on the ground. Through the crowd of people, Chapa could make out a disturbing scene of men and women tied to stakes in a circle. None of them, including Logan, were moving.

The medicine man in the middle of the ceremony shouted, "Tatanka Iyotake" as he hovered over Logan's body. Logan was struggling against the ropes and trying to yell as if he was having an epileptic fit. His features appeared to be aging, and it was obvious that something terrible was happening.

"We have to do something," said Erica. "He is killing Logan."

Chapa raised his shotgun and fired a shell into the air. The sudden "boom" startled the crowd assembled for the Ghost Dance, causing them to stop and turn in his direction.

Chapa yelled out, "Stop, BIA officer," and approached the crowd with his shotgun raised at eye level. He pointed it at the people in his way and they scattered, opening up a path to the Crow Keeper, who stood defiantly blocking his way to Logan.

"The boy is dead," said the Crow Keeper. "But his sacrifice was not in vain. You will now get to witness the resurrection of Sitting Bull."

As the old shaman pointed back to Logan, Jini swooped down from the sky and grabbed the headdress with her steel-like talons. The falcon snatched the decorative crown made of feathers as if it was snatching a mouse from a field, and carried it back into the sky. Without the headdress, the connection to the spirit world was broken and the transformation of Logan's body stopped. Logan's features immediately returned to normal, while his body remained limp.

A look of shock crossed the Crow Keeper's face as he realized his plan had failed. The Crow Keeper's shock turned to rage as he turned from Logan to face Chapa. Behind the BIA agent, Tia proudly held up the headdress with Jini perched next to it on her shoulder.

As quickly as it started, the eclipse suddenly came to an end, and sunlight flooded the courtyard. There was an eerie calm, as the crowd assembled for the opportunity to witness the history making Ghost Dance stopped and looked to the Crow Keeper for direction. Chapa slowly walked backwards towards the girls, keeping his eyes on the Crow Keeper, but increasingly becoming worried that the crowd would turn and attack.

"My friends," said the Crow Keeper, "These usurpers from the BIA have interrupted the Ghost Dance and violated our holy place. They have come into our home and destroyed everything we have been working to build. The BIA has murdered Sitting Bull again, just as surely as he was murdered once before by the BIA in Standing Rock. You know what happened to all of the Ghost Dance followers the last time, and they will do it again. If we don't fight back now, we will all be killed."

A wave of anger was building through the crowd as they turned and glared menacingly at Chapa and the girls. Chapa regretted announcing himself as BIA, and the Crow Keeper was cleverly using that fact to inflame his followers and remind them of history. If the crowd turned on them, they would be overwhelmed within minutes.

While the Crow Keeper was talking, however, Logan slowly began to regain consciousness. He opened his eyes and was momentarily blinded by the sun.

Erica was the first to notice Logan's movement and prodded Chapa in the side with her elbow. "Look. He is alive!"

*\*\**

It seemed like an eternity since Logan had seen light in the sky. The boy was filled with an overwhelming feeling of relief and joy to be able to again feel the warmth on his body.

There was an intense pain in Logan's hand where he had been cut by the Crow Keeper's blade, but the throb was subsiding. In fact, it was not just subsiding, it was healing. The jagged tear in the skin of his hand had already began to seal, repairing the wound.

His spirit was back in his body, but Logan felt different. Stronger. His head was no longer filled with the feelings and memories of his mother or the other descendants whose bodies still lay in the courtyard, but he knew their sacrifice in the spirit world had affected him somehow. They were now a part of him.

There was also something else. Sitting Bull had been in his head, and that had left a mark. Something cold and dark that he didn't understand.

Logan put those thoughts out of his mind. All he knew right now was that he had to start fighting back. Logan flexed his arms and pulled on the ropes binding his hands to the wooden post behind his torso. To his surprise, the rope stretched and strained under the pressure, then broke into pieces. With his hands free, he pulled the gag out of his mouth and up over his head.

"Logan!" shouted Erica. "We came back. I told you we would come back."

The cult members lining the courtyard noticed Logan's awakening and immediately lost their focus on the Crow Keeper's words. After watching the others die, no one could believe the boy was still alive. Gasps of shock filtered through the air, and some fell to their knees and started chanting, "Tatanka Iyotake."

The Crow Keeper looked confused and slowly walked away from Logan towards the entry to the cave at the edge of the camp. The Crow Keeper knew he was losing control over the confused onlookers, as they now wondered whether Logan was, in fact, Sitting Bull. The medicine man knew the Ghost

Dance was left unfinished, but he had promised the legendary war chief would take possession of the boy. His followers wanted to believe, and he had nothing to gain by convincing them otherwise.

While the crowd was distracted by Logan's apparent return from the dead, Mags emerged weakly from the forest. Her shirt was stained with blood from the deep cut in her side, but she was still able to walk. Logan was confused to see Magaskawee from the Blessing Way ceremony and had no idea why she was here with Chapa.

Mags shouted out a warning as she ran up behind Chapa and the girls: "Chapa, we have to get Logan out of here. Red Moon is right behind me."

"You're bleeding," said Chapa, ignoring her warning. He quickly inspected the blood-soaked homemade bandage and saw that Mags needed medical help quickly.

Mags pushed away Chapa's attention. "I will be fine. Get the boy."

The group rushed to Logan's side as he finished untying the ropes around his body. Erica was the first to reach Logan and grabbed both hands. "Logan, Tia saved you. Actually, it was Jini. She pulled that thing off your head and broke the magic."

Tia smiled awkwardly and held up Sitting Bull's headdress. "You can keep it as a souvenir."

"I'll pass," said Logan.

"I hate to break up the reunion," said Chapa. "But we have to go now. Mags fought Red Moon to buy us enough time to rescue you, but he is right behind her. She is hurt, and we are surrounded. We can't fight our way out of here."

The four of them walked with Logan out of the courtyard, through the rows of makeshift buildings back towards the trees, hoping to retrace their steps to the Crazy Horse Memorial parking lot. Chapa assured them there would be waiting police officers that would provide protection, but it soon became apparent they would never make it.

Red Moon and Adriel appeared at the edge of the forest, blocking their escape. A wry grin spread across Red Moon's face as he saw Mags, and the sun flashed off his knives, which were already drawn.

"Go back," Chapa said, waving his arm frantically toward the courtyard. Logan led Erica and Tia back to the compound, hoping to find a way to escape Red Moon. Before they could even make it back to the courtyard where the Ghost Dance took place, five *ozuye*, wearing the trademark black leather vests, stepped out of the crowd. Logan and the others were trapped.

# Chapter Fifty-One

Ever since he returned to his body after the Ghost Dance, Logan felt strange. It was a foreign feeling at first, and he wondered if it would wear off. With each moment that passed, however, he felt a growing sense of security that whatever happened was permanent. He didn't just *feel* different—he had actually changed.

Chapa's head was on a swivel, scanning the compound, desperately looking for some way for them to escape. He made clear he didn't want to fight his way through Red Moon or the *ozuye* in front of them. Instead, he found another way and announced it to the group. At the far end of the compound was a small dirt parking lot, with a collection of vehicles and motorcycles. All they had to do was make it to the parking lot without being killed, and find a vehicle with the keys still inside.

Mags and the girls led the mad dash towards the parking lot and Logan followed behind with Chapa. The *ozuye* from the compound saw the attempt to escape and began firing at the group as they ran between the wooden buildings. The screams of the fleeing men and women who were still in the area from the ceremony punctuated the chaos caused by the sounds of gunshots.

Logan looked over his shoulder and saw that Red Moon and Adriel had caught up to the *ozuye*. The combined forces were now following them along with Adriel's shadow wolf, which was running by his side.

He nudged Chapa. "Look," he said, pointing to the wolf. "We aren't going to make it."

Chapa handed his shotgun to Mags and pulled out his revolver. As they ran through the alleys between the buildings, he squeezed off a few rounds to slow down the pursuing *ozuye*. Although some of the men slowed to avoid the bullets, Red Moon and Adriel maintained their advance. The two were closing ground and were no more than fifty feet behind them.

Logan followed Chapa as they ran away from the compound, but something kept nagging at his mind. An inner voice was telling him to stand and fight. He had been running since the attack in Cortez, while everyone else around him risked their lives. He was tired of it, and this time it felt different. He was no longer afraid and knew what he had to do. Logan focused his mind on the knife given to him by Tia and recalled the weight and feel of the handle in his hand. Deep in the Crow Keeper's cave, the knife disappeared from its hiding spot in a wooden container near the prison cell, and appeared in Logan's right hand. Logan's confidence soared as he suddenly felt whole. He had almost forgotten how good it felt to have the weapon in his hand.

As Mags and the girls ran towards the last building before the parking lot, three *ozuye* turned the corner from the alley on the other side of the building in an attempt to cut them off. Before the *ozuye* could shoot, Logan threw his knife in a side-armed motion, striking one of them in the center of his chest and dropping him immediately. As soon as the knife found its target, Logan recalled the knife into his other hand and threw it at a second *ozuye*. The man managed to block the knife from hitting his head, but the weapon struck his arm, causing him to drop his gun and run away. Seeing his partners defeated by Logan within seconds, the remaining *ozuye* retreated back behind the building for cover as Chapa and the others successfully made it to the parking lot.

Chapa yelled at Logan, "I don't know how you suddenly turned into a bad ass, but it couldn't have happened at a better time."

He turned to Mags and the girls and urgently barked out instructions. "Look in the windows but stay low. Find one with keys and shout out to me and Logan."

The group fanned out through the parking lot looking through the windows of the parked cars, desperately hunting for one with the keys inside.

Most of the vehicles were old and some looked to be in questionable working condition. Logan worried that even if they were lucky enough to find one with keys, it may not even start.

Chapa crouched next to Logan behind an old sedan that was parked in a row of cars closest to the buildings. Logan peered over the hood, looking to see if Red Moon was still following them. Red Moon and Adriel soon arrived and regrouped with the remaining *ozuye*.

Adriel's shadow wolf was the first pursuer to run into the parking lot, and it was clear it was acting as a scout to flush them out for the others to attack. Logan looked at Chapa for guidance and the FBI agent waved his palm in a downward motion two times. Logan understood the unspoken direction—wait here.

Seconds later, Logan heard a muffled call from Mags, "We found one. Let's go."

The shadow wolf had now picked up their scent and was making a beeline in full gallop for Logan and Chapa's hiding spot behind the sedan.

Chapa grabbed Logan's arm as he heard an engine starting in the distance. "Now we go!"

The pair emerged from their hiding spot and ran across the parking lot, weaving between vehicles as shots rang out behind them. A bullet impacted a windshield beside Chapa, shattering the glass and throwing sharp fragments in every direction. Chapa kneeled down and covered his face to avoid the explosion, and the delay was enough to allow Adriel's wolf to catch up to their retreat.

The shadow wolf lunged for Chapa's neck but instead it caught his raised arm in its jaws. It began to drag Chapa out into the open towards his fast-approaching master, but Logan delivered a downward blow with his knife to the neck of the wolf, causing it to dissipate into small shadowy black particles that blew away in the wind.

Chapa ignored the blood on his arm and got back to his feet. He searched the parking lot for Mags and the girls and saw they had found a waiting pickup truck. Mags was in the driver's seat and had already backed it out and pointed it at the road away from the compound. All they had to do was make a run for it and jump into the bed of the truck.

Logan looked at Chapa confidently. "You go first. I'm right behind you and will keep them distracted." Chapa didn't need any prodding and, despite the pain in his arm, ran full speed towards the waiting truck. The wounded BIA agent jumped up onto the bumper and poured himself over the lift gate, expecting to see Logan right behind him. Instead, Chapa's jaw dropped. Logan had stayed behind.

The three *ozuye* with guns had initially focused their fire on the sprinting Chapa, and were caught off guard by Logan as he rounded the front of a parked car and punched one in the face with the butt of his knife. He held the first man as a shield and threw his knife from behind the man's head, striking another *ozuye* in the chest. Logan slammed the face of his human shield into the car's front hood, then jumped up onto the car dodging bullets from the remaining *ozuye*. Logan hurdled the roof of the car and slid down the back windshield, landing flat-footed on the top of the trunk.

After pausing for a second on the back side, Logan jumped over to an adjacent car. As he leaped between vehicles, he threw his knife in mid-air, striking the last remaining shooter in the neck, causing him to drop to the ground.

Red Moon and Adriel watched the blitzkrieg unleashed by Logan as they carefully stalked his location, staying low and moving between the cars. From a distance, Chapa could see the pair approaching and called out a warning, "Logan, Red Moon is on your left."

Chapa banged on the back window of the pickup truck and yelled at Mags. "Put this thing into reverse. Go back and get him."

Mags put the truck into reverse and pressed down on the gas pedal, lurching the vehicle backwards. The truck sped in reverse through the soft dirt of the parking lot towards Logan who was already sprinting to catch up and follow Chapa into the bed of the truck. Mags slammed on the brakes and the wheels threw dust into the air as she put the transmission back into drive, ready to accelerate as soon as Logan was safely on board.

Red Moon and Adriel ran after the streaking Logan, but repeated throws from Logan's knife caused them to slow their pursuit. The delay bought just enough time for Logan to vault onto the bumper and grab Chapa's outstretched hand.

Logan's knee landed hard on the bumper, but he didn't feel any pain and performed a forward roll over the lift gate, falling headfirst into the truck.

"Go," yelled Chapa as he slapped furiously on the side of the vehicle with his good arm.

Mags heard Chapa's instruction over the sound of the engine, and the truck accelerated as it sped away from the compound.

*** 

Watching the old truck speed out of the parking lot, Red Moon slowed down into a jog. He realized they had no chance of catching the truck on foot.

Adriel had his hands on his knees and sputtered his words through his quick gasps for air. "Should we follow them?"

"No. The police will be here soon and we need to be gone when that happens. I'm not going back to jail." Red Moon looked around at the chaos of people running into the buildings to gather belongings and vehicles hurriedly leaving the compound. The bodies of those sacrificed in the Ghost Dance could be seen in the distant courtyard, still tied to the posts where they were murdered by the Crow Keeper. "This is over for now."

Red Moon and Adriel mounted their motorcycles and sped off down a dirt road away from the compound as approaching sirens filled the air. They would be long gone from the scene when the police arrived, and Red Moon knew the Crow Keeper would flee to safety into the caves.

The hum of the motorcycle engine normally calmed Red Moon, but not today. Instead, he was slowly filling with rage as he drove through the Black Hills of South Dakota back to the Pine Ridge reservation.

The leader of the *ozuye* couldn't believe he had actually failed. Because of Logan, Red Moon's entire life had changed. His friend Mato was dead, and the Crow Keeper was in hiding.

Eventually, Red Moon's rage subsided as a new thought entered his mind. It was a thought that brought him both comfort and a new goal. Revenge.

# Chapter Fifty-Two

L ogan sat at a picnic table in the Crazy Horse Memorial parking lot next to Tia. The ride from the Crow Keeper's compound had been short, and everything was a blur once they ran into the army of state police and BIA officers who had swarmed the area after the fight at the Memorial went viral on social media. The old truck driven by Mags received a police escort back to the Memorial's parking lot, where Chapa and Mags were now getting medical attention at a newly established command post. Erica asked to borrow a cell phone, and Logan could barely make out the words through the tears as Erica exploded in emotion when she heard her parents' voices.

Taking in the scene, Logan could not believe how much his life had changed in the last few days. His life at the trailer back in Cortez with his uncle Hatani seemed like an eternity ago, but he missed it. He was ready to go home.

"Do you think it is really over?" asked Tia. "Red Moon may come for you again. What will you do?"

"I know Red Moon is still out there, but I am not afraid. Something has changed. I can't explain it, but I feel different. Stronger. I just want to go home."

"You could make a new home in Anasazi," said Tia slowly. "My father would let you stay if you want."

Logan smiled at Tia. "I appreciate it, but I need some time to figure this out. I have a life with my uncle and friends back in Cortez. I have to get back to school, you know. I can't just leave."

Tia smiled back. "Well, you are always welcome to visit... you can come see me anytime you want."

After a few moments of awkward silence, Jini swooped down, circled the pair and landed on Tia's shoulder before letting out a loud squawk. Tia slowly stroked Jini's chin and the bird's head snuggled against Tia's hand.

"She likes it here in the Black Hills," said Tia. "I think I am going to let her stay."

"What do you mean?" asked Logan.

Tears welled up in Tia's eyes and she took a deep breath. "She doesn't want to be locked in a cage again, and it is too far for her to fly back to Anasazi. I have thought about it a lot and it's time to set her free."

"But how will you see?" asked Logan.

"Logan, I am blind. It's who I am. Would you be friends with me if I couldn't see?"

Logan stammered, unsure of how to respond. "Of course. I mean... you know. I want you to be happy, that's all."

"Setting Jini free in this place makes me happy," said Tia definitively. The girl kissed the bird and stroked her hand down its back for one last time. Tia felt the familiar pressure on her shoulder as Jini launched herself into the sky above the forest surrounding the monument and circled the giant face of the Lakota hero carved into the mountainside. Tia could hold back the tears no longer and they ran freely down her face as she watched Jini fly away. The tears eventually stopped, and a smile formed on Tia's face. The light went out in her eyes, but it was as if she suddenly found newfound happiness in the darkness.

***

Across the parking lot at the Memorial, Chapa was sitting in an ambulance alone next to the body of Resnick. The state police had recovered his body and that of Mato from the rocks surrounding the Crazy Horse sculpture. Chapa pulled down the sheet that was covering Resnick's face and took one last look at his bloodied and bruised friend.

"Hey buddy, that was a pretty stupid move you pulled back there. Just wanted to let you know that we saved Logan and the girls. We couldn't have done it without you, and I am sure you wouldn't have it any other way. Always looking to be the hero."

Chapa hadn't known Resnick very long, but he had grown to respect him. Without Resnick's bravery, they would all likely be dead, and the Crow Keeper would have pulled off his resurrection of Sitting Bull. Chapa didn't understand what that would mean exactly, but he knew Logan would be dead like the others at the compound.

He pulled the sheet back up and covered Resnick's face. He knew this was the last time he would see his friend, so he took his time. He could never explain any of this to Resnick's family and he had learned long ago not to linger and dwell on the death of friends. You pay your respects and move on.

Chapa folded Resnick's hands onto his chest under the sheets and laid his own hands on top. Quietly to himself he again repeated his grandmother's prayer. Chapa smiled and rubbed his chin as he imagined that Resnick would approve of his send off.

"Goodbye and see you in the afterlife, my friend."

Chapa lingered for a few minutes then climbed out the back of the ambulance to search for Mags. He found her nearby being worked on by an EMT from the local fire department. The deep knife wound in her side had been stitched up, and she had an IV in her arm pumping her with fluids.

As he got closer, Chapa could hear Mags arguing with the EMT. "I'm fine now. Go ahead and pull out the IV. We are done here."

"But, ma'am, you had a deep wound. You need to get more fluids and rest."

Chapa walked up and flashed his BIA badge. "You can let her go and I will take it from here." He added with a chuckle, "Trust me, you were going to lose that argument anyway, man."

The EMT worked to remove the needle from Mags' arm as she glared at him, silently pressuring him to work faster.

"Just wanted to let you know I am going to be hitting the road soon. I have to get the kids back to Colorado," Chapa said.

Mags didn't answer as she continued to glare at the EMT who was furiously wrapping up his work. Hearing no response, Chapa decided to be more blunt. "You want a ride back to Anasazi or you staying here?"

"As much as I would love to ride twelve hours in that beat-up pickup of yours, I think I need to stay here."

Mags finally flashed a smile as the EMT finished his work. "Probably safer, too. You will be lucky to make it to Denver in that piece of junk."

"I understand," said Chapa. "You live here, so no reason to make the trip back. I will make sure Zuma knows what you did to save Tia and the others. To be honest, at first I didn't understand why he wanted you to join Resnick and I, but I'm glad you came to help."

"Thanks. I would love to go back to see Zuma but there is still much to do up here," replied Mags. "Red Moon is on the loose and the anger and desperation in the Lakota people will allow the Crow Keeper to rebuild his following."

Mags hopped down from the ambulance and pulled down her shirt sleeve. "I want to say goodbye to Logan and the girls before you leave."

Chapa and Mags walked over to his pickup where Logan, Tia, and Erica were already waiting. "We are hitting the road in a few minutes," said Chapa. "Mags is staying here and wanted to say goodbye."

Mags walked up to Tia and Erica and gave them both a big hug. "Where's Jini?" she asked.

"I set her free," replied Tia. "She liked it here, and after being imprisoned by the Crow Keeper, she didn't want to go back in a cage."

Mags smiled and squeezed Tia tightly again. "I am so proud of you. Never forget that feeling today of freeing Jini. Being able to see is a gift, but it does not define you. You are so much more, and I hope you now have a chance to discover that for yourself."

"And Erica," Mags said. "Keep an eye on Logan for me. I have a feeling he will find trouble again. He will need someone to talk to who understands the truth about what happened."

Logan was standing off to the side acting as if he was avoiding Mags for some reason. From the first time he saw Mags at the Blessing Way ceremony, he was intimidated. Seeing her here was still confusing and it was like Mags knew something about Logan that he didn't know about himself.

When Mags finally turned to Logan, he asked a question that had been burning in his mind since he first met Mags in Anasazi. "You said earlier that you knew my mother? Is that why you helped us?"

Logan's question took Mags off guard, and she hesitated for a few seconds before answering. "I helped Chapa because Zuma asked me to, and because it was the right thing to do. The Lakota are my people, and I had to do what I could to stop the Crow Keeper from starting a war."

Mags looked intently at Logan. "And yes, I knew your mother before you were born. She was an incredible woman and would be so proud of you."

She paused. "You *saw* your mother during the Ghost Dance, didn't you?"

Logan had not yet spoken about what he saw when he was in the spirit world. "Yes. I think I did. She somehow helped me resist Sitting Bull and stay alive."

Mags nodded as if she could see right into Logan's mind. "Logan, when you cross over into the spirit world, it changes you. Sometimes the spirits give you gifts."

Mags bit her lip. "And sometimes those gifts turn out to be curses. Whatever your mother did for you in the spirit world cannot be undone and it will change you forever. I don't know whether it will turn out to be a gift or a curse, but it will be what you make of it. Do you understand?"

Logan nodded his head. "I think so. Do you think I will see my mother again?"

"You will see her again in this world or the next," said Mags, as she grabbed Logan's shoulder. "I am confident of it."

"That's enough chit-chat," said Chapa. "You all have some family who are pretty anxious to see you again. Everyone, in the truck."

Logan climbed into the passenger seat while the two girls piled into the back seat. Chapa watched them all get comfortable and knew it wouldn't take long before they would be asleep.

Chapa held out his hand to Mags. "Take care, Mags."

Mags shook his hand, then pulled him in for a quick embrace. The woman whispered softly in Chapa's ear, "Next time you are up here, come find me... Safe travels."

Chapa climbed up into the driver's seat of his black pickup and turned the key, anxiously waiting for the engine to turn over. After a few spurts, the familiar roar of the engine came to life and it was like music to his ears. The truck was old and battle-scarred, but it had never let Chapa down. He slowly pulled out of the parking lot and adjusted the rearview mirror to watch Mags as he pulled away. Chapa saw the red glow of the evening sky above the Crazy Horse Memorial, and enjoyed the incredible sight that would forever remind him of Resnick.

The truck had barely made it back to the highway when Chapa heard snoring. He looked around the cab and noticed that all three teenagers were sleeping. *It will be dark soon, and they probably won't wake up for hours,* Chapa thought to himself.

No matter, he mused. Long cross-country drives were a specialty of Chapa and he relished the opportunity to have a night of peace and quiet. The only thing that would have made it better would have been Resnick by his side eating snacks and talking about UFOs. He pushed that thought out of his mind and focused on coming up with a story for Dawes once he got back to Washington. The boy was safe. Resnick was a hero. That was all that would matter in the long run.

THE DESCENDANTS OF THE GREATEST NATIV
AMERICAN WAR CHIEF TO HAVE EVER LIVED HAV
ALL BEEN KIDNAPPED – EXCEPT ONE – FIFTEEN YEA
OLD ORPHAN LOGAN HATANI. SPECIAL AGENT
CHAPA AND RESNICK ARE ASSIGNED TO PROTEC
LOGAN, AND SOON DISCOVER THEY ARE IN OVE
THEIR HEADS IN BATTLING A MOTORCYCLE GAN
LED BY THE VICIOUS RED MOON.

WITH HELP FROM ERICA, THE SMARTEST KID IN HI
SCHOOL, AND NEWFOUND FRIEND TIA, A BLIN
GIRL WHO CAN SEE THROUGH A PET FALCON, LOGA
EMBARKS ON A DANGEROUS JOURNEY REQUIRIN
HIM TO CONFRONT HIS NAVAJO AND LAKOT
HERITAGE. ULTIMATELY, LOGAN MUST PREPAR
HIMSELF FOR A BATTLE WITH A CULT LEADE
DETERMINED TO RESURRECT A SECRET POWER THA
HAS LAY DORMANT SINCE 1890. THE GHOST DANC
HAS RETURNED AFTER MORE THAN A CENTURY ANI
THIS TIME, ONLY LOGAN CAN STOP IT.

ISBN 9781737785903

9000

9 781737 785903